Darkness is dispelled by the
of characters so easy to love
profound, others daily, with the singular light of God's love for His children, the animals, and all the world. Filled with the flame of hope, *Surviving Carmelita* tells the ages long story that with God healing is possible, for the Creator's compassion will meet us wherever we run.

~LISA SAMSON, Christy award-winning author

From a Midwest suburb to colorful Key West, Susan Miura crafts a beautiful mosaic of Christ's redeeming love using the jagged lives of the most extraordinary characters. A book to be savored.

~PATTI LACY, author of *Reclaiming Lily*

Susan Miura crafts a compelling story of a loving mother who has many skeletons in her closet and many spiritual hurdles to overcome in the course of coming to grips with past and present realities. Her journey vibrantly demonstrates how the presence of God and the devil and lies and secrets intersect to provoke transformation and change.

~*Midwest Book Review*, Senior Reviewer D. DONOVAN

An inspiring tale about dealing with death and the transition from guilt to healing.

~*Readers' Favorite*, Reviewer VINCENT DUBLADO

Surviving Carmelita

Susan Miura

Susan Miura

ST JOSEPH, MISSOURI USA

For more information on Susan Miura, please visit — SusanMiura.altervista.org

Editor: Debra L. Butterfield
Cover Design: Carrie Dennis Design

Printed in the United States of America.

To everyone who has a heart for Christ
and lets it shine brilliantly in a world prone to darkness.

Chapter 1

Josie

My brass teapot gleams in a shaft of autumn sunlight, but as I pour juice for the kids, it fades in the wake of a hazy memory that creeps up my spine, lingering at the base of my neck. The cup overflows with the strawberry-mango mixture. It drips from my hand, down the counter, pooling on the kitchen floor. Instead of grabbing paper towels, I stand frozen, staring at the crimson puddle while trying to grasp that memory. Fog, a white shadow, flashing lights. Not a memory at all. It is last night's dream. A nightmare, actually. Void of details, yet the weight of it bears down on my heart like a tombstone.

"Earth to Mom."

Funny that I didn't hear Mitch come downstairs. His thirteen-year-old feet normally trumpet his arrival. I move into action, wiping the sticky mess as Ashley joins him at the table and pours herself a bowl of Life, scowling because it isn't the Choco Crunch I refuse to buy. Any minute now she'll tell me yet again that she's "the only nine-year-old on the planet who doesn't get to have it."

Instead, she pops a crunchy square into her mouth before dousing the rest with milk. "The grass is all frosty, Mom. What if it's still cold after school?"

"Then you'll just have to trick-or-treat with a jacket." I might as well have said Halloween would be cancelled.

The fourth-grade drama queen stops mid-bite as horror drains the color from her face. "That'll ruin everything!"

Kids. Don't they know it will all work out? By the time heads hit pillows tonight, bags of candy will crowd our kitchen counter, along with popcorn balls and plastic spider rings. Just like every year. I stash Rob's empty coffee cup in the dishwasher and join them at the table. "We'll check the forecast and go from there, okay? Now finish up. That bus will be here before you know it."

As I wrap sandwiches, Rob calls from the living room. "Josie, weather's coming on. You don't want to miss your boyfriend."

So predictable, but it doesn't stop me from laughing. The weatherman has been "my boyfriend" since I chaperoned Ashley's class tour of Chicago's NBC station and he told Ash she had a pretty mommy. My boyfriend. I smile to myself. As if my heart could ever stray from that goofy guy on the couch. "Be right there."

Weatherman Kurt says a warm southwest current will arrive in time for the afternoon's Halloween activities. Perfect! I leave to tell my soon-to-be zombie and hippie the good news while Kurt rambles on about cold, moist air moving in later in the evening. Doesn't matter, though. By that time, everyone will be safe and sound at home.

I return to the kitchen…and the usual montage of morning conversations.

"Where's my math paper? It was just here."

"Dad, can you fix my bike seat tonight?"

"Honey, did you see my keys?"

I pluck Ashley's math paper from the counter, which uncovers Rob's keys, and smile, knowing we'll do this all again tomorrow. Two hugs later, Ashley and Mitch traipse down to the corner as their big yellow "limo" pulls up. I grab my coat and head to my other world, the Riverbank Public Library, to start my three-hour shift in the children's department.

Maples shade the parking lot with crimson leaves that glow beneath the morning sun. I head through the main entrance framed by cornstalks and grinning pumpkins perched on haystacks. Even after all these years, it's still my privilege to work with books and children. Somewhere in life's blueprint for Josie Caruso, the word *librarian* is stamped in bold capital letters. And maybe that blueprint was drawn on crumpled paper, but no matter. The final plan led to a place where I can introduce children to the stories that formed a lifeline for a friendless, only child way back when.

By the time my stomach starts growling for lunch, I'm off to watch my kids in Lincoln Elementary's costume parade. The lot is packed, so I squeeze into a space better suited for a go-cart than my Camry, but there's no time to search for something wider. I make it work.

"Josie, we're here!" Ana waves me over to the sidelines, where parents ready their cameras and cell phones. She presses a granola bar into my hand—triple nut crunch with cranberries.

"I could never survive without you." I sink my teeth into sweet, nutty chewiness, my empty stomach dancing with joy.

Dressed in a silky white dress and feathered angel wings, Ana's daughter, Carmelita, wraps skinny arms around me. Her cubby bear hug sends waves of warmth to my heart, but lasts only a moment as she proudly spins to spread her wings. "Look, Mrs. Caruso! Look at me!"

A halo gleams. Wings sparkle. Neither outshines that Carmelita grin.

"Is that really you, Carmelita? I thought I was getting hugged by a real angel!"

She dances on tiptoes with an aura radiant enough to ward off the damp, dark night ahead. "Guess what, Mrs. Caruso. I got a kitten! Her name is *Pantera*. That means panther. Now you know a new Spanish word. Tell Mama what I teached you. 'Member? About the sky."

The child has more energy than a puppy on steroids. Her enthusiasm inspires me to make her proud. "Alright, here goes." I clear my throat dramatically. "*El cielo es azul*."

Ana claps. "Bravo. The sky is blue." Her eyes tear with giggles. "That will come in very handy, I'm sure."

As the double doors open, the crowd moves forward like a school of fish. Ashley, donning a tie-dyed shirt and peace sign necklace, marches proudly with her fourth-grade peers. Carmelita's halo bounces crazily as she waves wildly to Ashley. In her exuberance, she loses her balance, falling against her mother's protruding belly.

9

Ana catches her before halo hits concrete. "*Cuidado!* You bumped your baby brother and you almost got hurt."

Carmie kisses Ana's tummy. "Sorry, Juanito. Don't worry, you're safe inside Mama."

More pirates, pumpkin heads, presidents, and mummies march by before Carmelita's renewed bouncing tells me the eighth graders are up next.

"Here come Savanna and Mitchell!" She waves both hands to prevent the remote possibility of being overlooked by her big sister.

We raise our cell phones for pictures as our kids parade around the lot, pretending not to know us. My blond-haired, blue-eyed zombie couldn't have contrasted more drastically with the beautiful Savanna Gutierrez in her glittering gypsy dress. I watch them share a smile, wondering if their friendship has become something more.

Carmie squeezes my hand. "Mrs. Caruso, can Pantera meet Clover?"

The image makes me laugh. My bun is probably quadruple the size of her kitten. I hadn't taken the name of the breed seriously until Clover outgrew her first cage. Oh. Flemish *Giant*. "Sure, bring her over tomorrow. Then you can get the Barbie you left at my house."

Propelled by the good news, Carmelita becomes a human pogo stick. "Mrs. Caruso found my Barbie!" Boing, boing boing. "And Pantera's gonna meet Clover!" Boing, boing.

In a whirl of color and noise, the kids head back inside for sugar-loaded parties. Ana and I linger on the playground as Carmelita swings next to us, legs pumping madly as she strives to reach the heavens. As for me, no swing is necessary. The autumn sun warms my face, Carmie's laughter fills the air, and my kids are excited about the fun night ahead. Challenging days will ebb and flow, so I am savoring this little slice of paradise.

Dinner finished, Mitch heads out to pick up Savanna and his buddies while I drop off Ashley at a Halloween party. Driving home, I spot the Dobson twins leaning against their porch. Malevolent grins tell me they're plotting something and it better not be a repeat of previous Halloween escapades—tossing pumpkins from porches and blanketing the street in slimy orange mush. No doubt their parents are out for the night. Again.

Silence fills the house as I enter, broken only by the soft thumping of Clover's feet as she pads over to greet me. I scooch down to stroke her soft, furry patches of caramel and white.

"Come on, let's find some spinach." She hops along behind me on the well-worn path to the refrigerator. With the kids out and Rob at another late-night meeting, it's just the two of us. But as she's about to nibble her leafy treat, Clover's head jerks toward the living room. The bell rings and she runs to the safety of her cage as I grab the candy bowl and swing open the door.

"Trick or treat!" Miniature fairies giggle and prance, holding pumpkin buckets out for candy bars. Beyond their sweet faces, a pea soup fog obscures everything past our oak tree. I shiver. The last thing I want to do is drive in it, but Ashley's party is nearly done and it's only a half-mile, that's all.

Ashley sits in the back seat rustling through her pumpkin bucket while I inch through the dark mist. It has swallowed the moon and stars, reducing streetlights to muted glimmers incapable of accomplishing their task.

"Almond Joy, Mom. Your favorite. You can have that one." The residue of party giddiness still echoes her voice.

"Thanks, honey."

"Oh, Mom! A dark chocolate, your other favorite. I'll save that one for you, too."

Please let her always stay so sweet. "Ah, the perfect meal. Almond Joy for the main course, dark chocolate for dessert." I hope my levity is working. No point in Ashley joining this stress-a-thon as I strain to see past the front bumper.

A giggle from the back. "Oh, sure. You'd never let *me* have a dinner like that!"

The car's brights do little to provide visibility. As our street sign creeps into view, my fingers relax their grasp on the wheel. Almost there…finally. Gentle pressure on the pedal ups my speed to a whopping fifteen miles per hour. How I long for the safe harbor of my garage. Squinting does nothing to cut through that endless mist.

A flash of white. I slam the brakes, which grunt and groan as my Camry skids like a drunken hockey player. What is this? Ice? Oil? Why can't I…

Thump.

Tires finally grip pavement. The sliding stops. Silence envelops us even more densely than the fog.

For a moment.

"Carmie?" A voice cuts through the mist.

Goosebumps prickle my arms. Was that Ana calling from the sidewalk?

"Carmelita, where are you?" Her pitch and volume tangle together and rise. "Carmelita!" A shadowy figure appears at the edge of my headlights and stoops down, out of view.

Ana.

I can't move. Can't breathe.

A primeval sound, born of pure terror, rises from the ghostly silence to a full-blown scream so gut-wrenchingly painful it shrouds my body in chills. With hands frozen to the wheel and my heart pounding insanely, I stare into the murkiness, waiting.

"Mom?" Ashley's shakes can be heard in that single, whispery word. "Mom, what happened?"

I take a breath, unable to turn my head in her direction. Unable to move at all. "I don't know, Ash."

But somehow I *do* know, beneath skin chilled by the breath of demons, that whatever just happened will change everything.

Chapter 2

Preacher

Ah, the moon. It is crescent tonight, its sliver of light gleaming high above the Atlantic's black waters. Many a night this ever-changing view of the sky and sea has settled me, but that peace is not forthcoming as I stand at the bedroom window. Next to me, digital numbers glow 11:53 p.m. from the bedside table. Why am I awake? Today's work taxed my body as well as my brain. Cleaning out the barn, preparing Sunday's sermon for our little Florida Keys church, helping Rosa with her physical therapy. It felt good to slip into bed early with my Bible and notes, the mattress a blessing beneath my body. I had not recapped more than the first few lines of the new sermon before sinking into sleep's delicious embrace.

Now…this anxiety. It corrodes my stomach, hovering in the room like a restless ghost. I part the sheers for a clearer view of the starlit sky.

"You awake too, Manny?" Rosa whispers.

I turn toward the bed Rosa and I have shared for forty-three years. Her ebony eyes, aged now with crows feet that deepen when she smiles, are cloaked by darkness. But I do not need light to see her face. Every curve, every wrinkle, the oval beauty mark on her temple, are etched forever on my heart. "Go to sleep, *querida*. I'm sorry if I disturbed you."

A soft sigh. "It wasn't you. My dreams, they left me edgy. They had no meaning, no faces. Just trees rustling at night, like they were trying to tell me something. I struggled to understand. Afraid to know."

"Strange." A single light twinkles on the water. Probably a couple of *amigos* fishing, feeling the night breeze on their faces, now and then a tug on their lines. Such a feeling of peace out there in the darkness. It has been a long time since the sea has soothed my soul. *Soon, Lord. Soon.*

"Help me up, would you?" She tosses back the covers. "I cannot stay here. Too edgy."

I position her wheelchair next to the bed. She swings her legs over, turns and twists as I support and lift. Together we navigate the moves familiar for two years now. And still it breaks my heart.

Rosa reaches back, squeezes my hand. "What about you? Dreams?"

"Just a feeling. No reason that makes sense. Getting old, maybe."

"*Mi amor*, you are spry as the dolphins out there in the water. Sixty-three is not considered old anymore."

My eyes return to the window, searching for whatever has filled this night with trepidation. "Tonight I feel like a hundred and sixty three."

"Come. Let's check on everyone, have a cup of chamomile. Maybe that will settle us both."

I push the chair through darkness, knowing how to avoid each obstacle: the rocker in the corner, the mermaid sculpture our daughter made in high school. My fingers touch the doorknob, freezing, powerless to grasp. Rosa's face tilts up toward mine. Unable to see her expression, I know the question in her eyes. But I have no explanation for the fear that grips me in its jaws like a tiger shark. Night's cloak becomes murkier, heavier. I can't breathe.

The phone splits the night like cracks of thunder, causing us to jump in unison. Two strides get me to it. A beloved name glows on the caller ID, but instead of warming my heart, it ices my spine, stealing another breath.

My sister, Ana.

I cast a last glance at the Florida night before my soul cries out, *Oh, God, what is this?*

Chapter 3

Josie

The fog dissipated during the night as though it never existed at all. Those tiny drops of water came together for just a nanosecond in the history of the world, then disappeared, leaving in their wake tattered hearts and shattered lives.

I killed an angel. A cherub, really, considering her age. Carmelita Mariposa Gutierrez.

Such a big name for such a little girl.

But I'll be in kindergarten next year! I'll be a big girl!

A big girl.

No Carmie, you are eternally little. I saw to that, didn't I? It was *my* foot on the pedal, *my* car rolling down the street on that cursed foggy night. Reflected in every tear, I see those soft feathery wings clinging to wet, dirty pavement; that lock of curly hair lying across her silver halo. No breath, no pulse, no sweet Carmelita smile. In less than a heartbeat, she went from spunky, bright, and beautiful to limp and lifeless. Nothing else will ever matter again. Not to me...and certainly not to Ana and Emilio Gutierrez.

From the upstairs window I peek between curtains as morning welcomes a new day. *Welcomes.* Ha. My lips curl at the irony. Familiar faces gather in Ana's driveway, some holding flowers. Others carry teddy bears that will never be hugged or tucked beneath cozy covers, but lay instead at the base of a curbside cross made of white roses. So beautiful.

Can I have one rose from your garden, Mrs. Caruso? They are so beautiful.

Imagined midnight phone calls wrap around my mind like thorny weeds. Between inconsolable bouts of weeping, I'd conjured up hundreds of these conversations based on the sketchy facts I knew.

"Did you hear who did it? *Josie.*"

"Josie? The neighbor lady? *Dios mío!* She is Ana's *best friend.*"

"*Sí.* The new kitten ran into the street and our Carmie ran after it."

"Was Josie drinking? Or going too fast?"

"Some *muchachos* smashed pumpkins in the street. The car, it slid on the mess. They say Ana is hysterical, but she refused to take drugs. You know, because of the *bebé.*"

Drugs. Rob wanted me to take some after the police left. As I lay in a crumpled, soggy heap of unimaginable agony, he offered to contact our doctor for a prescription—or pull the ER midnight run. But no, I welcome the pain, want it to course through my veins and suffocate what is left of my heart.

But not Ana. She doesn't deserve this. I ache to wrap my arms around her in an endless hug and tell her I'll go back in time, undo it. I'll breathe life back into Carmelita. I will do *anything.* My mind drifts back to last night. Ana's grief-stricken face fills my vision, her eyes wide with shock as paramedics surrounded her daughter. Oh, Ana, if only I could take Carmie's place.

If only.

A van pulls up. Out comes a toddler, two teens, and Ana's older sister Ria with her husband Miguel. He wraps a comforting arm around his wife's shaking shoulders, kissing her head before returning to the van for Ana's grandmother. A nyloned leg appears, followed by another, while Miguel grabs a walker from the trunk. She dabs her nose before grasping it. Ria picks up her curly-haired girl and holds her tight.

The scene unfolds before my swollen eyes, with my mind and body drained from a night spent sobbing to the point of vomiting. Rob stirs on the bed, unaware I've slipped from the spot where he lay holding me throughout the night, saying, "I'm here, Josie, I'm here. We'll get through this. We'll find a way. It was an accident. You couldn't help it."

Such pretty words. Same ones my mom repeated endlessly thirty years ago when I ruined my best friend's life. Hardly a day went by without me and Roxy playing together, sharing secrets, pledging our everlasting friendship. Until I spotted our young, pretty teacher getting into a car with Roxy's dad. If I had known what it meant, I would have never said a word. But why go there when there's pain enough right in front of me?

Ana's grandmother says something to Ria. No, Ana's *abuela*. Carmelita taught me that. They both stop walking as Ria points to my house and abuela shakes her head. I get it. I am that woman in *The Scarlet Letter*, only instead of "A" for adulterer, I have a flaming "K" for killer emblazoned on my chest. Josie disappeared in the fog. I am forevermore "that lady who killed Carmelita." I wait for a fresh flow of tears to drench the clothes I've worn since yesterday, but a thin, protective sheet of ice has begun to crystallize my heart. No more tears. And anyway, Carmelita's abuela is crying enough for both of us.

The sheets shuffle and I turn back toward Rob, whose eyes are open now.

"Hey." It's that walking-on-eggshells voice. I know it well from the times I've used it myself with certain patrons at the library. The drunks. The mentally ill. The killers? "You doing okay?"

Staring out the window seems like a good alternative to answering, and so I do. Is he crazy? Will other people ask me, too? Who cares how I'm doing? All that matters now is the Gutierrez family. The answer to that question, for the rest of my life, will be "no." I am as far from "okay" as east is from west. "Okay" will never, *ever* be a word that applies to me again.

"Josie?"

"Yeah?"

Rob yawns and stretches. "I was thinking. You want to maybe talk to a pastor or somebody like that?"

"What?"

"A pastor, a priest, somebody like that. Maybe it would help. I could call the one from our church."

"*Our church*? The one we go to on Christmas and Easter?" The pastor's name eludes me. Not sure I'd even recognize him if we bumped carts at Target. Twice a year I hear him talk about a God who wants to have a "personal relationship" with the people He created. He talks of salvation and unconditional love, but none of that resonates with me. Not that I'm anti-God, I just didn't grow up with Him in the mix. Rob's folks are churchgoers, though, so we tag along with them.

"Yeah, well, I know we don't go much, but it's still our church, right?" He pats the bed and I step toward it, sitting on the edge.

"What would be the point, Rob? I mean, is he going to tell me that God will make this all better?" And how would that work, exactly? He's "up there" somewhere, that's about all I know, and that's worked fine…until now. If He's really invested, He could've jumped in to save a little girl.

He takes my hand, caressing my knuckles with his thumb. "I don't know, honey. I'm just trying to help. Honestly, I'm lost here. It seemed like a good idea."

Another car door slams outside, drawing me back to the window. What freakish curiosity lures me to those pained faces? Another teddy bear is added to the growing pile by the white rose cross put in place as the sun began to rise. I know, having been there to watch. A woman who looks vaguely familiar emerges from Ana's house and drapes a pink and black ribbon around it before surrounding the base with a ring of white mums. Oh, yeah, another of Ana's sisters. The florist.

"Josie?" Robs voice develops an edge. "Did you hear me?"

"Yeah. Sorry. The thing is, I don't really feel like talking to anyone right now. Especially a stranger."

"What about Aunt Theresa? She's always been your favorite and she volunteers with some sort of crisis team, right?" He swings his legs off the bed and grabs sweatpants from his dresser. "Remember, she told us about that? We could have her come over. I'll take the kids out so you two can talk."

Like I really want to talk to St. Theresa, fixer of the broken. I love Aunt Theresa, though. I do. She has this way of making everyone feel significant, like she's just happy you exist. But she'll ask questions. That's not what I need now.

"I'll find my own way, Rob. Really. No phone calls, no visitors, no holy therapy."

Let's talk about this, honey, you'll feel better. Mom's words failed to convince me. Even then, I knew talking wouldn't erase all the trouble I'd caused, or bring back my best friend. Temperatures had hovered in the upper 90s that week, so it was a happy me that put on my swimsuit for an afternoon in Roxy's inflatable pool. Mom said she'd drop me off right after a quick trip to get me new sneakers. That's when I saw them. Roxy's dad was placing a small suitcase in the trunk, while Mrs. Bartos leaned against the car, arms folded, eyes nervous. Mom didn't see them, and said I must have been mistaken.

"My Dad's gonna bring me back a surprise from his business trip," Roxy said when I arrived. Her mom stood next to her, pouring lemonade for us.

"Is Mrs. Bartos going with him?" I asked. "I saw them getting ready to leave."

A glass of lemonade crashed to the floor, its sticky liquid weaving pathways around chunky shards of glass. But Roxy's mom didn't bend to clean it up. She stood with eyes wide, mouth open, like she'd just watched the scariest scene in a horror flick. It was what writer's call a "defining moment." It would be years before I'd recognize it as such.

Ashley's bedroom door squeaks open. Little feet pad down the stairs as she heads for the kitchen. My baby. She shouldn't have been there. Shouldn't have seen.

"I'll get her breakfast," Rob says. "You stay here. Try to sleep. You look exhausted."

Yeah, I'll try to sleep while Ana's and Emilio's families arrive by the carload to grieve for the child whose life I ended.

"Thanks. And Rob..." My brain muddles when I think of my daughter. "Ashley...she was...she's been through a lot."

"I know." He kisses my forehead. "Don't worry, I got it. Get some rest."

He slips a T-shirt over his head. The bedroom door closes, leaving me alone to battle the fog that will once again descend. I am sure of it.

My intense yearning to attend the funeral is exceeded only by my desire to shield Ana from more pain, if that's possible. I ache to run to her, hold her tight, cry with her…beg forgiveness. But what good would it do, coming face to face with her daughter's killer? Seeing me would only make things worse. My mind transfers the memory of Roxy's hostile eyes to Ana.

"You ruined my life. You're the devil! I hate you forever!" Roxy blamed me completely for her parents' divorce. She adored her father, who showered her with gifts, called her Princess and bought her a giant heart-shaped box of chocolates every Valentine's Day. It was me who witnessed his infidelity, and to Roxy, that was reason enough for me to bear the blame. No amount of "I'm sorrys" made a difference.

Her loathing forged steel walls around my ten-year-old heart, and depleted me of all social contact. Quiet and shy, I had relied on Roxy to make friends for us. When we split, she got the girls, and I finished the summer solo. The school year wasn't much better. Loneliness seeped into my pores. My friends were books. My hangout: the library. In the years to follow, my heart-shaped fortress kept friends at a safe distance. Until Ana.

No. I can't face my Ana. She demolished those steel walls, leaving my heart bare-naked. Seeing hatred in Ana's eyes would dissolve it like battery acid.

Mitchell slips into his Reeboks, oblivious to the untied laces, and grabs a hoodie. "I'll go see how they're doing, and ask if it's okay for us to come to the funeral."

Someone has to play messenger if we have any hope of saying our final farewells to Carmelita. That someone should not be a thirteen-year-old-boy.

"No, Mitch. Let's just wait. I'll figure something out." What if they yell at him? Slam the door in his face? My sanity has truly left me. Ana and Emilio would never do anything like that. Not even now.

"Wait? The funeral's tomorrow, Mom. Anyway, I want to see how Savanna's doing."

Ah, there it is. Maybe seeing her will be good for him. For Savanna, too.

"Okay. Just hurry. Don't impose on them and their grief. Just ask if we can come to the cemetery. Say how sorry you are about..." my throat closes up, swallowing the rest of my words.

"Fine. Whatever."

My frustration and exhaustion combine in one sigh. Must I summon the energy for discipline...even now? "Don't use that tone, Mitchell." My words sound more tired than angry.

"Why? You're just feeling guilty because you were the one." He flips on his baseball cap before storming out the door. The chill of his tone hangs in the air as I collapse into a chair. I try to pull the icy dagger out of my heart, but it may as well be The Sword in the Stone. He doesn't understand that I'm doing this for her. My Ana. She doesn't want to see me any more than Roxy did all those years ago. I'm the cause, and the painful reminder, of her broken life. Fifteen minutes crawl by like an entire week before the front door opens.

"Well?" My pulse drums beneath the surface of my wrist. If I were to look, no doubt it would be grotesquely throbbing in and out, in and out. But my eyes stay fixed on Mitch, imploring him for a word-by-word account of his brief visit.

"Sorry about before." He slides his hoodie zipper up and down, focused on *it*, instead of me.

"It's okay."

"They were really nice."

"Good." Go on, go on. Talk to me!

He turns to head upstairs, but I need more. Anything.

"What else?" The words shoot out at a higher volume than intended as blood surges through my veins like raging rapids. My impending insanity is becoming painfully clear.

Mitch groans as if turning around is a monumental effort. "Mr. Gutierrez told me to wait at the door. He talked to Mrs. Gutierrez and then said we can come." Monotone words hold something in check. I don't want to believe it is anger, but the acid pooling in my stomach says it is. Please, Mitch, I long to say. Don't you see it was an accident? Don't you see this is killing me? I want to tell you how much I love and need you and your sister and Dad. I just can't.

Defeated eyes gaze into mine. He needs something from me, but there's so little of me left. Maybe, at the very least, I can muster an ounce of encouragement. "You did good, Mitch."

"Then Mrs. Gutierrez came to the door."

Ana! "She did?"

"Yeah. She looked different, though. Her face…she just looked older or thinner or something. Real serious. She asked how you were doing."

"She did?" Ana, what have I done to our lives?

"Yeah. I told her you stay in your room a lot and don't talk much."

"Did you tell her I'm so sorry?"

"No, Mom, I didn't. Don't you always tell us to say that ourselves? You need to talk to her."

I turn from my son's level gaze. Do I? Confusion whirls in my brain. There is no precedence for this situation. No guidebook for killers of little girls.

"Anyway," he continues, "it was kind of good that I went because I was sorta afraid of seeing them, but now that I did, it's like the next time won't be so bad."

"Good," whooshes out of me. I'm so proud of him. My boy. Should it have been *me* at Ana's door? *Me* saying I'm sorry? Would she want that? Ana loved me like a sister.

Loved me. Past tense. Before my crime.

"But just so you know, Savanna didn't come to the door." Frost ices his words. "That's pretty much the whole story. We can come to the funeral, Mr. and Mrs. Gutierrez don't hate us, but Savanna does. Can I go upstairs now?"

And there it is again. I try to will my arms around Mitch, but they just hang awkwardly at my side.

"Savanna doesn't hate you." My voice squeaks with pain as I imagine what this is doing to my son. "She's grieving."

"Yeah, because *my* mother killed *her* little sister." Frost gives way to a blizzard wind that whips at me, blinding me with a white-out. An avalanche can't be far behind.

Footsteps clump out of the office, startling us both.

"That's enough, Mitchell!" Rob's volume silences whatever else my son next planned to pummel me with. "This conversation is done." He extends his arm, pointing through the office door. "In here…now!"

My son slogs forward. No, Rob, don't yell at him. He's just hurting. I hear Rob hiss, "How dare you," and, "We're not going to," before the office door slams shut.

The obnoxious honking of a car alarm wakes me at six-thirty. It only takes a heartbeat for a single, uninvited thought to come crashing into my head. Funeral day. Thank goodness everyone else is sound asleep. I need time alone before they rise—time to think, or just go blank, over a steaming cup of coffee. It has been my sustenance for three days. Quivering hands slide through the sleeves of my robe as I glance at a stranger reflected in the closet door mirror. Eyes permanently puffed and shadowed beyond anything makeup can cover, clothes roomier than they've ever been. I should eat, but knowing it's the right thing to do doesn't provide any incentive to do it.

In the kitchen, the coffee has just stopped brewing. Rob must have set the timer last night; a simple act for which I am profoundly grateful. My hands embrace the hot mug, but unlike all those mornings before my world unraveled, I take no pleasure from the coffee-scented steam wafting into my nostrils. On the table, a ticket peeks out from under yesterday's mail. The officer had given it to me the night of the accident, but I never even looked at it. Nor do I want to, fearing the words will read "life imprisonment," or maybe even "death by stoning." Instead, I see what must surely be a sick police joke: "Failure to reduce speed to avoid an accident." Under "fine" the handwritten amount reads $200. Some atonement. The whole ordeal has been whittled down to nothing more significant than a fender bender. At the bottom of the ticket, bold letters state, "For questions, call 555-3700."

Questions. I have enough to fill the Grand Canyon, but the police cannot answer them. No one can. Instead, an ache fills the abyss where answers should be, creating in me a driving desire to pour out my guts to someone who could offer some hope, some guidance…something. But the only one here is Clover, gnawing her cage to let me know she wants out. I open it and lift her, burying my face in that mass of soft warm fur. Together we sit on the couch and stare at the empty room where Carmie's orphaned Barbie lays face down on the carpet.

The sky mourns Carmelita by blocking the sun with pewter gray clouds. We gather in the cemetery. Father Martinez says, "Blessed are those who mourn, for they will be comforted," but gazing at the grieving crowd, I don't see anything that even remotely resembles comfort. He preachifies again, turning to his Bible. "We are hard pressed on every side, but not crushed; perplexed, but not in despair; persecuted, but not abandoned; struck down, but not destroyed."

Who is he kidding?

He talks about the "bright-eyed beauty, loved by everyone who knew her." I stare at distant gravestones, trying not to imagine those dancing eyes, stilled forever. He says Carmelita is with Jesus now, beginning an eternity of joy beyond our comprehension. The group prays. A white casket with pink roses etched into the lid is lowered. It is far too small to be covered in dirt for eternity.

Tearful friends and family form a procession, tossing flowers into the grave. We are not among them. The four of us stand off to the side, watching as Emilio wraps both arms around Ana. Face in hands, her body shudders with sobs that faintly reach me. She pushes away from him and walks toward the grave. The crowd parts. All the world holds its breath as a mother looks down at her little girl's casket. Ana crashes to her knees, wailing with a pain as old as the earth, then disappears from view, surrounded by the people who love her. Except for me, here by the trees.

An unexpected image forms in my head. Mary at the foot of the cross, watching her bloodied Son breathe His last breath, like I've seen in paintings during our holiday church forays. If there's any truth to that story, why would God kill him off? What was the point of that? Or in killing Carmie? If He's everything Aunt Theresa says He is, then a five-year-old angel would be spending today playing with her kitten, not…this. He could have saved her.

But He did not.

The pain starts in my throat, where I struggle to contain quiet hysteria. It spreads throughout my body, tearing at me like the devil's own claws as I watch my friend fall into shattered pieces of inconsolable grief. I did it. I killed her daughter. I fight back tears, opening my mouth to suck in air, but there isn't any. The bones in my legs slowly dissolve. My knees betray me, incapable of bearing weight one moment longer. Darkness encircles me. I let it suck me under without even reaching out for support.

"Mom!" The dreamy voice comes from some far-off place outside the darkness, but I am already falling into oblivion.

If I am lucky, very lucky, I will never come back.

Chapter 4

Josie

She's been there for a whole week now; down there in that pretty white box. I stare at my bedroom ceiling, where a thin layer of dust lines the left edge of each ceiling fan blade. Four more hours before the children return with backpacks, homework, and stories of the day. Ashley will look at me with those hazel eyes and say, "Are you better today, Mom?" I'll say, "Yeah, honey, a little," then return to my sanctuary and hibernate. It's the best I can do. Lids close over eyes that prefer darkness more than light… until the phone shatters the silence of my room. I don't want to answer it, but the caller ID screams the words Lincoln Elementary.

"Hello?"

"Mrs. Caruso? This is Linda Shurden, the nurse at Lincoln. I have Ashley here with a stomachache. Can you pick her up?"

Pick her up? My pounding heart fills the telephone silence.

"Mrs. Caruso, are you there?"

"Yes."

"Can you pick up Ashley? She's in tears. Miserable."

Say something, Josie. My hands shake, just thinking of the cold touch of the steering wheel—the wheel that set into motion a living hell. Here in my room, it is dark, safe. No one stares at me with accusatory eyes. At school they all know who I am…and what I did. But Ashley, my baby. She needs me. I have to do something.

"Yes, someone will pick up Ashley."

"Is that someone on the list?"

The list. I can barely process the basics. "Yes, her father. My husband."

I tap the red dot on my phone, wondering if my racing heart will survive the next few minutes without exploding from my chest, then call Rob. He answers on the third ring.

"Josie, you okay?"

How I loathe the question. "Ashley has a stomachache. She's in the nurse's office."

"And?"

Oh, Rob, if only you knew how much I want to take care of my baby girl the way I always have. The words fight to stay inside…and do. "So you need to pick her up."

"Josie, you're five minutes away from the school. Are you kidding?"

"I can't, Rob. It's just…I can't."

"It's a forty-five-minute drive for me. You need to do this, Jo. You'll be fine. You're the girl who reinvented herself, remember? You've got more guts than most people I know."

I'd gone away to college, determined to leave the lonely years behind me. I slapped on a friendly smile and strode into that dorm room with the resolve of Jane Eyre, the fortitude of Hester Prynne and the confidence of Elizabeth Bennet. It was an act, of course, but in time, the act became my reality. I made friends, dated, and after speaking at an Earth Day rally, tripped while exiting the makeshift stage and fell into the arms of Robert Caruso.

"You backpacked through Sicily and climbed Mt. Etna," he continued. "Fought off a would-be purse-snatcher just last summer. You can do this."

What happened to that fearless woman? My heart heads toward a full-blown meltdown. A little girl happened, that's what. A dead little girl. "I can't." When I finally form the words, they are shriller, louder than I expect. "Don't you get it? I…cannot…do…this!"

"Calm down, honey." It is his Ashley voice, the one he uses when she is crying or can't figure out her homework. But I'm a grown woman. Or was. "Listen to me. It's just four blocks. Nothing will happen." His soft voice washes over my heart like warm chocolate, slowing my pulse. "I know you can do this because it's for Ashley."

For Ashley. Yes. I have a new mantra. For Ashley. Then I think of that steering wheel.

"I love you, Josie. We're going to get past this. You're going to get better."

"I don't know, Rob."

"I've got a client waiting, so I have to go. Call you later to see how it went."

"Okay."

"Love you."

Click. Rob is gone. The moment with him is behind me, with Mt. Etna looming ahead. And here am I without any climbing gear.

I slip into jeans, run a comb through my hair, and grab my keys. My skin shrinks at the touch of the cold metal. Outside, the scent of decaying leaves wafts through the air, whispering to me that the world keeps turning, seasons change, life goes on. Life. On days like this, the rich aroma of simmering stew would drift through our house, or I'd have warm, gooey chocolate chip cookies waiting when the kids got home. A lifetime ago, when the world was sweet and beautiful, and a little girl would skip up my steps to play with her favorite bunny. That was life.

Despite the November breeze, my shirt glues to sweaty skin. I turn the car key and try to breathe deep as the motor comes alive for the first time in over a week. It's just a few blocks. I'll walk inside, tell them I'm there for Ashley Caruso. I won't look at them, won't let their poisoned darts pierce my armor. I exhale. My jaw tightens. This might take everything I've got, but somewhere inside this shell, I'm still a mom.

I grip the wheel and turn on the radio, but the effervescent announcer grates my nerves before the car leaves the driveway. Click. He's gone. Just like Rob. He doesn't understand how hard this is, but I'll do it for Ashley. For Ashley. Somehow my mantra carries me to the school and through a brief conversation with the nurse.

Home again, my daughter's tear-stained face reminds me I'm failing her, minute by agonizing minute. She sits quietly on the couch, arms crossed over her hurting tummy. I've always been there to catch her when she falls, make her life better, brighter. But I don't know how anymore, not from down in this dark, cold place.

The faint jabberings of kids in a cooking show reach me through the bedroom vent. Laughter bubbles from Ashley, who bounced back to healthy with a bit of ginger ale and a nap. All is well for the moment, but what will tomorrow bring? Her giggles are cut short by the ringing of our land-line phone. I jerk, then relax. It must be a friend or family member, because Ashley chatters away in a happy tone. Too soon, the talking stops and her feet fly up the stairs. No, not the phone. Not a conversation.

A pig-tailed head peeks through my bedroom door, eyeing me as though her presence might shatter this new china teacup version of me. I mumble a "Hi, honey," prompting her to enter. Ashley covers the receiver, whispering. "It's cousin Tina," before holding the phone out to me.

I shake my head. She presses the phone into my hand, anyway.

Cousin Tina. Always making me laugh. Always ready to listen. The perfect proprietor for her qaint little Key West bed-and-breakfast. "Hi, Tina. How are you?"

"Good, Josie. Still running my humble island inn. Still ending my days with sunsets that fire up my soul."

The words are typical Tina. The tone is not. Gone is the lilt, the laughter behind each word. It could only mean one thing.

"How about you, cousin? How's my Josie?"

Damaged. Dying. I open my mouth to speak, but silence fills the void between us.

"Josephine Maria Caruso." She speaks my name like a prayer. Soft. Loving. Her comforting warmth hugs me all the way from the island. "Rob called me from work. Sweetie, why didn't you tell me? Haven't we always shared life's troubles, as well as the joys?"

Troubles. Accident. Grief. Words that don't come within an ocean's depth of this nightmare.

"Josie? Talk to me, honey. Tell me what's going on inside that pretty head of yours."

The darkness creeps from deep within the chasms of my soul. It slithers through my veins, wrapping around my heart until I can no longer open it to the cousin I've loved since childhood. Words stay imprisoned in my mind. She waits.

"I can't, Tina. I'm sorry."

She sighs her disappointment. "It's alright. Rob told me you haven't said much since it happened. He sure wishes you would get some counseling. Not a bad idea, you know."

"He's been taking Ashley."

"You need it, too."

I nod. It's all I can muster.

"Listen, Jo, I have an idea."

My stomach cringes. Here we go—another fix Josie strategy. I take a deep breath, knowing she loves me and that whatever she says next will come straight from her heart. But that doesn't mean I want to hear it. "Okay."

"Starting next week, I'm booked pretty solid through April. Problem is, my front desk clerk, Rebecca, is moving on. Finally leaving that lying, cheating son of a hockey puck. Good for her, I say. Bad timing, though. How about you come down for a few weeks? Help out while I'm interviewing for her replacement? It's a win-win, Jo. You need to get away. It'll do you good. Rob thought so, too."

So, Rob's in on this. "I don't know."

"Aunt Theresa can watch the kids."

"You talked to her, too?"

"Yeah, well, I wanted to get all the ducks in a row before I suggested it. She was pretty excited, actually. You know she's crazy about your munchkins."

Fixing Josie has become an it-takes-a-village project, but there isn't a village in this world big enough. Still, Tina is trying. I can't fault her for that. Watching out for me like she's been doing since I was a toddler and she was just starting high school. How can I tell her I'm not fixable?

It would break her heart.

"I don't expect you to answer right this minute. No, siree. You think about it. Talk to that handsome husband of yours. Let me know when you're ready."

I shove away the possibility of yet another change. Tina holds a treasured place in my heart, but the best I can give her now are polite, meaningless words. "Okay. I'll call."

"All righty." Her words fall short of the cheery tone she attempts. "You take care."

I would do that, truly I would. If I just remembered how.

The coffee maker drips its last drop. I pour a cup, knowing the kids need breakfast, wishing I could blink away the next forty-five minutes and be alone again. I take on my tasks, working in silence as Mitchell comes into the kitchen without the "Hi, Mom" I used to get every morning. Before. He gets the milk without my asking. I warm up muffins, grab an apple to cut up.

Ashley sits prettily at the table, her hair in crooked pigtails. "Morning, Mom."

"Morning." I try to smile, unaccustomed to forcing it.

"I did my own hair. Daddy said me and Mitch need to do more stuff for ourselves now."

"Oh." My heart winces.

"Is it all right if I visit Mrs. Gutierrez on the way home today? She's usually sitting out there waiting for Savanna."

Ana? She wants to visit Ana? I core the apple, peeling off the skin so it won't get stuck in Mitch's braces. The paring knife slips, its tip nicking my thumb, which instantly drips blood. A tiny crimson puddle forms on the counter. No, please. Not the images...again. They batter my brain, thrusting me back to that bloody street. Ana screaming...

"Can I, Mom?"

Ashley has thrown me a lifeline. "Um, I don't know." I wrap a napkin around my thumb before setting the apple slices in a bowl.

Mitch gulps milk, his eyes shooting a question. "Why not, Mom? Just because you can't talk to her doesn't mean Ashley can't. People like to know their friends care about them, you know?" His voice rises. Eyes narrow, darken. "Except for Savanna. She just turns away every time I try, because now I'm the kid whose mom killed her sister."

Just like Roxy did to me all those years ago. Only Mitch doesn't deserve it.

"The worst part is, you're not even bothering to make things right."

Make things right? In what alternate universe can anything be right ever again? "Mitch." Blood thunders in my ears, deafening my thoughts. Though I labor to express what's in my heart, jumbled words and phrases will not connect with any coherency. I shake my head, saying nothing.

Ashley stares at me, awaiting my response to her question. "So can I visit her, Mom? Just for a minute? I think maybe she'd like it."

I have neither the energy, wisdom, nor desire to pursue this conversation. "Sure, I guess so."

Mitch shakes his head. "You can do whatever you want, Ashley. Mom doesn't care."

My daughter's eyes widen. "Yes, she does!" Her gaze fixes on me, awaiting confirmation, but I stay focused on the apple. "Mom's heart is just sick right now. Daddy said she'll be all right again pretty soon."

"What about you, Mom? Are you going to talk to Mrs. Gutierrez?" Mitch asks.

Is he crazy? I cannot trod down the driveway where Carmelita played, walk past that curbside memorial, and torture Ana with my presence.

"I don't think so, Mitch," I finally manage.

"Why not?"

I hold my breath, fighting not to scream the words. Because I killed her daughter! Hazy fog fills my head. I grab the counter's edge, holding tight for support.

"Mom? Are you okay?"

No, Ashley. Mom is not okay. Mom is not even Mom anymore.

33

Silence has descended on the house for more than an hour. I get up for a drink of water and see Mitch's forgotten phone on the kitchen counter. I zero in on the unopened text message, confused by my compulsion to open it. Normally I wouldn't intrude on his private conversation, but "normal" was part of another life where things made sense. Maybe, just maybe, this message will offer a peek into Mitch's heart—a heart barricaded from the mother who loves him beyond reason. Such an insight would more than justify an invasion of privacy. Then again, that could lead to conversations—a Herculean effort for me these days. I press the screen.

"Where will you live?"

An unseen force sucks the air from the room. Why would someone ask him that? He lives here, with me and Rob and Ashley! There's no turning back now. I scroll up to Mitch's comment. "Gotta get out of here. Packing up tonight when they're asleep, then out the window and onto the roof. Pretty sure I can jump to the deck from there."

It only takes seconds to see the whole conversation between Mitch and his friend Chris.

Another kid chimes in: "Your Mom kill anyone today or is she taking a break?"

I click off the phone. It has become something evil, toxic. I close my eyes and journey back in time to a pastel birthing room where I squeezed Rob's hand as labor pains surged through my body.

"Josie, you have to push really hard this time," the doctor said far too calmly. "The baby is not in a good place right now."

Fingers gripped bedrails. I pushed with the strength of a heavyweight wrestler. Pain sliced through my insides, ripping parts that weren't meant to be ripped and nearly causing me to black out. Would I live to see my baby? But if he was "not in a good place," nothing else mattered. Not the pain, not even my life. I didn't realize I'd been holding my breath until they said the head emerged. Drawing in a lungful of air, possibly my last, I pushed again, thereby sending the baby from my warm dark womb into the neon brightness of the hospital room.

Silence. Something was wrong. I didn't know much about motherhood, but a silent baby could only be bad. The doctor scooped up my newborn's limp blue body. I looked at Rob, his shocked expression confirming my worst fears. I couldn't breathe. Couldn't speak. Would my greatest joy become my most unbearable pain?

Our Mitchell had entered this world on the edge of life itself, whisked away from me, placed on a table surrounded by masked strangers, touched by latex hands. I couldn't even see him. Couldn't hold him. But moments later, the most amazing, melodious sound graced my ears. My son was crying! With each shriek, he announced to the world he was here to stay. A smiling nurse handed me a healthy, pink baby boy, and I breathed in his newborn scent, more lovely than roses, then nestled him to my breast.

Thirteen years later, he is running away. He can't take living here with me anymore. *Me.* I don't blame him. Because of me, he lost Savanna. Because of me, people say cruel things to him. His text says getting away from me will make things better.

Collapsing on his bed, I sob loud and long, hopelessly trapped by grief and guilt in the darkest corner of hell. No light, no hope, no way of ever coming back to what was. When the last tear falls on that soggy patch of sheet, I know what I must do. The plan ferments. I send an email to my boss at the library, then drag a suitcase up from the basement. A phone call, a note, and a bunny hug complete my mission. It is a plan born of desperation—the only one I can think of that will allow my son to survive. Help all of them to heal. I hang onto that thought and get out of my son's room before fragmenting into a million pieces.

Chapter 5

Preacher

Sun flickers on the water as I head north, leaving the Keys behind. Traffic is light on our side of the Overseas Highway, heavier southbound with the snowbirds heading for their winter perches. Rosa searches her purse for a lemon drop, knowing I enjoy them on these long rides. Just half an hour left before we arrive at Miami International. Nine days ago we drove this same route, hearts sinking in darkness like the lead weight on a fishing line. Silence filled the car. Nine days since we stood in that damp, chilly Illinois cemetery beneath a sky the color of gravestones. Nine days without Carmie in this world. The pain still stabs like a red-hot dagger.

I dreamt of her last night. Big brown eyes. That infectious little-girl giggle. Her weight on my shoulders as she stretched to reach a coconut.

I got it, Uncle Manny! I got it! Now me and Auntie Rosa can make coconut pie.

The memory tears my eyes, thankfully covered by sunglasses. My pain must be held in check, for I refuse to diminish the joy of the honeymooners stealing a kiss in the back seat. I reach back and smack my young assistant pastor on the leg. "Get a room, you two."

Owen jumps. "Oh, sorry."

"I am teasing you, Owen. Kiss all you want. That is what honeymoons are for."

"Okay. I mean, we will later. When we get there. So who's picking us up? You or Mike?" Owen tries to veil his fear of flying beneath the casual tone.

Calm him, Lord. Fill him with Your peace. Please bless my shy assistant with a happy, well-deserved vacation. And thank you again for sending this faithful man to help me lead my flock.

I pluck a lemon drop from Rosa's palm. "Mike will get you. Rosa gave him all the information."

"Think he'll remember?" Owen grabs the top of my headrest. I feel his weight against the cloth seat. He, too, has burdens, I realize. But not a niece in the grave. "He gets pretty busy at his clinic. Tends to forget things. We were supposed to go fishing last week. He never showed. Had a German Shepherd with a bowel obstruction."

"Si, our veterinarian has a full schedule, but we will make sure he remembers. Three weeks is long enough without my assistant pastor."

"So you're admitting you need me?"

I harrumph in jest. "Nothing of the sort. I am simply saying some people in the congregation, perhaps one or two, might miss you."

Elena laughs, her happy face gracing my rearview mirror. What a perfect bride for the shy Owen. The Sunday school children adore her. And that voice. Worship songs will not be the same without our lovely songbird leading the way. Rosa and I were overjoyed when they announced their engagement on Valentine's Day. Will I feel such joy again? Logic tells me I will. God has more in store for me, I am sure of it. If only my leaden heart agreed. Though grief's thorny vines wrap around me, I refrain from choking up until my friends are out of sight.

"Maybe I'll just stay in Idaho until you admit you need me."

"And do what, grow potatoes?" Little does he know I would be lost without him. "Who honeymoons in Idaho?"

"Are you kidding? It's perfect. Snake River Canyon, Twin Falls, Craters of the Moon. We're going to see it all."

"And the rock," Elena adds. "He wants to see a big rock."

He has told me all about the amazing scenery over the past few weeks, but still I tease. "I think the big rock is in his head."

Elena and Rosa giggle. Mr. Serious does not. "It's balanced, Preach. And it weighs forty tons. Look." Owen tosses a brochure onto my lap with photos of the geological phenomenon. Rosa grabs it immediately.

She hates when anything distracts me from the road.

"Oh, now that is really something!" My wife gives Owen the response he desires.

My newlywed friends fill the remainder of the ride with three weeks' worth of sightseeing plans—a welcome distraction. As we enter the airport jungle, traffic noises increase, but quiet has descended on our car. Rosa glances at me. Our thoughts join. Our hearts worry for Owen, who has been dreading this moment since the day he reserved the flight. I ask the ladies to stay in the car as we unload the suitcases.

Owen struggles to unlock the trunk, a task he could do blindfolded. I grasp his shoulder. "Look at me, Owen." He complies, fear darkening his blue eyes. "You will be fine. Many times I have flown. Across the country. Over oceans. Look at this as a new experience, an adventure. Trust me, it is less scary than getting married."

He laughs. "Yeah, I guess you're right. Thanks."

We unload the matching suitcases—a wedding gift from me and Rosa.

"Manny?"

My name sounds foreign coming from my young friend, who rarely calls me anything but Preacher. "Yes?"

"You going to be all right? I mean, I know Carmelita's death has been really hard on you. It's a bad time for me to be leaving. I should have cancelled this…"

I hold up my hand. "Stop. Cancelling a honeymoon? This is a celebration of life, Owen. Go. Be happy. Staying here would be a waste. There is nothing you can do about my grief. It is part of life. Perhaps the hardest part. God and I, we will journey through it together."

"I just thought…"

"No more thinking. Go open the door for your beautiful bride, and let the kissing begin."

Southbound now, Rosa and I drive in silence as we cross onto Key Largo. The highlight of our drive comes next—visiting our son.

Another mile or so and we will see the leaping dolphin on his dive shop sign. We cruise past the Waffle House, where old Eli waves at our car as if knowing the precise moment we would pass. Rosa waves back, mumbling "unbelievable" as always. No explanation necessary. The white-haired, wild-eyed Eli has been a fixture at the Waffle House since before we married, and was as wrinkled then as he is now.

Rosa reaches for my hand. Fingers entwine, resting on my thigh. "Let's take Alex to Bayside Grill. He likes their mahi-mahi sandwich."

I nod.

Thank the Lord she understands my silence. Rosa is not one to insist on analyzing, dissecting. We will talk later. For now, my head and heart are filled with prayers for Owen, Ana, and Rosa. Always Rosa, whose legs still cannot bear her weight, despite years of therapy. The Spirit whispers there is another who needs my prayers, causing my left hand to tighten on the steering wheel. When the paramedics arrived at Carmie's funeral, my attention was on my sister, crumpled at her daughter's gravesite, but I glimpsed the woman, lying on the ground, before her family surrounded her.

They say she was Ana's best friend. They say she loved our Carmie. They say it was an unavoidable accident. But how can I pray for the one who killed my niece? I tell myself again that through God, all things are possible. He carried me through every mission trip, even when we were surrounded by AIDS-afflicted children. He guided me through Alex and Dulce's teen years, through Rosa's hospitalization after the collision, through my brother Roberto's death. For every challenge, every painful experience, I poured out my heart to Him in prayer.

But for this woman who killed our Carmie, no prayers will come. I turn on the radio to drown out the Spirit's whisper, though I know the Spirit will not be so easily muffled.

Chapter 6

Josie

The steering wheel mocks me as I settle into the driver's seat. I would rather wrap my hand around a Burmese python than grab hold of that black vinyl, but grab it I must in order to remove the toxin that's been poisoning my family these past weeks: me. My breaths come fast as I turn the key that will, in seconds, reduce my home to a reflection in the rearview mirror.

I drive right past that white rose cross without a sideways glance. My eyes don't dare veer toward the colorful array of bears, ponies, and bunnies, or the ghostlike votives that glow brightly every night. Yes, I've seen them from my window, illuminating the cross so it stands out like a lighthouse on a midnight ocean. I've stared at it for hours, asking the universe "why?"

But the universe has nothing to say.

I do not glance at the porch swing where Ana and I sat many an afternoon, coffee in hand, waiting for Savanna, Mitchell, and Ashley to come home from school. "Our spot," where no topic was left untouched. Family, jobs, global warming, politics. And once, just after she'd knocked down my walls and entered best friend territory, I told her about Roxy and my years of having only books and middle-aged librarians as friends.

"Couldn't you make new friends?" she'd asked.

"Small town, and I mean dot-on-the-map small. Roxy was queen bee of our class and graced that pedestal through high school. The boys loved her and the girls wanted to be her best friend. And when you're the queen bee's enemy…"

"I see," she had said, compassion softening her eyes. "But I don't understand. That's not the Josie I know."

I told her about this bookworm's metamorphosis in college. How I summoned up the guts of those strong women in literature and discovered my own suppressed leadership qualities. And that I could be funny. Express opinions. Encourage people.

"Good," she'd said. "I like this version better. And for the record, this best friend isn't going anywhere."

But what probably brought us closer than anything was the phone call. We were laughing over my parent-teacher conference faux paus when her cell went off. She smiled and said, "It's my brother Roberto," but seconds after her cheery hello, her face wnet white. It was not her brother, it was her niece. It would never be her brother again.

"*Mi hermano*," she sobbed. "A heart attack. He is gone." I did the only thing there was to do. I held her tight out there on that porch swing, letting her sobs soak my T-shirt until the last drop fell.

I shake my head in an effort to lose the memories. Just keep driving, Josie. Gold and crimson treetops line the side streets as the distance grows between me and my house. Lincoln Elementary appears in the windshield. Within those walls are nine years of holiday shows, PTA meetings, science fairs, and bake sales. Memories threaten to swallow me up, forcing me back to my cozy brick house in the shade of the oak we planted a decade ago. No, I have to do this for Mitch. And Ash. It is the only way. Until this moment, I didn't know it was possible for the fiery pain inside me to blaze even hotter.

Is there no limit?

Carol, the secretary, offers no comments about the beautiful autumn leaves or the upcoming craft fair. We are now polite strangers. Using words like "imperative" and "crucial," I hand her the envelope. She promises it will get to Mitch immediately. The note inside says it is extremely important he come home after school. There is something on the table he needs to see. If nothing else, the part about his cell phone on the bed will bring him home. Once he sees my message, he'll know he doesn't have to run away. He can stay home without me there to ruin his life.

A night in Atlanta and ten more hours of driving leaves Miami's bright lights in my rearview. Reflectors lining U.S. 1 illuminate the road ahead. Soon there will be nothing but the Atlantic on one side and the Gulf on the other, swallowed by a black, moonless sky. I should have already stopped for the night, but something in me needs to get off the mainland before another sunrise. Please let there be a cheap place to stay in Key Largo. Next to me, a brown and white stuffed bunny, soft as Clover, leans back against the passenger seat.

Say it for Mama, Mrs. Caruso. Tell her you can say, "I have a bunny."
Tengo un canejito.

I'd walked into a gas station just outside Miami, and there it sat, looking sadly displaced amidst fuzzy manatees, sea turtles, and dolphins. Stuffed-animal delights. For a heartbeat, a blessed, happy heartbeat, I forgot. Smiling, I reached for the Clover-sized bunny, thinking it would be perfect for...

Oh.

With quaking arms, I crushed it to my chest, thinking about the child in the ground for two weeks now, and the family I'd left less than forty-eight hours ago. When had they read the letter that tried—but surely failed—to explain what I was doing?

I love you all so much. Please forgive me for what happened, and for leaving. By the time you get this, I will be on my way to stay with cousin Tina. It's what's best for everyone. I'll come back. I promise.

Would they want me back?

Before walking away from the life I could never have again, I'd called Aunt Theresa...with everything inside me rallying against that decision.

"I'm doing more harm than good here, Auntie. And I can't talk to Rob. This is too...it's so...complicated."

She understood, of course. She always understood. She assured me she loved the opportunity to watch the kids and affirmed my decision. "You know we all love and support you, sweetie. You do what you have to do, and make sure the good Lord is part of that equation." She knows He is not. "I'll take good care of your family. Don't you worry."

Don't worry about my family? It would be easier to *crawl* to Key West. But all that mattered was that my kids and Rob would be loved. Cared for. No doubt she was there before the last school bell rang.

Few cars make the southerly trek on this November night. Key Largo's Mile Marker 118 welcomes me as I enter a part of the country I'd only read about. Soon 117, 116…a strand of pearly islands linked with bridges will help me count down to Mile Marker 1 in Key West. After that, there will be nothing but ocean.

My bleary eyes scan the roadside for hotel signs, something like a "Dew Drop Inn" where the rates won't deplete my sparsely-filled wallet. Ah, "Shelly's." An illuminated "vcncy" sign beckons me toward a small gravel parking lot. The burned-out letters look like they haven't glowed in years. Just past the happy manatee mailbox, a large pink conch shell sculpture abuts the door, where a woman about my age is turning the office's outside lock. She looks my way, shielding her eyes from the headlight's glare.

I lower the driver's side window, allowing warm, ocean air to satiate the car's interior. "Excuse me, can I still check in?"

She walks toward me, shaking her head but smiling all the same. "Now what is it about closin' time that always brings folks around?" A clip-on nametag introduces her as Zara. I can't decide if sounds European or Martian.

"Sorry. I'll go…if it's too late." Translation: please, please, please let me stay.

"Nah. It's okay. Pull over there behind the office and I'll put ya in number two." She points into the darkness. "Down there's the beach. Not too big, but real pretty at sunset. Other side of the island gets the sunrise."

I grimace, but manage to nod. Can I face more sunsets?

The gravel road is lined with boxy duplexes, each with two numbered doors. Peeling paint coats the weathered buildings, except for bare patches where tropical storms have stolen the last flake. Two doors are clearly marked 1 and 2. I park and head for the office, breathing in the heavy tropical air, tasting a hint of salt and sea life.

Paperwork complete, Zara hands me a key. A real key, vintage 1970s, attached to a plastic disc with a hand-painted two.

"Anything else I can do for you tonight, hon?"

Not unless you can raise the dead. I shake my head, shoving the receipt into my purse.

"You've come a long way, haven't ya, now?" She looks into my eyes again like she is trying to figure something out. Maybe she sees the scarlet "K" burning a hole in my chest.

"Yeah."

"You drive all the way from Illinois by yourself?" She pronounces the "s" at the end of Illinois.

"Yeah." I swallow, but the saliva strains to get past an unexpected lump.

Zara nods with an "Mmm hmm," as if she'd known. "You sure you don't need anything before I go?"

"No, I'm good." The irony of my words is lost on Zara.

"All righty, then. Goodnight. I'm open at eight tomorrow."

Half a turn of my retro key swings the door open far too easily. A tiny lizard scampers across the doorframe, and thankfully, to the outside wall. Inside, a dorm-size television rests atop two wooden orange crates covered with blue burlap. The bathroom sink is usable only by first closing the door. In one window, a rusted air conditioner unit rests in peace, allowing the night breeze to do its job.

Oh, man…the Bates Motel. Good enough, though, for what I paid.

I set my suitcase on the small dresser, my purse on a chair. Hopefully, no crawlies will tack up a "Home Sweet Home" sign between now and tomorrow morning. Everything appears clean. No complaints there. And really…all I need is a bed, which appears functional enough. The door, not so much. Not sure it will stand up to a large madman with an axe… or even a small one. I slide a chair across the room, jamming it under the doorknob, TV drama style, then freeze to listen for outside noises.

The song of night critters fills the silence, accompanied by a distant engine rumbling down U.S. 1. Sun-faded curtains, standard issue with every haunted motel, rustle with a small sea breeze.

It's just one night. Okay, so no one knows I'm here, which is slightly creepy. And if a madman does get me, well…it will end all this torment. That isn't going to happen for two reasons. One, this is not a Freddy Kruger movie, and two, there's nothing in the dark that isn't there in the light, just like I always tell Ashley.

Footsteps on gravel. The crunching intensifies, unmistakably moving toward my door. I hold my breath, longing for Rob's protective presence. Has the sound stopped, or is my heartbeat drowning it out? I stand, taking a step toward the chair securing the door, fearing I may need to hold it in place.

Loud raps on the flimsy door send me banging into the chair.

"You okay in there, hon?" The voice on the other side of the door could only be Zara's.

"Fine. Just stumbled." Hopefully my words aren't as shaky as the rest of me.

"You left your license in the office. Here, I'll just slide it under."

A picture taken when the man said "smile," when I could smile, appears beneath the door.

"Thanks."

"You're welcome. See ya in the morning."

Soft golden light illuminates a cyan sky and tranquil Gulf waters. Probably not as dramatic as the sunrise on the island's Atlantic side, but powerful nonetheless. I slip off my gym shoes, easing toes into grainy sand already absorbing the warmth of a new day. Wisps of blue hover over the horizon line as if someone painted them there.

Are You up there in Your ivory tower of clouds? Can You do all the things they say? Did You make this ocean and fill it with everything from plankton to whales? I scream the words inside my head, not wanting to awaken sleeping tourists with wild rants. *If You did, then You're able to stop a car... or a kitten...or a child. With only a blink. But You didn't! You didn't!*

No one hears my mental tirade. Not the gulls, not the ragged dog loping down toward the water, not even the guy having a smoke outside his cabin. No, only One is meant to hear these words. But am I talking to Him? Or are my words simply dissipating in that golden blue expanse? Throughout my life, I never once considered speaking to Him. Never asked for anything, never had those little prayer conversations like Ana does. Hardly gave Him a passing thought. But if people like Ana and Aunt Theresa and Rob's parents are right, then He needs to hear.

You obliterated the life of a sweet little angel. Devastated a family and shattered the best friend I ever had. But that wasn't enough! You had to put me behind that wheel. Not a drug dealer or a rapist, oh no. Josie. The soccer mom. The librarian. This is who You chose to destroy.

The wildfire sweeping through me blurs my vision with its fierce heat.

"Hi, lady."

A shadow darkens the sand in front of me. My jaw clenches as I raise my head.

He is just about Carmelita's age. Tow-headed, freckle-faced. Squatting next to me, he doesn't notice my shock as he scoops warm morning sand into his plastic bucket.

"I'm Noah. Me and Daddy are gonna build a sand castle. The biggest one in the whole world." Little arms stretch to form a circle that will embrace the universe.

He oozes Carmelita's joy...before that night.

"Oh. That's nice." Fighting resentment, I snap the words as if saying, "get off my beach," but the boy is heedless of my attitude. My rudeness. Shame follows the final syllable.

"You can watch us if you want."

"Thanks." I force warmth into my tone. "I was just leaving."

"Where are you going?"

My tongue feels sandpapery as I am forced to confront what I have done. "To visit my cousin," I rasp. "Wh—where's your parents?"

"Mommy's getting dressed and Daddy is somewhere. I'll go find him." Good idea.

He takes off running, looking everywhere but right in front of him, where a large piece of driftwood lies in his path.

"Hey! Watch…"

The tangled wood catches his leg and sends him flying.

"Daddy!"

His shriek worries two gulls from their crab snack. As I hurry forward, they ascend with their own high-pitched screams. A man reaches the boy as my knees hit sand.

"Okay, Noah. Daddy's here. I've got you." He scoops up the wailing child, holds him tight. Noah's arms wrap around his daddy's neck in a chokehold.

Walking away might be rude at this point, but it's what I want to do. Still…

"Is he all right?" I manage.

The dad smiles. "Oh, sure. He'll be fine, won't you, Noah?"

Noah sniffs his answer and groans. He raises his head from his father's shoulder. "Where were you?"

"Right there." He points to the shade of a palm tree not ten feet away from where the boy and I had been talking. Funny how I never noticed him.

"You were?"

"Yes, silly. What do you think, I'd leave you here all alone? I was watching you the whole time. I saw you talking to this nice lady."

He does not see the scarlet "K" beneath my shirt.

"Okay." He sniffs dramatically. "My knee hurts, Daddy."

"I know, buddy. Come on; let's go show it to Mommy. I bet she has a bandage and kisses to make it all better. Say goodbye to the nice lady."

"Goodbye, lady."

They walk toward one of the strange boxy cabins, Noah's head resting on his father's shoulder. I hope nothing ever happens to that boy that can't be fixed with a bandage and kisses.

His eyes bore into me from across the aisle as I focus on a steaming cup of Waffle House coffee and a half-eaten blueberry muffin. Please let it be my imagination. I glance his way, then down again. No such luck. Those crystal blue eyes peer out from a century of wrinkles, lasering my shattered heart. That wild white hair hasn't seen a comb since the Nixon Administration. A crazy's homed in on me. So much for finding myself in solitude.

"More coffee, ma'am?" The smiling young waitress stands poised to pour, her white "Maddie" nametag tilting at an angle on her shirt.

"Thanks."

"So you staying on a bit or hitting the road?"

She means well. I bite my lip. She really does. "Hitting the road."

"South or north?" She whips a notepad out of her uniform pocket, tallies up my tab, and hands me the bill.

"Key West."

"Oh, you'll have a great time there for sure. You ever been?"

"No."

"It's a real party town. You just missed Fantasy Fest—it's always in October. Talk about wild! Pirates in Paradise is next. Plenty of artsy stuff, too. You stayin' long?"

No doubt she considers this a simple question. When was the last time I didn't know where I'd be on any given day?

"Not sure." I glance toward Mr. Blue Eyes again, only to find his gaze hasn't wavered one bit.

Before I can look away, he speaks. "Key West is too far!"

Several customers pan looks in the silence that follows. Blood flushes my cheeks.

Maddie bends down toward me. "Don't you mind him," she whispers. "He's harmless enough. Just hangs around here and mutters. Kinda strange, but nothin' nasty."

"Key West is too far!" Louder this time, causing a dozen or so customers to stare—some at him, others at the target of his words. Me.

Maddie turns toward him. "Oh, now, Eli, Key West ain't more than a couple hours from here. Not that far at all."

He slowly raises his hand, blatantly pointing his finger at me.

"The sky is far enough," he says, thankfully quieter this time. It doesn't matter, though, as everyone surely is listening as they pretend to eat their breakfasts. Maddie rolls her eyes and whispers "See what I mean?"

"Okay, Eli, she got it." Maddie also utilizes her pointer finger and aims it at the strange man. "The sky is far enough. Why don't you go back to drinking your coffee now?"

To my surprise, his eyes lose their focus on me, as though someone flicked a switch. He obediently picks up his cup and sips. A soft breath escapes me, one I didn't even know I was holding in.

"He's been hanging around here since I was just a munchkin." Maddie bends in my direction again, whispering her words. "He was old then, too. Folks around here are just plain used to him. Maybe he's talkin' 'bout that nasty storm comin' our way. Weatherman said it should hit in an hour or so. You'll have to find a place to stop. You know..." Maddie squints her eyes, taps her pencil. "Seems to me he said that before, to a girl 'bout eighteen. Couple months back. She was heading to Key West, just like you." Maddie jabs the pencil stub behind her ear. "Oh, well...that's just Eli being his crazy old self."

Clouds laze across the sky, but there's no sign of a storm...except the one in my soul.

Maddie catches the direction of my gaze. "Oh, I know what you're thinking. Blue skies and all smiles. Well, one minute, it's slather on the suntan lotion. The next thing you know, wham! That rain's beatin' down like a monster. Know what I mean?"

"Yeah." For the first time since leaving home, the words flow right out of me. "I know exactly what you mean."

The strange man gazes out the window, cup in hand, no longer commenting on my destination. A subtle movement of his head locks our eyes. I can't look away. His face softens. Time stops. A slight nod, an affirmation, but of what? He refocuses on the view outside, leaving me hanging in the Twilight Zone.

"Ma'am?" Maddie touches my shoulder, breaking the spell. "Anything else?"

"No, but thanks."

I pay the bill and make a right out of the lot, knowing it will be my last turn until I hit Mile Marker 1.

It's a real party town.

What was I thinking? That each day of changing B&B sheets and greeting customers would be followed by the peace of a golden sunset? My image of secluded beaches serenaded by the soft rustle of palms gets waylaid with raucous music and noisy bars. Of course, Key West is Margaritaville. Everyone knows that. It's like Daytona during spring break, only year-round. But there has to be someplace there for me, some secluded patch of sand where I can hide away and think.

I cruise past Shell World, the biggest seashell store I've ever seen. Ashley's eyes would bug right out of her head if she were with me. Mitch would have loved the shark jaws and pirate swords window display. No way would we haven driven past it. I ache to go in and buy them something, but I continue on, southward bound, right past the welcome sign for Islamorada. By the time I hit Duck Key, the storm front is moving in like the "monster" Maddie described. Palm fronds swish crazily as the line of black clouds creeps forward with menacing flashes of light. Maybe Weird Eli was right. Key West might be too far for today. But there is still time before it hits full force, and I want to get as close as possible. It's rain, not fog. As long as I can see, I can drive.

A few more bridges fill my rear view mirror before I pass a wooden sign with words painted in bright blue: "Welcome to Cielo Azul Key." It takes a few seconds for the words to sink in.

El cielo es azul.

So I'm in Blue Sky Key. Pretty name, but not appropriate for today. Slate gray clouds tumble overhead like atmospheric bullies in the eastern sky. Daylight turns to dusk within minutes. The gusting wind grabs everything in its path, taking paper bags and palm fronds for a sky-high ride. A short distance away, waves pummel the shore like cymbals with saltwater sprays. Bring it on, Mother Nature, I don't care. Key West or bust. I switch the windshield wipers to hurricane mode. My foot remains steady on the gas.

Smack!

Something hits my car.

I scream. My heart careens as wild as the wind. Could it be—?

I floor the brakes. Squeeze the wheel with both hands. A branch tumbles over the hood and disappears. Just a branch. A sob escapes. I am back in that car. That foggy road…

Mom, what happened?

I don't know, Ash.

I shake my head to fight the shiver that wracks my body with pain. I need to get out. Now. I close my eyes. Images permeate my brain. The haunting fog, screams in the night, crimson blood pooling on the street. Breathe, Josie, breathe.

Relief eludes me.

Okay, there is no one here but me. I have to fix this…fast. I suck in a breath and put the car back in drive, switching to high beams.

A fence and gravel driveway loom ahead. I tighten my grip as the car crunches over crushed shells, past a white sign. "Help Wanted, Inquire Within." I stop in the driveway, hoping the homeowners don't mind if I wait it out in the car. Possibly not the best plan. Those black clouds clearly have volatile intentions. At the rate they're moving, they couldn't be more than ten minutes away. Huge drops pelt the windshield, like someone up there is crying a million tears. Rumbles emit from deep within the bellies of the thunderheads, sending a brown and white dog racing for shelter under the house porch.

My plan, exactly. Only my porch is a Key West bed and breakfast.

Chapter 7

Preacher

Melissa's hand ponytails her blond tresses to keep them from whipping wildly into her country girl face. Ah, such a face, that one.

Her gentle beauty is but a reflection of the heart within. She will make a fine mother, despite her youth and unfortunate circumstances. Eighteen and single is no way to start out, but God is with her, and she is surrounded by more love than she realizes.

We step off the porch, instantly pelted by fat raindrops. To my left, a wooden sign bangs against the fence—a sign that says far more than its words. Despite the rain, I stop to look at the girl who arrived here frightened and broken just three months earlier. She turns to face me.

"I put the sign up, Preacher, just like you said to do if I ever decided to go back." Melissa swipes raindrops from her cheeks. "I've thought about it. Our talks and stuff. Then that letter came."

She looks down at the water making rivulets through the sparse sea grass. I wait.

"My parents said all this stuff about family and love, working things out." Her voice thickens. She sniffs. "I don't know…it just got to me. Lately I've been missing autumn in Michigan, the colorful leaves, Mom's caramel apple pie. And Dad." She laughs, perhaps at a memory. "You should see him fussing over his peach preserves. Fall out here just feels kinda like more summer, you know?"

"I see." And I mean it. I have experienced the wonder of autumn in the Midwest—the scent of wood burning in fireplaces, gold and crimson treetops set against a clear blue sky. God does some of his best work there, but I do not believe it is truly what Melissa misses.

"Are you mad?" Her forehead crinkles. "I know it leaves you shorthanded. Maybe someone else will come, you know, just like I did."

My heart does not know whether to plummet or soar. It is what I have wanted for her. What I have prayed for. And yet...there will be such emptiness. For Rosa, as well. We have watched her faith take root and blossom; witnessed her transformation from a scared, runaway teenager to a nurturing mother-to-be. Grown to love her.

The rain strikes harder, gusting as the sky darkens. I put my arm around Melissa's shoulder and head for the barn. "Mad? Have I not told you to consider this all along? You are blessed with parents who love you, and someone else who aches for your return."

"Yeah, well, it didn't feel that way before I left. All that yelling and preaching. Telling me how to handle, you know...my situation. Dad got so angry when I said I wanted an abortion, I thought he was going to kick me out."

"But he did not. He has been a good father, no?" A white flash over the Atlantic prompts us to pick up speed.

"Yeah. I guess it was *me* that kicked me out."

I smile to myself, knowing well how that feels. "Your parents were scared, Melissa. Just like you. They feared you would make a mistake that would haunt you the rest of your life." Children do not understand how we fear for them. Thank goodness my Dulce and Alex are grown and doing well, but still...there were times. Finding marijuana in Alex's room when he was nineteen. Dulce wanting to marry that...that boy. Thank goodness she finally saw him for what he was and married Andy instead. "They love you beyond measure. Enough to give you the time you needed here, even though it was killing them. Enough to write those letters and call every other day."

"They did?"

"*Sí.* I kept my promise not to tell. Until now." Secrets. The weight of them bears down on me daily. Keeping them is part of my calling, but God forgive me, sometimes it feels like a curse. "Go home to them, Melissa. Perhaps you will consider giving that David another chance, too. After all, he is a big part of this picture."

"Yeah, I know." She looks out to sea as a rumble emerges from the belly of a storm cloud.

"Since I am unloading secrets today, I will tell you another. David called me, too. Many times. He loves you as much as you love him... and do not tell me differently." I have never met Melissa's David, father of her child, but I like him. Whether the two will reunite and form a family...this is in God's hands. I cannot help hoping it will be so.

"Really?" Her eyes widen, hopeful. "You think?"

"Sí. I know." Another flash and crash make us both jump. "Come on, it's getting dangerous out here, and Connor is probably scared." We run the last few steps.

"Maybe we still have a chance," Melissa yells into the wind. "I'll see him first thing...when I get back."

"And send me some of those peach preserves. We need something to remind us it is truly fall, not just bonefish season." I grab the door handle and we enter the welcome refuge of the barn.

"You got it." A smile glimmers her words.

As my eyes struggle to adjust to the muted light, a small hand grabs my arm.

"Where *were* you guys?" Connor holds tight, sending a wave of guilt my way for not getting here sooner. "I was waiting *forever*."

"You were waiting less than ten minutes, *chico*." I sweep my free arm toward the barn's many occupants. "And you had plenty of friends to keep you company, no?"

"Yeah, well...it's just that we have to get the others inside. Diego and the donkeys are still out there."

"Ah, you were not frightened, then?"

"Course not." He lets go of my arm, straightening his shoulders like a Marine. "I'm eight now. Not a little kid anymore."

Melissa covers her mouth and turns away, coughing to hide her laughter. I shake my head and smile, until a ghostly howl fills the barn—a warning this storm has dishonorable intentions.

"You two stay put while I bring in our rain-soaked llama and his two *amigos*. Comfort those who need it, like the goats and rabbits. And our new arrival, of course." We all turn to look at Lightning, slumped against his enclosure. That colt is going to need a miracle, but I keep that thought inside.

"I want to go, too." Connor implores me with his eyes. I expected nothing less.

"Stay puts means stay put. The animals need you, and so does Melissa." I decide to add an incentive. "You can be the boss while I'm gone."

Connor's fist punches the air. "Yes!"

I grab some halters and head outside. Darker now, the sky sends wind-whipped rain at an angle. Diego and the donkeys wait at the pasture gate, their eyes telling me I should have done this sooner. They are right, of course, but sooner was not an option. Rescuing Lightning was no easy task. We spent an hour getting his frail body into the trailer. My muscles have not forgotten the effort.

"Okay, okay *animales*. I am here. Come." I slip a halter around each head. Even Diego cooperates, anxious to get inside. "You will soon be safe and dry." As I lead them out, a black streak catches my eye.

"Lily, Lily, come back!" Connor flies from the open barn door, pursuing a Newfoundland triple his size.

"Connor, get back here!" Melissa runs after him.

Ay yi yi. Does no one listen to me? I trot with my hoofed entourage, yelling for the kids to get back inside. Connor reaches the dog and grabs her collar.

"Go, go, go!" I shout, my words stolen by a gust. No matter, they head back at a frantic pace. We reach the door, Melissa grabbing the donkeys as I struggle with a suddenly obstinate Diego.

"*Váminos*, you stubborn llama." Diego ignores me, staring past my shoulder. I follow his gaze. Someone is crouched by the outer fence that runs along Highway One. I close my eyes. Take a breath. *Oh, Lord, what have you brought me on the winds of this storm?*

Chapter 8

Josie

Somewhere out in nature's mayhem, a baby is crying.

Where is its mother? Why is an infant out in this storm? I strain to listen, hoping to locate the mournful sound. It begins again, somewhere close by, and I will my eyes to see through the watery onslaught. This is crazy. What's wrong with this world? I grab the door handle.

Flash! Crack! I jump at the lightning. Its illumination reveals the "baby."

"Oh, that poor thing," I say to no one but the stuffed bunny in my passenger seat. I shake my head, because the fact that the "baby" is a miniature goat stuck in the fence is still going to get me soaked. Probably fried by lightning, too. But my heart won't let me stay put with that critter getting pelted.

I fly toward the fence, drenched in the seconds it takes to reach the pathetic goat. A loose rope sags around its neck. Newly budded horns curve backward, just enough to let its head slip into a makeshift stockade. My approach only serves to make its escape efforts and bleating more frantic than before.

"Looks like somebody lost you."

It answers with a loud bleat.

"Okay. Okay. Shhh. Let's get you out of there." Another bright flash scares us both, but lights up a strange scene I hadn't noticed when I drove past. Beyond the house, a family is scurrying around a large fenced-in area, trying to coax a menagerie into a barn. Is that big one a llama? Behind it walk a donkey and a moose-sized dog. Where am I? No time to think about it now. The goat's hysteria increases with each passing second. Coming at this from the other side might be best. Once it's free, I'll be able to grab the leash and get it to the barn.

The nearby gate is, amazingly, unlocked. Within seconds I am inside the large enclosure.

"Okay, critter, here we go." Despite the rain whipping my face, I keep my tone calm, hoping it knows I mean no harm. "Bear with me here." I shout over the wild wind. "My goat experience is rather limited."

A little muscle is enough to widen the gap in the wire fence. I gently angle the goat's head, wondering if goats are prone to biting people. I've heard they eat anything, even metal, which means bones would be no challenge at all.

"Come on, goat, we're almost there." One nubby horn eases through the opening, followed quickly by the second. Rain pelts us like bullets now as I grab the leash and head toward the crazy scene by the barn. The next crash shakes the earth, sending my newfound friend and me running across slippery sea grass at breakneck speed. Through the blur of water, a weathered sign, Rosa's Haven, stands out above the barn. Beneath it in smaller letters are the words *Refugio de Rosa*. A young woman and boy are running inside with their animals, but the man and llama stand still in the downpour, watching our approach.

"Inside! Quickly!" He shouts, pointing to the barn door as another flash and crash spurs us on. "Vaminos!"

I need no further encouragement. We run in, followed by the man and beast. He shuts the big wooden door, stares at me. I must look a sight, standing there dripping, still holding the goat leash. He just shakes his head.

"Another lost lamb, I see." He says the words quiet as a prayer, with a lovely accent a bit stronger than Ana's and golden brown skin a shade darker than hers. Which makes me think of Carmelita. No, Josie, don't go there.

I point to my critter. "Not a goat?"

He smiles. Oddly enough, that too reminds me of Ana...and

Carmelita. But his smile is older than Ana's, with crinkles around the edges that match the crinkles around his eyes. Thick salt and pepper hair perfectly frames his distinguished, weathered face. Kind eyes reflect a goodness within, but something sad looms just beneath the surface.

"Si, she is a goat." He laughs. "Definitely a goat. Her name is Lucy. My mischievous Lucy, always wanting to see the world. It was kind of you to return her. *Muchas gracias.*" He wipes his wet hand on his jeans and holds it out. "Manuel Delgado. Call me Preacher. Everyone does, except my wife."

I return the gesture. "Josie." My attempt at a friendly expression is foiled by a low growl from a big black beast less than ten feet away. Its thick, wavy fur cannot hide the hundred or more pounds of solid muscle. One mighty chomp from that wide muzzle and I'm history, but intelligent brown eyes glare into mine. Seeing through me. Seeing the killer inside. It knows… and it's here to deliver justice in the most painful way possible.

"Oh, Lily, stop. She is a friend." Preacher walks over and squats down by the furry beast, talking to her in a warm buttermilk tone, petting the giant head. "Please, *señora*, if you do not mind. Slowly reach out your hand so she may sniff it. She will not harm you."

He's got to be joking. Against whatever reason I still possess, I reach out my hand, firmly believing it will be the last time I ever see it. The big black nose sniffs my fingertips, my palm, then partway up my arm. A giant pink tongue appears. Within seconds I'm slobbered from the elbow down…and surprisingly happy about it.

"There. That is settled. Now you are friends. Newfoundlands are very good-natured, but wary of strangers. She just had to know you were not a threat. We do not normally take dogs and cats, but Lily here was a special case. I fear Frisco, our other pooch, is still outside. He came to us on his own. I wonder where he is waiting out the storm."

Tell him, Josie. Tell him you saw a brown and white dog run under the porch. Why is every word such a struggle?

"Under the porch." I hadn't meant for it to come out as a whisper.

"Pardon, señora. Did you say something?"

"The porch. A brown and white dog ran under it."

"Ah." He sighs, then shakes his head with a smile. "That would be Frisco. A bit of a gypsy spirit in that one."

Leathered hands reach into a storage closet, emerging with towels. He places one around my neck as though we are old acquaintances. The friendly gesture warms my rain-chilled skin.

"This should help make you a bit more comfortable," he says, then turns toward the others. "Here. Get some towels. The animals can wait for just one moment, no?" He tosses one to the boy and teenaged girl before turning his attention back to me. "How about some coffee? We get stuck in here every now and then, so I put in a coffeemaker."

"Stuck?"

"You know, sometimes a storm, sometimes a sick animal or a late-night birth. That is how your young friend Lucy was born. She came into this world at two in the morning." He bends down to gently scratch Lucy's neck. "Been causing trouble ever since, haven't you, *chiquita*?" She nuzzles his arm in response. Oh yeah, she's a real troublemaker.

"Come on, Lucy girl. Let's get you back with your mama." The man holds out his hand for me to relinquish the leash. Walking between the goat and llama, he stops in an area where a bigger version of Lucy munches hay.

The smell of wet fur mingles with those of musty hay, sweet oats, and damp wood in a primordial scent that swirls about, intoxicating me with each breath. It seeps in, easing tense muscles. Outside the storm beats the island like a heavyweight champ, but in here, there is safety and peace, even amidst the animal chaos. I close my eyes, breath deep. For just a heartbeat...all is well.

At the other end of the barn, the boy—probably younger than my Ashley—plops onto a stool, drying himself before turning to the monstrous Lily. She could munch him like an oyster cracker. Instead, she obediently raises each paw at his command. The girl, possibly his sister, looks to be college age. She hustles animals into pens as I attempt to dry off. The boy's red hair flies as he chases three crazy chickens, eventually corralling them into a large coop. I think of Ana and how she would giggle at this scene, then shove that thought from my mind. Desperate to refocus, I watch mismatched sheep and two ostriches lay claim to the pen against the far wall. Next to it, another pen holds the smallest pony I've ever seen, accompanied by a pair of donkeys. But it is the pathetic creature opposite them that tears at my already shredded heart.

The scarred and skeletal appaloosa barely clings to life. It leans against a wooden post, head hung low, seemingly oblivious to the surrounding activity. I glance at the other animals, checking for signs of abuse. All appear healthy...until I see scars on the donkeys' backs. But all receive nothing but kind words and gentle touches from their caregivers.

Next to me, a large Siamese cat licks rain off its body, sniffs the hay, and circles, exposing the tail I hadn't seen before. My hand flies to my mouth. Mangled pink skin and a few sparse patches of fur are all that survived some horrendous accident...or abuse. What kind of place have I stumbled onto? I stroke the cat's head; she purrs like a jet engine.

"I see you have met Charro."

I jump. Hadn't heard Preacher approach, even with that llama beside him.

"She is one of our permanent residents. You would not have wanted to see her the day she arrived." He runs a gentle hand over the scorched and mangled tail. "Poor *gato*. Got caught in a fire. Please excuse me while I get Diego and the others settled in, then we will have proper introductions." He turns to the buck-toothed creature at his side. "Ah, Diego, you smell like a stinky wet beast." A sweet tone belies his words, and Diego surely considers himself complimented. Gesturing toward stacks of hay, he says, "Please, have a seat. It is not quite an easy chair, but it is the best we have here in the barn."

My heart tells my head to say the words that used to come easy before the world crashed and burned. I suck in a breath. "I can help."

"Really? Muchas gracias. I see a wayward rabbit there." He points to a narrow opening between two bags of grain. "Would you feel comfortable picking her up? That is our Sunny."

"Sí. Tengo un canejito." I don't know why it comes out in Spanish.

I know exactly two Spanish sentences, *two*, yet the words fly out as though it were my primary language.

He stops, eyebrows raised, and smiles that Ana smile again. "*Hables Español?*"

What was I thinking? "No, I don't really speak Spanish. I was just beginning to learn."

"And the first thing you learn is 'I have a bunny'?"

I hadn't considered the oddity of it until now. "Yes."

"Very unusual. *Bunny*, not rabbit. Hmm." Mumbling to himself, he leads Diego to a stall. "Very unusual."

Peeking out from behind the grain bag, the floppy-eared canejito eyes me suspiciously. I extend my hand, speaking soft and low, hoping to gain its trust. "Come on, little bun. I won't hurt you. Come on." The rabbit takes two steps in my direction; enough for me to get one hand under its front legs and slide it forward. Placing my other hand under its back feet, I lift. Her soft warmth against my chest floods me with images of Carmelita.

Can I hold Clover, Mrs. Caruso?

I am going to teach you Spanish, Mrs. Caruso. Say 'tengo un canejito.' It means, "I have a bunny."

I made this picture of me and you and Clover, Mrs. Caruso. That big heart means I love you.

My throat thickens as I set Sunny down in the oversized rabbit hutch. What am I doing here? This is not where I belong. These are not my people. Sunny hops over to her buddies, like Ashley did that night of the Halloween birthday party. Then I picked her up. In the fog. And the kitten ran into the street.

Stop it, Josie. *Stop.*

And that's what I'm doing in a stranger's barn on a storm-drenched island, fifteen hundred miles from everyone I love.

A white flash, an ear-shattering crack. Demonic rumbles give way to utter darkness. The storm has swallowed our light. Something smacks against the outside wall, but it is another chilling sound, just half-a-second later, that quickens my heart. Shattering glass, crunching metal.

"What the heck was that?" The girl's voice quivers from just a few feet away, her outline slowly forming as my eyes adjust.

"I am not sure, Melissa." Preacher's voice comes from a different direction. "Sounded bad, though. Something got damaged out there, that is for sure."

Yeah, and I bet I know what.

Despite his words, the man's voice is a comfort in the darkness. "Is everyone okay?"

"I'm all right, Preacher." The boy's trembling tone betrays the confident words. "I'm just sitting here with Lucy and mama goat. Lucy's scared. She's shaking. I'm petting her to calm her down."

"God job, Connor. You stay with the goats and I will find my way over there in *un momento*."

"What about my dad, Preacher? You think he's okay? You think he'll know there's a storm? He had it bad last night."

Unless he's blind *and* deaf, it would be pretty hard not to notice.

"Do not worry, Connor. Your father has lived on this island a long time, has he not? He has been through many storms. Perhaps too many. He is in a nice, sturdy trailer. We will check on him when the storm passes."

"All right."

"How about our unexpected visitor? How are you faring, Señora?"

Glad for the darkness, actually. No one here needs to see my pain. "Fine, but my car…

"Hmm, yes. It is too crazy out there to open the doors right now. We will check on it soon. At least we are all safe. I thank God for a small crew today. My wife, Rosa, is in the house cooking. I sent home the gift shop staff when the storm clouds appeared in the distance. It is just us and our furry friends."

"And the ostriches, don't forget them," Connor adds.

And what about that skin-and-bones horse barely clinging to life? No one seems too concerned about that one. My eyes strain to see him through the darkness, but the darkness wins.

"You think Dr. Mike will still come, Preacher?" The girl's voice emerges from the donkey pens. "He has to get here *today*. It's really important."

"He knows the situation, Melissa. He will crawl here if he has to. The storm, she is moving quickly. It will not be much longer. In the meantime, I think we should introduce ourselves to our guest. You still with us, Señora?"

"Yes."

"All right, then. That voice you heard from the goat pen belongs to Connor. He and his father live down the road in the trailer park."

"I'm in third grade," Connor pipes in. "I'm an official member of the Sea Turtle Rescue Squad."

"Sí. It is true."

"Rosa's the leader," Connor continues. "That's why she's cooking."

"True again, Connor. My Rosa founded the squad years ago. Tomorrow is their potluck dinner."

Next week is the Girl Scout potluck. I was down for lasagna. Ashley and I were going to make it; her mixing the ricotta with egg and Parmesan, me making the sauce. Together.

"Hi, I'm Melissa." The dark shape waves to me.

"Hi."

"Melissa is from Michigan," Preacher explains. "Her father owns an orchard up there. She is visiting awhile, helping at the barn and gift shop. As for me, I am pastor of Living Word, a small community church next to the trailer park where Connor lives." A violent wind gust rattles the windows up in the hayloft. Preacher pauses until the noise subsides. "My wife and I own this crazy shelter, along with the gift shop and a section of beach. Well, part beach, part bird sanctuary. We call it Rosa's Haven. I will explain more in the next day or so, but that should be a good start."

"Thanks, but I'm not staying."

A sound comes from Preacher's direction. Something like a muffled laugh, but maybe it was one of the animals.

"Tell her about Owen and Elena." Connor's voice bubbles with personality. "Owen's my friend."

Preacher laughs. "As you can see, Connor does not suffer from shyness. Owen is my associate pastor. Often my handyman, too. He has been living in the guest quarters attached to our house. Ah, but love found our Owen. He and Elena married last week. They will be living down the road after their three-week honeymoon."

Three weeks. Must be nice. Rob and I only had seven days before he had to return to work. Still…it was wonderful.

"I think that covers everyone except Mrs. Cohen, who works in the gift shop. Very nice lady. You will meet her Monday."

"She's *really* old."

"Connor!"

Shuffling noises come from the boy's direction. "Well, she is," he mumbles.

No need to repeat that I'm not staying. He'll figure it out when I leave. Such a nice man, though, introducing everyone like that. Something friendly on my part would only be right. "I'm Josie," I say to the kids. Turning to Preacher, I add, "Thanks for letting me use your barn."

"You are most welcome, Josie. Now, that is not a name you hear a lot, but it seems to me I have heard it recently. Let me think. Josie, Josie. Hmm. So familiar. Where did I hear that?" The miniature horse stomps while Preacher considers the answer to his own question. Lucy lets out a bleat.

I wait for more. Only rain battering the barn fills the silence.

"Oh," he says at last. "It is nothing."

Then why did "it" pervade the dark, empty space between us and feel very much like *something*?

Bright light flashes through loft windows. Thunder cracks and booms. Utter darkness reigns.

"Preacher, can you come here? Now?" Fear shrills Connor's voice. "Lucy's scared. She'd feel better if you were here."

"On my way, Connor. Give me un momento. I mean, you tell Lucy un momento." Preacher's slow, steady footsteps thump against the wooden floor as he maneuvers through the dark barn. "All right, Lucy. Here I am. Don't worry, storms never last forever. You just have to be brave until the skies clear again. Remember, rain is a good gift from God. It gives critters like you and people like me water to drink, and helps the plants grow. This is true, Connor. No? There is nothing for Lucy to be afraid of."

"Well, what about the dark?"

"There is nothing in the dark that is not there in the light."

The comforting words, so familiar, confirm my initial instincts about Preacher. I am in good company, here. I am safe. I just hope he doesn't start sermonizing while we're stuck in this barn. My acting skills aren't honed enough for me to "amen" the God who destroyed everything I held inside my heart.

"It is still just us and the animals," he continues. "But if it bothers you, talk to the One who can make you feel better."

"So you think I should ask God to help me not feel scared of the dark?"

"I do. He likes to hear from you, you know. He likes when you talk to Him about anything, and He *really* likes to help you feel better."

And here we go.

"Even in this barn?"

"Anywhere at all."

"What about the bathroom?"

Leave it to a boy.

"Bathrooms work too. Anywhere, anytime."

"What about in my dad's bar when the drunks are fighting and I'm hiding behind the parrot cage?"

The innocent question speaks volumes about the boy's life. A weary sigh escapes Preacher. "I think perhaps that is the best place of all."

Clucking, munching, and swishing tails join the howling wind and pounding rain to provide a natural symphony of sounds. It pervades the surrounding darkness. In the midst of it all, Connor prays. I know this not because of his silence, or Preacher's suggestion. I know this because I can feel it there in that damp, earthy barn. I can *feel* it. Squeezing my eyes shut, I shake my head. No, I will not bear witness to this divine communication. I want no part of it.

And yet…there it is.

Flash! A glimpse shows the boy, hands folded, head bowed, with Preacher standing nearby. Thunder booms, though now subdued to a rumble. Feeling the presence too?

"See that? Already she moves past the island. It will not be long now." His words flow like a soft breeze.

Through the small loft windows, midnight black slowly fades to twilight blue. The shapes and faces of my companions gradually come into focus. Lightning flashes again, but far less brilliantly than those that came before. Distant rumbling echoes from somewhere over the Gulf, leaving the Atlantic side at peace.

Preacher was right about the storm skittering away. Twenty minutes ago I'd thought a hurricane would obliterate this barn and everyone in it. The world brightens with each minute that ticks by. Pounding rain diminishes into a drizzle as the storm travels west, carrying our combined tension out to sea. Charro stretches, yawns wide enough to swallow a rat, then curls up on the barrel and closes her eyes. Clearly the danger has passed.

Until Melissa shrieks.

"Nooo! Preacher, the horse! He's down! We need Dr. Mike here *now!*" All three race to the pen where the emaciated horse had been standing before the lights went out. He lay flat on his side, each rib visibly pressed against his skin. Curiosity draws me toward him, though I keep my distance. He lays with half-closed eyes, too weak to take notice of his audience. But my suspicions about Preacher and the gang have blown away like the storm. If someone mistreated this animal, it wasn't them.

Tears slide down Melissa's cheeks, silently plopping onto the hay-covered floor. She kneels next to the horse's head and softly strokes its neck.

"No, Lightning, you have to hold on. We're going to make you better. Please don't die."

Lightning?

Preacher whips out a cell phone, makes a call, then kneels by the whimpering girl. "Calm down, Melissa. It is not good for you to be upset. Not good for the baby, either."

I glance at Melissa's belly. Between the chaos and darkness, I hadn't noticed. A soft roundness, protectively covered by her hand, balloons her T-shirt. A miracle in the making. But oh, she is young and, I'm guessing, single as well. It doesn't matter. Soon I'll be heading south again, leaving behind these strangers, the tortured horse, the dog with a heart bigger than its massive head. Soon I'll be free to ponder my own situation.

Won't that be lovely?

"Lightning is going to be fine," Preacher continues. "Dr. Mike is on his way." He puts his arm around her. "No more crying, *querida*. Lightning will live up to his name, you will see. We will shower him with prayers, love, good food. Dr. Mike will give him medicine. A month from now, no more bones will be sticking out. He will run around the paddock like a wild thing."

Lightning heaves, ribs stretching taut skin as a wheezing sound emanates from his throat.

That's some faith you've got there, preacher man. Some crazy faith.

Chapter 9

Josie

The vet stands, brushing hay fragments from his cut-offs. Mid-thirties, I'd guess, though it's hard to tell with his thinning hair. His six-foot frame matches my Rob's, but his features are lighter, his face rounder. Preacher and the kids had watched in silence as he examined the skeletal horse. Now for the verdict. No doubt his next words will crush all three, for this bundle of bones begs only one thing: death. How well I understand every heave of this creature: every labored breath, every rattle. Put him out of his misery. Let him go. I hover near the rabbit hutch and listen.

Dr. Mike shakes his head. "This is a tough one," he says. "But the colt's got the will, that's for sure. His heart is still beating strong."

"So he's going to be okay?" Melissa's eyes glisten. Hopeful words beg for only one response.

"I can't promise you that. Sorry." The vet shades his head, shoos a fly from Lightning's face. "Fortunately, horses can lose up to thirty percent of their body weight and still survive. However...he's going to need huge amounts of TLC, fresh water, good hay. Mash it for the first few days. If everything goes well, grain in a couple weeks. He'll need supplements, too. I've got those back at the office. The fancy hay is in the truck. Figured you might be needing some. It's pricier than the regular stuff, but it's just for awhile. Consider today's batch a donation."

"Thank you, Mike." Preacher pats the vet on the back. "You are not

69

nearly as terrible as everyone says you are."

The vet grins like a mischievous boy. "Hey, now, don't go spreading that around."

They are friends. Good friends. They talk to each other like Ana and me...the way we used to.

"Tell me, why is he lying down?" Preacher kneels, his hand gliding softly over the protruding ribs. "Do you think he can stand?"

"He's very weak," Dr. Mike explains, reverting to veterinarian mode. "The starvation reduced his muscle mass, which means it'll be easier for him to break bones. With the hay mash and vitamins, he should gain strength every day."

"So he *is* going to be all right?" Melissa methodically caresses Lightning's back. "I mean, if we take really good care of him?"

Dr. Mike sighs, clearly wanting to say what she longs to hear. "Like I said, can't promise. He's in bad shape. But if anyone can bring him back, you three can. And Preacher, you might want a word or two with you-know-who about this one."

Preacher nods and smiles. "God heard all about it during your examination. Though, of course, He already knew."

The vet nods his agreement. I am not so easily convinced. "Another thing. Don't expect immediate results. *If* he recovers, it could take months for him to look healthy. It may take awhile to gain his trust, too. He obviously isn't used to humans treating him well."

"We'll make him better." Connor's tone and expression reflected a resolve worthy of a determined parent. I push away the thought.

This Dr. Mike guy is a bit too generous in handing out hope. Despite the "if" and "I can't promise," he still made it sound like this near-dead animal could make a miraculous recovery. Are they all blind? Can't they see the colt does not want recovery? Can't they see he just wants life to be *over?* I sigh my resentment toward this man, louder than intended. Four sets of eyes look my way.

"Poor thing." I mean it in ways they wouldn't understand.

Preacher stands up, gesturing toward me. "Mike, this is Josie. She came by during the storm."

"Ah, a new arrival, huh? You'll be seeing me around a lot the next few weeks, between Lightning here and Lily, just about to have her first pups."

So the colossal beast is a mother-to-be. Go figure.

"Actually, I'm leaving."

"Not if that's your silver Camry out front."

I fly to the door, sliding the wooden bar holding it shut, and swing it open. Heavy tropical air floods the barn with its earthy scent of saltwater and rain soaked palms. The world before me glistens as the sun peeks between storm cloud remnants, but in this moment, the beauty is difficult to appreciate. "My car!" I'd forgotten. "What happened to it?"

The vet saunters over to the doorway, shaking his head. "It's kinda like this. Tree verses car. Tree wins."

Connor and Melissa stay with Lightning as Mike and Preacher join me outside to examine my storm-beaten car. A large mangrove branch lays sprawled across the hood. The windshield is little more than a gaping hole, it's pebbly glass covering the driver and passenger seats, glittering beneath the emerging sun. The battered hood could easily belong to a demolition derby loser, but what lies beneath it concerns me even more. I can't even afford a new windshield at this point, much less a new engine. This was not in the plan. Not at all. The stupid branch couldn't have fallen on the trunk, or just a foot to the left or right. No, of course not.

I stand and stare, unable to speak. Now what? My funds are limited, and I really don't want to impose on Tina—she's got enough challenges. I have to call the insurance company, tell Rob, buy a car or rent one. Confidently handling adversity was part of my other life. It did not follow me into this one.

Preacher walks around the car, inspecting the crushed metal, brushing glass off the hood. Shaking his head and saying, "*guau!*"

"Well, if that means 'wow,' then yeah, guau is right," Mike says. "Grab an end there, Preacher. Let's get this thing off and see what's under it."

And then what? It's not like I'm going to hop in and drive away.

They swing the branch off the car, exposing the huge dent and countless ugly scratches. The guts of my car could not possibly have survived.

A door slams. We simultaneously look toward the house where a woman in a wheelchair rolls toward us. Small gusts, weakened now that the storm has passed, scatter leaves around her wheels. An empty McDonald's cup rolls in front of her. She stops, bends to pick it up, and drops it into a mesh bag attached to her chair.

"Manuel, where are the kids?" Wrinkles crease lovely skin. "Is everyone all right? I have been so worried!"

"Everyone is fine, *mi vida*. The kids are in the barn and all is well, except for our guest's car."

The woman's eyes widen. Her face turns from Preacher to me and back again. "So we have a new guest? Did Melissa put out the sign?"

"Sí. Did you know her plans?"

The woman nods. They exchange sad smiles. She looks at the damaged car, then to me. "Oh, dear. I am sorry about your car." Extending her hand, she beams a radiance that attests to a soul bathed in joy. It emits from her smile like soft sunbeams, warming something within me. "I'm Rosa. Welcome to our sandy corner of the world."

Cocoa eyes invite me in, revealing a heart overflowing with love, friendship, and something more. Stuck in that wheelchair, Rosa reflects a peace that emanates from deep inside. I want it like an addict wants heroine, but it isn't for me to have. I killed a child, left my family. Peace has dissipated like the fog that night. I want to smile for her, but my lips refuse to cooperate. I want to tell her how I ran for cover when the storm hit, how thankful I was for the shelter of the barn. Instead, I extend my hand to meet hers.

"Thanks. I'm Josie."

"Hello, Josie." A small wind blows wavy auburn tendrils into her eyes. She runs her fingers through it, shaking her head. The strands fall obediently into place in neat layers that end just below her ears. She turns to survey my car…what's left of it. "What a mess! You may stay here, of course, while your car gets repaired." She surveys the Camry from hood to trunk. "If that's even possible."

Preacher looks at me, gesturing toward his wife. "You heard the lady. She is the boss."

"Thank you." I stammer, because I cannot leave as I had hoped. Yet I cannot stay. Can I? "You're very kind. I wasn't expecting to stay."

Preacher and Rosa exchange a glance, followed by a small laugh.

"No, I'm sure you weren't." Rosa picks leaves off the hood and tosses them onto the ground. "That is often the case."

Meaning?

"Do you cook?" she continues. "I'm a bit behind on preparations for tomorrow's potluck. It is a fundraiser for the Sea Turtle Rescue Squad."

This road I'm on keeps heading in places that are way off my preconceived map. Sea turtles? I've participated in my share of fundraisers over the years, but this is a first. What would Ashley and Mitch think? Awesome. That's what they would say. Awesome. Who doesn't love a sea turtle?

"Yes. Happy to help."

"Gracias!" Her smile could push a storm to Canada. "Did you say your name was Josie?"

I nod.

"Manuel, haven't we heard that name recently?"

"Yes, but no matter." He telegraphs a message with his gaze. If only I could translate. Obviously it does matter...but why?

"Let's focus on getting rid of this mess." He sweeps his arm over the parking area and animal pens, where a menagerie of windblown objects lay strewn about. A small tree made kindling out of part of a fence. Preacher heads toward it. "Come on, Doctor, show me what you've got."

"A whole lot more than *you,* old man!" The vet slaps Preacher on the back with a laugh as they walk toward the fallen tree.

"Hey, who are you calling old?"

"Weren't you one of the original twelve apostles?"

They position themselves on either side of the tree, each grabbing an end. The dirty, wet wood leaves dark smudges on their arms and clothes.

"Less talking, *chico.* Save your strength for the tree."

"Hey, who you calling boy? I just turned thirty-two."

Preacher smiles. "Si. Half my age, that makes you a chico."

Counting to three, they lift the branch, dumping it near the side of the road. A lone coconut rolls onto the dirt parking lot. Mike soccer kicks it to Preacher, and the two continue the game along the gravel driveway as they return to the barn.

"Bravo!" Rosa claps, her face lit with another angelic smile. "Who needs the World Cup when I have you two? Now shall we turn to more serious matters? What are you going to do with this car?"

Three faces turn to me. My stomach crunches, partly due to the unified attention, and partly to the stress of dealing with insurance agents, car dealers and all the decisions linked with my newly demolished car. They wait for me to follow up on the headshake with actual words, but a hardy "woof" pulls me out of the limelight.

"Frisco!" Dr. Mike pats his thighs as the brown and white dog I saw earlier races like a thoroughbred down the stretch. Frisco leaps, nearly knocking down the laughing vet. The prodigal dog has returned.

"Oh, boy, someone needs a good bath." Rosa rubs Frisco under his chin. "Just look at the muck in that soggy fur. Silly dog. You're supposed to come home before a storm."

Frisco puts a muddy paw on Rosa's wheelchair and licks her arm.

Beam me up, Scotty. Something about the aura of devotion in this place makes everything hurt inside. Memories of a life filled with love weigh on me until I can hardly take a breath.

There must be some way to get to Key West. Public transportation doesn't appear to be an option. Haven't seen a bus. A taxi would cost a small fortune, but that may be the answer. Tina could pick me up—should be just an hour or so—but my poor cousin has enough to handle right now.

Tina. I better call. She's expecting me this afternoon. I excuse myself from my new acquaintances and scurry out of hearing range.

"Josie! Are you okay? Tell me you weren't driving in that storm."

Forcing a casual tone, I tell her about finding the goat and meeting Preacher and Rosa, waiting out the storm, then finding the car. Or what's left of it.

"Oh, sweetie. We gotta get you here and I'm so very stuck right now. The wind whipped a hunk of driftwood at the living room window. Glass everywhere, and the couch and carpet are soaked. I've got five guests comin' in the next hour, *and* I have to help Mary Lee with dinner. I'm so sorry. How about a cab? My treat. I just…I don't know what else to do."

Tina's words are embedded with frustration. I need to take that weight from her so she can handle her own challenges without dwelling on *me*. "It's fine, Tina. Seriously. I absolutely can't come right now, anyway. The car's a mess. I need to get it towed, call the insurance company. You know the gig." A rain-washed breeze blows the hair from my face like a tropical kiss. Its scent carries a hint of hope. For what, I do not know. My heart is lifted, not into a brighter place, but just enough to make me consider that a brighter place exists. "These nice people invited me to stay. I'll just hold up here until you can come."

"All righty, then. If you're sure. You change your mind, you just grab a cab and come over."

"I will. Promise. Take care, cousin. See you soon."

"Now hang on a minute. I got a truckload of news." Fast words end with a laugh. "Everything's changing. You simply won't believe."

More changes. There have been oh-so-many. "Fill me in."

"Remember I told you about Rebecca, my front desk clerk, leaving her scummo husband? Well, I talked her into not letting him have the house. Not after all he's done. All those women. All those drunken nights. No, sir, that house should be hers." Tina pauses for affirmation.

"Absolutely."

"Anyway, we went to a lawyer armed with plenty of evidence. Long and short of it, she's staying, he's leaving, and she's going to be my partner with the inn. It's a win-win, Josie. She's tying up some loose ends and coming back in a couple of days. So when you come, you don't need to work. You can just relax."

But I do. Need. To. Work. I stand on Gumby legs, wishing there was something to lean on. Anything. "That's great. Wow. Really great…but you know I can still work." Can she hear the begging in my voice? "You might need some extra help with the snowbirds."

"No, Josie. Don't be silly. You come and rest. Clear your head. I'll take care of you. Help you get past this."

I close my eyes. I don't want her taking care of me. Don't want to relax and think. Especially think. How can I go there, knowing she'll be trying to balance running a business and fawning all over me?

"You still with me, Jo?"

"Sorry. Got distracted. Hey, I'm glad it all worked out with Rebecca. I'll call you in a few days."

"Sounds like a plan." A door shuts in the background. Footsteps. "Ah, customers. Gotta go, sweetie. You take care, now."

Key West is out. Home is out...for now. Possible alternatives? My head fills with visions of camping on the beach, fishing for my dinner, and sleeping under the stars. Surrounded by nature, away from accusatory eyes, maybe life would start to make sense again. Maybe I'd find that elusive inner strength people talk about.

I don't have a tent...or a pole. Don't even know if it's legal to live on the beach. Reality battles desire and wins. My temporary home will be the sunny guesthouse attached to Preacher and Rosa's four-bedroom Victorian. Well, sort of a Caribbean-style Victorian, painted in the colors of sea and sand. Soothing...in most cases. I run my eyes across the place as Rosa accompanies me to the guesthouse, with its whitewashed porch facing the sea.

Rosa amazes me with her dexterity as she gives me a tour, pointing out the microwave and fridge, the cozy loveseat where Owen and his fiancé probably snuggled up and watched movies, like Rob and I used to do.

"This leads into our house." Rosa points to an oak door in the bedroom I will pretend is mine. "Melissa has her own room there. Connor too, on nights when it is necessary." She doesn't elaborate. I remember Connor's comment about drunk men fighting at his dad's bar. Not too difficult to fill in the rest.

After mashing hay and feeding Lightning, my new housemates head out to buy horse vitamins. I stand by my annihilated car and watch as Connor climbs into the back of the pick-up, grinning, wind ruffling his hair. No seat belt. In fact, no seat. That would never fly in Riverbank. They would get pulled over and ticketed after half a block. It's not safe. But look at him…so free. He waves to me until the truck disappears from view. I return to the guesthouse, now sheathed in a cloak of silence, and stare at nothing.

I am alone.

My suitcase lies on the bed, its contents waiting to surprise me. I have no memory of packing. Beyond the window, a patch of coarse sea grass separates the house from the beach. Mid-afternoon sunlight traipses across the Atlantic's baby waves with no hint of that raging storm. Soft tropical sounds float around me. Seagulls. Swishing palms. I picture her out there, barefoot on the beach in her Hello Kitty bathing suit, carefully choosing the most special seashells to place in her bucket.

Want to see my seashells from Florida, Mrs. Caruso? This one is called a sand dollar. It is a present for you.

Fists pummel the front door, crashing through my sweet Carmelita memory. Breathing ceases. My heart beats at the speed of hummingbird wings. The pounding comes again, battering the door like Spanish bulls. Charging, ramming, determined to crash through.

"I know he's in there!"

The angry words slur with booze and a southern accent. Deep. Loud. The kind of voice that emerges from someone big enough to rip the front door off its hinges.

"Open up or I'll smash this conch right through the window!"

This *what*? My panicked mind races to process the word. Conch. An image forms of a peach-colored shell. Thick spines. Heavy enough to make shards of that beautiful bay window. I grip the bed's white-washed footboard, my knuckles matching the wood's hue. Surely my hammering heart will explode in anticipation of the crash. Any minute now. Any minute.

"Open up, Preacher. I ain't kiddin'. You give me my boy! I'll burn down that barn of yours and all the stupid animals, too. Got my lighter right here."

The conch hits the house with a thunk. I wince, then let out a sigh.

The maniac—Connor's father?—spared the bay window. So far.

"Fine. Have it your way. Time for a barbeque." He laughs heartily at his joke. "A barbeque and a bonfire! Ha! Got any marshmallows in there?"

Oh God, oh God, oh God. This cannot happen. I force my feet to inch into the living room where the window provides a full view of the barn. He hulks toward it. A red ponytail swishes across his shirtless back. Think. Find a telephone. I hope these island people have nine-one-one. My eyes sweep the room and land on the wicker end table. Yes! Next to the phone, a laminated placard lists numbers for Manuel, Dr. Mike, Ben, Hospital, Pharmacy, and Sheriff. I dial.

"Sheriff's Department. What's your emergency?"

My hand shakes so hard, the phone raps against my head. "He's going to set the barn on fire!"

"Try to calm down, ma'am. Where are you?"

"It's an animal shelter on Cielo Azul Key, right off Highway One. Don't know the address. Please, hurry!"

"Rosa's Haven?"

"Yes!"

"Is it Ben?"

"I don't know! Hurry! He's going to burn the animals!"

"A unit is on the way, ma'am. Is he a big guy? Long red hair?"

"Yes." My eyes stay fixed on the monster outside, terrified at what the next minute might bring.

"Does he appear intoxicated?"

"I don't know. Maybe."

Big Red bends down, plucks hay from a bale next to the barn door. Pulls something small from his pocket. I creep closer to the window, squinting to focus. A lighter.

I am their only hope.

Holding tight to the receiver, I fly out the front door screaming like a crazed banshee. My arms wave wildly to complete the picture. Distraction. It's what animals do when they have no natural defense.

"Stop it! Stop it!"

A tinny, distant voice travels through the receiver. "Ma'am, please don't attempt to confront him. Ma'am? He may be dangerous."

Too late. The lighter's flame snaps something in me. I fling myself at him like a fly ramming a humpback whale. He may have expected Preacher to stroll out of the house, but certainly not craziness personified. He stumbles backward. I collapse onto his hulk, falling with him. The lighter tumbles uselessly to the ground. Massive hands grab my arms as the man's confusion gives way to rage.

I'm dead.

"What the…who are *you*?"

I have no idea.

Whiskey-soaked curses pummel my face. The man rolls over, pinning my arms to the wet, coarse sea grass. His scarlet face strains from the anger and booze igniting his blood pressure. Wild eyes shoot daggers at mine. Fueled by adrenaline and my own shocking surge of hate, I push against his hands. A roar and a shove answer my groans. Despite jabs and writhes, I remain pinned like a dead butterfly in one of those sad exhibits. As a postscript to my helplessness, a lizard skitters over my arm and disappears into the grass.

"Answer the question! Who are you? Tell me before I snap your skinny arm like a chicken bone!"

I shudder, knowing he is more than capable.

Sirens blare down Highway One. Big Red tightens his jaw…along with his death grip. Get here before he kills me! Two units burn rubber. Screech. Yes! I tell myself I am safe now. Safe. But the terror remains. A door opens not three feet from my head. A mammoth of a man emerges from the car.

"Off her, Benny!" he booms. "Let her go."

"She attacked me!" He screams in my face. "I swear!" His hands still grind my wrists into the sandy dirt. "I was just standing here, and this crazy broad comes flyin' at me."

I strain to breathe.

The officer draws his gun. Oh, God, this is not the help I wanted. I wait for the explosion, the crush of weight. A bead of sweat trickles down my hairline.

"What's with the gun, Johnson?" His shouts make my ears ring. "Arrest *her!* I got my rights."

A female cop sprints over. "I'll kill you, Benny. I swear I will." Dark eyes flare, confirming the conviction of her threat. "Move. *Now!* I'll blow your 'rights' all over this parking lot!"

Ben releases his grip, rolls off. Dammed-up blood rushes through my veins, into my hands. I gasp, unaware I'd been holding my breath. No longer captive, I wobble to my feet and stumble backward. My eyes remain locked on the maniac, just in case.

"You all right, ma'am?" the big cop asks.

"Yeah." Do they see it, the red-hot "K" burning inside me? Do cops instinctively know when they're in the presence of a killer? I avoid eye contact by brushing dirt and sand off my arms.

They sandwich Big Red, each grabbing a tree trunk arm, and jerk him upright. In a flash he shoves the woman cop, nearly knocking her off her feet. Anger blazes her eyes again. She holds onto that arm with one hand and grabs her stun gun with the other. "Go ahead, give me a reason. I'd like nothing better."

He shakes his head, fear-laced curse words spewing like lava, eyes glued to the stun gun aimed at his chest, then finally says, "No. Fine. Just put it away, Sullivan. I hate that thing."

"Soon as you cooperate. And I'm actually hoping you don't." Words escape the officer's clenched teeth, the determination in her eyes as deadly as the gun in her belt. He would have to be a complete idiot to mess with this woman.

"She'll do it, Ben," Johnson says. "You know she will."

"All right, all right, you..." Again, he curses. "Just put the thing away." Ben puts his hands behind his back.

Sullivan keeps her eyes and stun gun fixed on Ben until the cuffs click, then returns it to her pocket.

Unable to gesture with his hands, Ben nods in my direction. "You gonna arrest her or what?"

"First things first." Sullivan points toward the ground. "That your lighter?"

"No."

Liar!

The big cop saunters over, bends down, stares at the lighter without touching it. "It says Benny's Beach Bar."

"So what, Johnson? That don't prove nothin'."

"Come on Ben, even drunk, you can't be that stupid, or think *we're* that stupid. I don't have to dust this to know your prints are all over it." Next he examines the bale of hay. "What a surprise. Hay's charred. It's only by the grace of God this didn't ignite. If it weren't for that storm, we'd have had an inferno on our hands. And a bunch of dead animals. I can only imagine what that would have done to Preacher. Rosa. *Connor*."

His punch hits its mark. Anger drains from Ben's eyes. He stares at the charred hay as though seeing it for the first time. "I just wanted my kid. I didn't want to hurt nobody. They got no right to take Connor."

Connor. Sweet. Spunky. Praying in the barn. *This* is what he gets for a father?

The woman cop shakes her head, disgust oozing from every pore. "Your boy comes here of his own free will. If it wasn't for Preacher and Rosa, he'd be in foster care and you'd be in jail. Why they've kept you out is a mystery." She looks at her partner, who nods his agreement, then glares back at Ben. "I can tell you this…it's not going to last. Your time is coming, Benny. And I'll be there giddy as a lottery winner when they lock you behind bars."

Tires crunch over gravel, causing the four of us to glance toward the long driveway.

"Oh, man." Benny shakes his head. "Man, oh, man."

"You got that right," Sullivan says.

Frisco runs up from the beach at the sound of Preacher's pickup, long furry ears flapping against his face, tongue hanging out to the side. I give him my best evil eye. *Now* you decide to show up? Where were you when Big Red was trying to incinerate your buddies?

Preacher's truck stops in the parking area. Melissa and Connor fly out before he cuts the engine. With a "be right back" to Rosa, he steps out and joins our little party.

"Dad!" Connor runs to his father, hugging the man who, moments ago, tried to roast his beloved animals. "What's going on, Dad? Why are you in handcuffs?"

My hatred for Big Red is amplified by the pain in Connor's eyes as he clings to his father. If ever a man didn't deserve that title…

Preacher eyes Ben, shaking his head before turning to the police officers. "Please tell me what happened."

They instant replay the ordeal. Ben chimes in with the part about the "crazy broad" attacking him.

Three strides bring Preacher to my side. He wraps his arm around my shoulder as though we've been friends for years. "Are you all right, Josie? Did he hurt you?"

The simple touch transforms me from human to statue. It is not a familiar state. I've grown up with an Italian family and married into one as well, so any form of affection is second nature to me. *Was* second nature to me. My frozen state isn't lost on Preacher. His arm drops down. My eyes focus on the space beyond him. "I'm fine."

Liar!

"You can't just take my kid, ya know." Ben's angry words are dulled by a softer tone. Connor's presence must be melting something inside.

"Have you gone completely *loco?*" Anger knits Preacher's eyebrows. "How dare you say such a thing!" He peers at Ben, steps closer and shakes his head. "Oh, Ben, I see it is the alcohol speaking. Will this never end?"

Connor grabs Ben's massive arm with both hands. "Dad, I told you I was going with Preacher to rescue a horse, remember?" The boy's head tilts up to meet his father's eyes. "When the storm came, I tried to call, but you didn't answer. Then we had to get medicine for the horse. Rosa said I could stay for dinner. Can I, Dad? Please?"

"You ain't never comin' back here, Connor. You belong with me."

And you belong in prison…is what I want to say, but I stand to the side, silently witnessing the father-son exchange.

"Dad, noooo! Please!" Hurt saturates his words, spills down his cheeks. It is possibly the worst threat anyone could have made.

Where is his mother? Why isn't she here to comfort him?

The big cop jerks Ben's arm, causing him to stumble. "Take it down a notch, Ben."

"You think you're so tough. Take these cuffs off and we'll see what you're made of, Johnson!"

"That's enough!" Rosa's voice booms from the car, where she'd maneuvered out of her seat. All heads jerk in her direction. Leaning her forehead against the truck's door, she drapes both arms inside the open window for support. Not likely she can hold that position very long. Still, she copes with her challenge in ways I cannot fathom.

"I'll not have you upsetting this boy more than he is already!" She shifts her weight in order to face the cops. "Officers, may I have a word with Ben? Privately?" The police nod their agreement, stepping away from their prisoner.

"And please, take those ridiculous handcuffs off. Benny will not hurt me."

"Prefer not to, Rosa."

"Officer Sullivan. Mary. Please."

That voice. I've never heard anything like it. Firm words draped in plush velvet.

"In all these years, has Ben ever once hurt me *intentionally?*" Rosa's eyes turn from the officers and blaze toward Ben. "Benny!" Steel replaces velvet. "Tell them you will cooperate."

Ben stares at Rosa, shame shadowing his face. He mumbles something to the officers, who shake their heads and remove the cuffs.

Really?

Officer Sullivan dangles the cuffs from her hand. "I'm doing this for you, Rosa, but it's a bad move."

I couldn't agree more.

Rosa gently squeezes her arm. "Gracias, Mary. It will be fine. And you give your mother my best. I hope to see her at the potluck."

Ben walks toward Rosa. So does Preacher, his shorter legs moving twice as fast to keep up. "Querida, wait. I will get your chair. Then we can talk to Ben together."

Ben waves him off. "I got it." He clumsily pulls the wheelchair from the pickup's bed, banging it off the bumper. Rosa winces. I watch as the maniac from moments ago eases Rosa into her chair as though she were a china teacup.

"Thank you." Anger infuses the courteous response. "Come. Over by that tree. I want to know what put the devil inside you."

"Yes, ma'am."

We watch the scene unfolding before us like mesmerized theater goers. Ten minutes ago this man held a match to a barn full of animals. Five minutes ago he had me pinned. And now…

"I will be right there," Rosa says. "You go ahead." She turns to Preacher as Ben lumbers away. "Manny, please let me have un momento with Ben alone," she whispers. "Sometimes these conversations are better one-on-one, no?"

"I do not like it. He has been drinking and you know well how he gets under those conditions."

Warm brown eyes gaze into his and say what words might not. Preacher responds with a subtle nod. She wheels first across gravel, then sea grass, to reach Ben. The distance between us muddles the words from their conversation, but that doesn't stop us from staring. Under the dappled shade of a sand pine, Rosa shakes her head while Ben hangs his like a disobedient puppy. She gestures toward the barn and then to Connor. We turn our heads simultaneously in a pathetic attempt to act like we aren't paying attention.

Preacher clears his throat. "All right, everyone. I think it is clear that Rosa can handle it from here…as usual. Officers, I thank you kindly for arriving so quickly. If the hay had not been wet, I shudder to think what may have happened."

With palms turned up, Johnson gestures his disbelief. "Come on, Preach. You can't tell me you're not going to press charges. This guy almost…"

Preacher's hand shoots up like a stop sign. "Please, Officer Johnson, I am sorry to interrupt. Let us not discuss this in front of the boy. Melissa, I would appreciate you and Connor checking on Lightning. See if he needs more water. Talk to him gently so he knows he has amigos here."

"Okay. Come on, Connor." Melissa waves him over and together they trudge off.

Officer Johnson waits until they disappear into the barn before resuming his tirade. "This guy almost burned down your barn. He could've killed your guest! We could be hauling a dead woman and crispy critters out of here right now." He shakes his head. "Ben's way out of control. Should've been tossed in jail two years ago, Preacher. You know it's true. Makes no sense. Didn't then, doesn't now."

There is some heavy history here. Something horrible. I cringe at the awful thought. The old me would have been curious as a reporter at a murder scene. Now...I am content to simply blend in with the sand.

Preacher nods. "You are correct in that our decision today, as in two years ago, defies logic. Please hear me out. For two years this man has been sober, only slipping now and then. Connor's life has greatly improved. I do not know what happened today, but surely Rosa is finding out as we speak. Please, officers, another chance. The boy has no mother to care for him. He needs a father."

Officer Sullivan nods in Ben's direction. "Not *that* father."

"He is a decent man, a good father when he is not drinking. You would be surprised. You only see him under the worst conditions." Preacher glances toward Rosa and Ben, then back to the officers, imploring them with hopeful eyes.

Officer Johnson mulls over Preacher's words, queries Sullivan with a look. She shrugs her answer. "You can press charges, you know." Her comment is directed at me. "You're the witness. And the victim."

Preacher's message to me needs no words.

My desire for anonymity has charged down the same wayward path as my desire for a happy, normal life. I do not want to press charges... or answer this police officer...or stand here for one more minute.

You have to answer, Josie. They are waiting. They are staring. Soon they will see the flaming red "K."

I shake my head. "No, but thank you for coming. I'm grateful."

Our two uniformed visitors exchange a disgusted glance. Go ahead, think what you want. Your judgment of me could never descend to my own. It's not even on the same radar screen.

"All right, then," Johnson says. "Come on, Sullivan, we're done here. But Preacher, just so you know, next time we'll press charges, even if you don't."

"I understand, officers. Muchas gracias…for everything."

Officer Sullivan and Preacher shake hands. "You're welcome." Her words are barely out when a deep "woof" bellows from behind the barn door. Connor opens it from inside and Lily bounds out, heading straight for Sullivan. I tense, expecting her to draw her gun, but instead she extends her arms as the furry beast leaps up to slobber her face. The same mouth that's been tight-lipped since arriving breaks into a child-like grin.

"Lily, stop. You silly dog." Her words infused with laughter, she scratches Lily's massive head and back. "You're getting my uniform all hairy again."

Preacher grabs her collar, straining muscles to get her under control. "Okay, you big baby, that's enough. Down, girl. I said *down*." Lily complies, but only after the two of them push her paws away.

Officer Johnson continues stroking Lily's head. "So when will the pups be up for adoption? And what's the fee? I'm thinking of getting one for my nephew in Minnesota. I'm going up there end of January."

"You are interested? Wonderful! Dr. Mike says she is due in a few days. Minnesota would be an excellent location. And the timing is perfect—they will be over two months old. Whatever donation you make to the shelter is up to you."

She looks at him like he has three heads. "Preacher, you do realize these are *purebred* Newfies, right? Those pups will be worth a small fortune. You could raise a nice chunk of dough for the shelter or church. Online they're going for nine hundred! Not that I could pay that, but don't just ask people for a donation. They'll give you five bucks and call it a day."

"Goodness! I had no idea! But for you, officer, my deal stands: whatever donation you see fit. Please do not spread that around, though. I like your idea about using the money. There are people in our congregation going through hard times. Still, there is more to this than money. We will make sure the puppies get good homes."

"Sounds like a deal. And a good one at that. I'll drop by after the little buggers are born."

The officers drive off, leaving Preacher and me in a dome of silence. Over by the tree, Rosa reaches out her arms. Ben leans down for a hug, then straightens, swiping both cheeks.

Preacher turns his gaze back to me. "Thank you, Josie. I know you are unaware of all that has gone on the last few years, but it was important that Ben not get arrested today. I greatly appreciate you trusting me in this."

Who wouldn't trust those saintly eyes? His words hug my heart. I may not have said more than three syllables to the cops, but at least I chose the right ones. Now I just need to find the woman I used to be and get her back, before Preacher, the cops, and the kids learn someone much worse than a drunk resides in this sunny slice of Eden.

Chapter 10

Preacher

I slip the last of the framed photos inside a cardboard box. The shelves on both walls are now completely void of her images, yet my mind's eye clearly sees each one. Posing on a chubby pony, holding her bucket of shells, smiling for a school picture. Is that everything, then? I glance around, my eyes landing on my cork bulletin board. There, above the list of next month's sermons, hangs a crayoned rendition of Rosa and myself next to a blue donkey.

There wasn't a gray crayon, Uncle Manny, so I made him blue. Maybe somewhere there really is a blue donkey. Do you think so?

Her name is clearly printed on the bottom, each letter inscribed in a different color. I sniff, swiping my eyes with the back of my hand. As though handling the *Mona Lisa*, I remove four push-pins from the masterpiece and lay it atop the stack of frames. Beneath it, her preschool photo begs one last gaze. It may be awhile before this opportunity comes again. I attempt to brand the image in my brain. The impish grin, bright eyes. What a fool am I. That imprint was made permanent long ago.

A soft tapping on the door tells me Rosa has arrived for our afternoon coffee break. I lay the photo on top of the colored picture, close the flaps, breathe deep.

One's heart can only ache if one has loved deeply. I know this, Lord, and I'm grateful for having loved her. But sometimes it is more than I can bear, especially when I think of my poor sister and the pain she must endure. Please comfort Ana, Lord. She needs you desperately. I pray her pain will not hurt the new baby.

Rosa wheels in, a container of homemade oatmeal raisin cookies resting on her lap. She fumbles to get the lid off while maneuvering her wheelchair. "I made your favorite today since I haven't baked for weeks. Some for the potluck, some for my Manny." She flicks the plastic lid and looks at me. Into me. Seeing the places concealed from the rest of the world. "Oh, Manny." Her eyes instantly pool at my sorrow, as well as her own. "I know, I know. She was much too young. This is too much. Too hard." Her chair cruises closer so she can cup both her hands around mine.

We smile weakly at each other, comfortable in our moment of silence while the aroma of oats and cinnamon faintly emanates from the plastic container.

"Your heart is aching, *mi amor*, but there is something else."

I gaze at our entwined hands, hers small and delicate, a few wrinkles proudly reflecting years of honest work, raising children, helping others; mine leathery and creased from the Florida sun and countless hours caring for our *animales*. Her eyes caress my face, but I know the synchronized gears of her brain are turning, meshing, as she struggles to understand my weary heart.

Rosa sets the container down and opens the box. "Why would you hide these as if there is shame? This is not like you, Manny. You still hang Roberto's photos, and he's been gone two years. *Por qué*?"

My Rosa, barely able to take one step, but blessed with the ability to see souls. She cannot fool me by calling it "good observation skills." No, it is more. Much more. I reach for a cookie, doomed to dissolve in a stomach laced with acid. The long day has been hardly more than a prologue for the long night ahead. Ben and Connor are staying for dinner. We will have to discuss the annual visit from Connor's mother. Will Naomi really try to gain custody after all this time? With no job and an arm spiked with track marks? No wonder Ben fell off the wagon.

And now this Josie. Many have come here with heavy loads, but I have no frame of reference for what God has sent this time. My head tells me to trust in the Lord. My grief-laden heart, however, is not quite ready to comply.

Father God, why? I faithfully shepherd all You send my way, but this...I will surely need you to steady this cup as I drink it.

"I will explain later." I decide to stall, wanting first to hear Rosa's impressions. "Mmm, this cookie is *delicioso*. You are the oatmeal raisin cookie queen, *querida*." I speak the truth. The soft, warm cookie soothes the turmoil. I reach for another. "So tell me, what did you see with those gifted eyes? What is going on inside our quiet visitor?"

Rosa sighs. "So much pain. I think this Josie is a very different person than she used to be. Something tore her apart, I am sure. Despair surrounds her like a force field—see the terms I learn from watching those *Star Wars* movies with our Alex? She is lonely in her despair. But these are just observations, nothing more."

"What do you mean by lonely?"

"Something is rotting her heart, and I think she is keeping it all inside. It is killing her."

I shake my head, avoiding her eyes.

"What do you know, Manny? Tell me."

It is time for her to know. "I wanted to hear your thoughts before telling you. Forgive me this little deception. The name sounded familiar to me, as it did to you. Then I remembered, saw the vehicle sticker, and confirmed it on the Internet."

"Oh, no, is she a criminal? A fugitive?"

"Josie is from Illinois, Rosa. *Riverbank*, Illinois."

Revelation lights her eyes. A gasp escapes sweet lips. "No! It couldn't be! It can't be true."

I turn my computer screen to face her. Another gasp, louder this time. Her face blanches as she scans the article in the *Riverbank Herald*, where the name Josephine Caruso jumps out from the second paragraph. Carmelita's preschool photo smiles at us from the screen. The sight of it waters Rosa's eyes.

"I cannot do this, Manny. To have her as our guest, knowing she is the one…it is too much."

"My first reaction as well. But querida, she was sent to us like all the others. The reason may elude us, but we are people of faith. Perhaps…" I tap the desk, wondering how crazy my next words will sound. "Perhaps in helping her heal, our wounds will also begin to mend."

"Your faith has always been a rung above mine. I don't know if it is in me to do this." Rosa covers her face with both hands. I wait, listening to the hymn of the sea as its waters fall upon the shore, recede, and return.

Rosa's hands drop back to her lap. " Does she know who we are?"

"No."

"When will you tell her?"

I reach for another cookie. "Not today. I have not even talked to Ana yet. Telling Josie I am Ana's brother may have undesirable consequences."

"I would not wait too long. Hiding it from her could have undesirable consequences as well."

I turn the computer back to its original position, gaze upon my niece's pretty face before closing out the screen. The punch of a button does nothing for my memory. Our Carmelita. Forever happy now with Jesus. Forever gone from this earth…and our lives.

Maybe there is still hope for the one who killed her. But do we have the strength…the grace…to help her find it?

Chapter 11

Josie

Roast chicken and a colorful array of sautéed vegetables fill my plate. I push them around with my fork, setting it down occasionally to sip water. A rapid-fire discussion has everyone talking at once. Thankfully, no rehashing of the police scenario takes place with Connor at the table. He sits next to his Dad, tearing off the last tidbits of meat from his chicken leg. Coffee, a shower, and time have washed the booze out of his father's system. Ben's apology just prior to dinner was sincere, but unnecessary. They don't get it—I don't care. Transformed, the ogre bent on torching the barn this afternoon sits across from me. The transformation is one thing. Weird, but I get it. People can assume completely different personalities when drunk. The true mystery here is that the guy's attempted arson got him an invitation to dinner.

Connor gulps root beer, then stands. "All done, Rosa. It was real good. May I be excused?"

"You certainly may. And I'm glad you liked it. There's oatmeal raisins in the cookie jar. Help yourself."

"Best cookies in the Keys!" Preacher winks at his wife. She rewards the compliment with a sunbeam smile.

An image of Rob munching my warm, melty chocolate chip cookies right from the pan makes my heart wince.

Mmm. Best cookies in the Midwest, Josie. No one makes them like you.

Preacher turns his attention to the boy. "Connor, would you and

Melissa please feed the animals tonight? Rosa and I would like to speak with your dad."

"Sure thing. We can handle it. Right, Mel?"

Her mouth full of broccoli, Melissa nods.

"The feed list is posted in the storage room—you know where to find it, yes?"

"I know." Connor tugs on Melissa's arm. "Come on, Mel. You done?"

"Mmm hmm." She picks up her plate and water glass. "All except the cookies. We can grab those on the way out. Preacher, don't forget we're calling my parents later. We are, right?"

"*Absolutamente!* That is one phone call I have been anxious to make. Thank you both for filling in for this lazy old man. I will join you shortly to see how our skinny Lightning is doing."

The back door slams. Time to excuse myself and head for the welcome solitude of my room. Before I can stand, however, Ben clears his throat and tosses his napkin. Another rage?

"She's comin', Preacher. That sorry excuse for a mother. I got just over a week to figure this thing out. I'll probably need me a bottom-feeding lawyer who'll suck up my bank account—what's left of it. I know I been a sorry excuse for a dad, but that drugged-out you-know-what ain't taking my boy and ruining his life."

Not the best moment to excuse myself. Much as I want to. And I do.

Preacher reaches for the salt, despite Rosa's disapproving glance. "Calm down, Ben. No one is taking Connor. I've already called my attorney friend in Marathon. He is a good man, you will see. A busy man, too. But it seems a client cancelled and he squeezed us in for next Thursday at nine-thirty."

"In the *morning*?"

Preacher's eyebrows arch a silent response.

"Morning it is," Ben says. "I'll be here at nine."

Rosa grasps the saltshaker, placing it out of Preacher's reach. "Manny, you are taking Melissa to her doctor appointment Thursday. Remember? I have early therapy before opening the gift shop."

"Ah. Too many things always happening. Mike is coming to check on Lightning that day as well." Preacher shakes his head. Weary eyes gaze at his wife, but he says nothing more.

I take advantage of the pause to make my escape. "Thank you for the delicious dinner." Standing up, I grab my plate, planning to wash it and anything else by the sink…until Preacher motions for me to sit. My stomach tightens. The three bites of food inside me squeeze into a leaden lump.

"Sit, Josie. Please. Here is what we can do. If you would be so kind as to accompany Melissa to the doctor, I can take Ben to the lawyer. Rosa can meet with Mike. Please forgive me for imposing when you have only just arrived. We are in a bit of a situation, as you can see."

But I'm not planning to stay. By next Thursday I'll be…where? Where will you be, Josie Caruso? Home, where you can't even function as a mother? Where your son will take one look at you and run away? Key West? Where your cousin will dote on you, even though her hands are full with guests? I settle back into the chair, ready to consider Preacher's plan.

"Melissa can drive the Caddy." As if on cue, Preacher continues. "We keep it for guests. It is old and rusty, but then again, so am I." He chuckles. I should laugh along…but seem to have forgotten how. Rosa rolls her eyes. "As I was saying," he continues, "if you go with Melissa, I would be most grateful. She likes to have someone with her."

My words stop in my throat and will go no further. Melissa is a sweet girl and all, but I'm not sure I'm the best choice for the job. An image floats into my head. Melissa alone in the doctor's office, waiting, nervous. Dwelling on the heavy load that is single motherhood. Everything inside me says I'm far too messed up to help sweet Melissa. But my heart shields the words from my mouth, thrusting them into oblivion. Something has to come out, though, because a haze of silence is sucking the air from the room. Preacher and Rosa await a response. Ben fixates on his roast chicken.

"Sure." Exhaustion must be making me crazy. It has been such a very, very long day.

Rosa releases her grip on her water glass, leans back in her chair.

"Excellent," Preacher says. "We're all set, then. Good thing you came by when you did."

He looks for a response. I eek out a smile and stand again. Nothing short of that Taser-toting cop will stop me from getting my body through the kitchen door. I must busy myself washing dishes, doing something, anything…to keep from getting further involved with these lovely people. What would they think if they knew what I'd done? Why I'm here?

Just say good-night, Josie. I squeeze a thousand emotions into my gut and mutter a "good night" to the trio at the table.

"Good night, dear. Let us know if you need anything."

"*Buenos noches*, Josie."

"'Night." Ben gazes down at his plate. "Thanks again for not pressing charges," he mumbles. "I'm so sorry. So very sorry."

I shake my head, wanting this moment to end. "It's all in the past."

Double-swinging doors lead me into a world where Rosa clearly reigns as queen. Utensil drawers barely reach my waist, as does a table holding a matching blue blender and hand mixer. I wash the dishes, taking care not to clink anything together as they talk. Not that I care about Ben and his situation, not at all, but what can it hurt to overhear a sentence or two?

"Ah, Ben." Preacher sighs. "When will you figure out the answer is not at the bottom of a bottle?"

"I know, I know. But man, it just feels better for awhile. Anyways, I'm sorry. I can't say it enough. I'm so sorry. I don't know why you keep putting up with me after…you know…after everything. I want to tell you it'll never happen again, but you've heard that before."

"Sí. It will keep happening until you hand the reins over to the One who can take away the stress. Your bottle does not do this, Ben. It is like blinders the devil puts on you to hide the truth. Do you know why? Because he can. Because you let him. Replace that bottle with faith, and God will give you a spirit of strength and peace. It is true."

Strength and peace. Nice words for a gospel song, but not something I've felt since…I can't remember when. Life was good enough, though.

Good enough for me. As for the devil, I didn't let him do anything. So whether it was him or God or just the way of the world, I don't know. What I do know is this: Ana and Emilio will never recover. Rob lost his wife and the kids lost their mother. As for me, I lost them all. *So if you are up there somewhere, Mr. Almighty, you sure aren't doing your job.*

Morning dawns. Watercolor shades of pink and gold wash streaks across the sky. Outside my bedroom window, an elderly couple strolls along the sand, wrinkled hands entwined like ivy vines. A small breeze catches her sun hat, lofting it to the water's edge. He bends to retrieve it, brushing the damp grains off the brim and lovingly replacing it on her silver curls. How long have they shared joys, heartaches, laughter? Will this scene ever play out for Rob and me? Will our footprints hollow the sand twenty years from now…or ever again?

They share the sun-kissed beach with squawking gulls and sandpipers skittering along the shore. And Frisco. He sits and stares at the water as if contemplating his future. Maybe he's onto something. Sitting out there might clear my head and help me figure out what's next.

A light rap on the door disrupts my thoughts. Rosa.

"Josie, would you like some breakfast?"

"No thanks, I'm fine." I'm fine, I'm fine, I'm oh so fine. Could anyone be finer than me?

"Now, Josie, you hardly ate a thing last night. Manny and Melissa are with the horse. I hate to eat alone. Please come and join me."

Oh, how I wish I'd headed out to that beach ten minutes ago. But my chance is gone, for who am I to say no to Rosa? As if anyone could.

"Okay."

Now what? A conversation? This is going to be the epitome of awkward. I suck in a breath and head for the kitchen.

"Ah, Josie. It is a lovely day, no?" She hands me a large cup that looks as though it had been spun on a potter's wheel. Another Rosa talent? "I brewed it with cinnamon. I hope you do not mind. There is cream and sugar on the table."

The scent of cinnamon and fresh-ground coffee beans swirls around my head, warming my face, warming everything inside. The first sip floods joy to my senses. My eyes tear at the utter simplicity of this unexpected contentment.

"Thanks."

She fills an equally large mug for herself, looks straight into my eyes. I add some cream and stir long enough to dissolve a rock.

"I think I know something about you."

My spoon freezes in place. The heat pulsating through my body no longer comes from the steaming mug. What was I thinking, settling in here? My heart roars in my ears, pummeling my chest from the inside out. No words come forth. Cinnamon spirals swirl slower and slower on the coffee's surface, then lay still.

"There is much sadness in your eyes, Josie. I ask myself why a nice woman like you would be so far from home. Alone. Why would she leave her husband and children?"

I nod to show I'm listening. I get it. I would wonder too, but I also wonder how she knows about my husband and children. Is it the wedding ring? Something about my face?

Rosa spreads cream cheese on a bagel. "Something happened to you. Something bad. Now maybe I am just a nosy woman, but if you would like to talk, I will listen."

Don't look at her, Josie. Don't do it. Ah. My eyes betray me.

She draws me in like a fire's glow on a frosty night. A soft Mona Lisa smile graces her face. She reaches out her hand, still warm from holding the coffee mug, and lays it on my arm.

"You are a wife and mother, no? You have a wedding ring. Your heart necklace has four birthstones. Something made you leave."

So that's how she knew. I reach up, fingering the cool metal and gems of my pendant. There's a garnet for Rob, an opal for me, an emerald for Mitch, an amethyst for Ashley. What a snowstorm we had the day she was born. Traffic at a standstill, Rob shot onto the shoulder. All I kept thinking was, "Not here, not here." Ashley emerged pink and healthy just thirty minutes after they settled me in a room. Later that day, my parents arrived with the pendant, Ashley's amethyst birthstone twinkling with the purple hue that became her favorite color.

Rosa smiles through the steam rising from her cup. "I bet you have a beautiful family."

I open my mouth to suck in a breath. She's killing me. "Yes. It's just…I don't, I can't…"

A gentle squeeze accompanies a soft smile. "No pressure. You can tell me when you are ready. Maybe now is not so good." She takes a sip. I do the same. "How about a little something?" she repeats. "There's raisin toast, bagels, eggs, and English muffins. There's also the fiber cereal that Manny and I eat. Oh, and Connor's Choco Crunch."

Why can't we have Choco Crunch, Mom?

Would it kill me to buy it now and then?

I shake my head. "No, thanks."

"Now, Josie, I will not have someone starve to death in my own home. Half an English muffin, for me? You must try it with the Damson plum jam I got from my friend Nancie."

Guess what, Mrs. Caruso. You can make baby pizzas with English muffins. My auntie does that. They are delicioso!"

It isn't intentional. This is no hunger strike or slow suicide. I love food. Well, the old Josie did. My desire for it died with Carmelita. Now everything tastes like cardboard. But worry lines furrow Rosa's brow. Can I choke down half an English muffin for this sweet woman? I will try. "Okay. Thank you."

While the toaster glows its heat into my English muffin, Rosa fills the minutes with the story of meeting Manny. The tale begins with her proud Spanish parents, descendants of Juan Menendez de Aviles, who established St. Augustine.

Okay, Mitch, what is the oldest European city in the United States? I hold the study sheet, trying to telepathically send him the answer.

I don't know. Saint something.

It's a month, honey. A summer month.

Saint July?

Rosa's lilting voice draws me back. She says her wealthy Spanish family hired a small crew of Mexican gardeners to keep the grounds of their estate neat, green, and flowery. Falling for one of them was out of the question. Forbidden. Taboo. Even the handsome one, fresh from Mexico, who was working his way through seminary. The one with the kind eyes and easy laugh who kept gracing her dreams.

"Well, now, I will not bore you with the whole story. Let us just say there were secret meetings behind the greenhouse, stolen kisses, notes left under the big rock. But love made us bold. We got careless. One evening after dinner, we met behind the barn." Her eyes grow distant— gazing into the past? "I was just eighteen, lost in passion, kissing the only man I ever wanted to kiss for the rest of my life. Suddenly, my father yelled my name. Oh, how we both jumped! Father's face was flame red, eyes glaring like an angry bull. Next to him, my mother stood with her hand to her mouth. 'No, no, no!' she screamed. She called me a disgrace."

Rosa spreads butter onto my English muffin. It melts into the crevices, dripping down the side. She grabs the jar of jam and slathers its sweet, sticky contents onto the toasted muffin. To my surprise, I look forward to taking a bite.

"You see, in their eyes, a Menendez girl was better, higher class, than a hired hand from Mexico. My future husband would come from their circle of Spanish friends and business acquaintances, or he would not come at all. They fired Manny on the spot. I cried until there was not a drop left in me. Have you ever cried like that, Josie? Until you thought you would just die from all the crying?"

I nod. She has no idea.

"Now where was I? Oh, yes. A few days later I was walking through the garden when one of the workers mumbled something while trimming a bush. 'Perdóname?' I asked. Without turning from his work, he said, 'Look under the rock.' Well, I ran so fast I tripped and tore my stockings, but I found my treasure: a note from Manny saying to meet him at the fork in the horse trail at three o'clock."

She stops, taking a bite of muffin. I do the same. For the first time in weeks, I enjoy the flavor, the texture. I take another bite.

"After lunch, I changed into my riding attire and nearly exploded out of my skin while waiting for the groomsman to saddle my white mare, Estrella. She was a beauty. So sweet. *Estrella* means 'star,' you know."

Gardeners? Groomsmen? I never would have guessed Rosa had a silver-spoon past.

"I headed down that trail at full gallop," she continues. "There he was, just like he said. But I was not prepared for what happened next. He helped me down from Estrella, bent on one knee, and held out a thin gold band." Rosa stops to gaze at the worn band around her wedding finger, rubs it with her thumb. "We got married that very day."

She had transported me to that Spanish villa, taken me down the wooded path to where her love awaited. "What about your parents?" The question flows out, surprising me. I want, *need* this answer of how Rosa faced a choice.

"Ah, well. That was not so good. When Manny proposed and I hesitated, he said 'they will forgive you. They love you and they will forgive you.' He was right, but it was many years before they accepted Manny into the family. Even then, we had strained relations with them for a long time. Things improved once our children were born. Thank goodness Manny's family did not have the same prejudices toward *me*. They were warm and loving…and so many of them!"

A breeze flutters gossamer curtains, carrying the scent of the sea into the cozy kitchen. "One by one they moved from Florida to other states. Manny and his brother Roberto were the last of the bunch to immigrate to the U.S. Roberto stayed in Florida for about ten years before moving to Arizona."

Roberto. Arizona. A misty memory creeps along the edge of my brain and lingers. What is it? Why has it suddenly put a wall between me and Rosa?

Rosa stops, her eyes saddened with the hint of tears.

"Do your children live nearby?" I force the question, knowing children are the universal language of mothers in any situation.

"Alexandro, our oldest, runs a dive shop in Key Largo. We see him every few weeks." Saying her son's name brightens her eyes again. "Our baby, Dulce, moved to the Panhandle when her husband got a good job there. They have a baby girl who just turned one. It is hard being so far away. They were all here for Manny's birthday last month. They will be back for Christmas, too, but I will miss them terribly at Thanksgiving. Dulce will be with her in-laws. Alex is going to meet his fiancé's family in St. Petersburg."

"Oh." Her melancholy tones tells me this will be her first Thanksgiving without her kids. I understand…and must change the topic before my cover crumbles like the remnants of my breakfast. "When did you decide to open the animal shelter?"

A small smile. Thank goodness. "Oh, querida, we did not decide. God's hand was in that for certain. It began when my parents died. My sisters and I each received one-third of the estate. But the rest of that story I will save for another day. My mouth has been going like a motor. It is your turn now. Come, tell me about Josie."

Who put this woman in my path? Her soft brown eyes invite me to open up my heart and soul. But I can't. I can't. Because that would mean letting her in, the way I did with Roxy all those years ago, then Ana. And letting people in is dangerous.

"Josie, are you all right, querida? Do you feel like talking to me? Just a bit?"

The toxic waste of terror, pain, grief and guilt threatens to flow out like a raging river. I long to tell her how I adored Carmelita, the spunky little girl who laughed like a bubbling brook and loved with a heart the size of Mexico. How her mother was my best friend and our lives were beautifully entwined in a world full of husbands and children, barbeques and birthdays, soccer and swimming lessons. Sitting on the porch, sharing life. How I single-handedly shattered that world when I killed Carmelita.

But that is not a burden to be shared.

I startle. How long had I stared into the past as memories crashed through my brain? I look at her and shake my head.

"I am so sorry." Her words float just a step above a whisper. "I did not mean to upset you."

"No, it's my fault." I stand, leaving the still-steaming mug on the table. "Please forgive me. I have to go." The screen door thumps shut as I head down the sandy path to the endless blue Atlantic. Behind me, chains forged on that foggy night drag gullies through the sand. Will they weigh me down forever? Is there no one who can snap the iron links and set me free? I trudge toward the horizon, hoping somewhere out there is an answer.

Chapter 12

Josie

Rosa has not knocked on my door for three days, except to announce Tina's arrival. My cousin dismissed my repeated assurances that I'm doing fine, and drove up from Key West to see for herself. By the time she left, *she* wanted to move into Rosa's Haven.

A grimace tightens Rosa's face as she strains to place a ceramic vase on a shelf in the gift shop. I fight my instincts to rush over and help her. Each time I've tried, she says "no, Josie, I need to do these things myself. To get better, I must go past my comfort zone." From where I stand, she spends more time out of it than in it. She shines her smile when she knows someone is near, but I've seen her when she's unaware I'm watching. Frustration furrows her forehead when her wheelchair can't maneuver over uneven ground, or something she needs is out of reach. Each time she tries to stand, pain etches her eyes.

And adding to her burden, a silently sullen guest who has rejected every opportunity to spill her guts. I do what I can to earn my keep: stocking shelves in the gift shop, setting out beach chairs in the morning, washing dishes after meals. But disclosing the reason I'm here…no. Cleaning stalls is easier…and far more preferable. Today, after the beach chairs were set up and all the new merchandise shelved, Rosa shooed me out.

"Go," she said. "Take the rest of today off. You need some quiet time to figure out whatever needs figuring. Go and pray, querida."

Pray. My eyes turn heavenward. I doubt what I have to say would be considered a prayer.

Azure waves lap the shore, propelled by a barely there sea breeze. Sandpipers skitter a safe distance in front of me as their long, skinny beaks peck the sand for insects and tiny crustaceans. Food and shelter. It is all they need, with both plentiful here in the Keys. How nice for you, little birds. God takes care of you while we humans flounder in a storm-tossed sea.

I feel for the cell phone that has found a permanent place in my pocket since turning onto that southbound highway five days ago. That first night, Rob's messages wound their way through wires and circuits, reaching my heart in that Atlanta motel. "Come home," he'd said. "We can work it out. We love you, Jo. We'll help you through this." The second message came thirty minutes later. "Honey, please call me. We all want you home." Three more messages broke the silence of that dismal room. I longed to hear his voice, to ask how Mitch was doing. To tell Ashley it's better for all of them this way. But their voices would have only drawn me back like a sailor to the sea. Back to a home where a family walked on tiptoes around the dysfunctional zombie in the bedroom. I steadied my resolve, leaving a message the next day after they'd left the house.

Rays of sun blaze directly through my sea-breezed hair onto a scalp unaccustomed to hours of fierce heat. High noon in the islands. At some point I'd abandoned the beach for sidewalks. Must have been hours ago.

Blistered feet cry out for rest, aching for the familiar comfort of shoes. Until those demands are met, they are going on strike. I am oh so many miles from Rosa's Haven, but in a place where the water-to-land ratio heavily favors the water, I should be able to find refuge. A sign announcing Sunnyside Beach beckons me to trudge on. Maybe there's a water fountain, a shady place to sit. I limp toward the beach, watching ghostly waves of heat rise from the deserted street. The intelligent life forms are inside air-conditioned buildings or frolicking in cool ocean waves.

Sunnyside is nothing less than paradise. My tortured feet get me to the restroom and water fountain, where I drink like a Death Valley refugee. And then they are done. I turn to face the ocean. Images of that lovely water washing over my parched skin spur me forward. From one patch of shade to another I run until reaching the water's edge. Setting my cell phone at the base of a palm, I dash straight into that salty blue heaven.

It is everything I need and more. Cool, wet, life-giving. It soaks into my skin, my spirit. At waist level, I fall forward, floating in a sea of tranquility until my need for air exceeds my need for water. A couple of breaths and back to silent submersion. Hidden from the world. Perfect.

Water sated, I grab my soggy waistband, hold my shorts in place, and head for a patch of sea grass under a large palm, snatching up my cell along the way. A soft breeze kisses my damp skin, rustling the palm branches overhead. A snow-white egret lands majestically on the shore, feathery wings shimmer in the sun. I long to feel the softness of those shimmering feathers beneath my fingers, no less so than decades ago when I was just a munchkin on a Florida vacation.

The kids would love this place. Donning snorkels and fins, they would skim the surface for hours, switching to Frisbee and shelling later in the day, watching the sunset. My babies. Rob would love it, too. Maybe here the sand and sea would call him to come and play, eroding the years of work and stress. Beneath the palms, we could dance together again.

The cell phone stares up at me from its cradle of grass. Maybe now would be a good time to leave another message. I've been choosing the moments strategically, so as not to actually make contact with anyone.

"You have five new voicemail messages," the cheery voice chirps in my ear. I enter my password, hold my breath. A jogger runs by in a Speedo that probably fit him a couple of decades ago. Tummy bobbing, he pounds the sand along the water line.

"First message."

Rob again. Same for the next. He wants to come and get me. Hates it that I'm with strangers instead of at Tina's. He doesn't get it. Bringing me home is not the answer. Tina is not happy with me either. When she visited, she tried a hundred ways to bring me to her island inn.

Next up is Ashley. "I love you, Mom. I miss you. Please come home." A cracked goodbye freezes my throat in mid-swallow. Blues, greens, and tans blur in front of me.

"I can't, sweetheart," I say to no one but the sandpipers.

Mom's aged voice fills the number three spot. Same spiel as Rob, with the addition of assuring me no one blames me. It was, after all, "just an accident."

Aunt Theresa wraps it up. "Josie, dear, please listen to me. You can't do this on your own. You're in a very dark place right now. We love you, dear. We've been glad to get your messages. The kids are fine. Missing you, of course, but fine. Call your mother."

I scroll past the names of people I long to hold and click on "home."

"Josie!" Aunt Theresa's voice nearly sends the phone flying out of my hand. "Oh, how I've been hoping you'd call when I was here."

"Auntie." I grip my cell with whatever strength I have left. "I wasn't expecting you. I mean, um…"

"I've been staying here most weekdays. Sometimes overnight. But tell me about you, dear. What's going on with you?"

"I'm okay. How are the kids?"

"Well, they're very worried, you know. They miss you, sweetheart. Rob, too, and your mother. I know you're going through a horrible time, but this is when you need the love and support of your family."

And this is why I didn't want to call.

"I know. Please just tell them I love them. Tell Mom I'll call her soon. Very soon."

"I will, dear. I certainly will. And we're all praying for you. Every day."

"Oh. Thanks."

Was my demolished car an answer to someone's prayer? Crazy Benny trying to burn down the barn? I shiver. Could both things somehow be true?

"Why aren't you at Tina's?"

I give her the rundown on Rebecca becoming co-owner of the inn and me not wanting to burden Tina at her busiest time of year. That I'm safe, living with a nice family. "I have to go now, Auntie. Thank you so much for staying with the kids."

"No, Josie, wait."

I pretend not to hear, press end, hating myself for shutting out the person who's caring for my family. I lean back against the trunk of a palm, closing my eyelids, which do little to contain the warm drops rolling down my cheeks.

My eyes open to a world of sunlight, squinting until they can adjust. How long had I slept? The picnic table where a family gathered earlier stands barren of the tote bag full of soggy beach towels and floaties. Teens toss a Frisbee around in the shallows, their backpacks grouped together on the grass. Must be after three o'clock. I sit up, head woozy from the unexpected nap, lips parched from a day spent outside with nothing more than a few sips from a water fountain. What I would give for a cool glass of sweet, tangy…

"Lemonade?"

A paper cup appears in front of me as though conjured by a genie, fragrant with the citrusy scent of fresh lemons. Clearly, I am still asleep and dreaming. I shade my eyes to see the man behind the voice. Windblown hair, the color of bittersweet chocolate, falls in waves to his shoulders. Probably a musician…or just a beach bum. The stick man on his faded gray T-shirt proclaims "life is good." Weathered sandals look like they've walked a thousand miles for a thousand years. It's a wonder they still hold together.

"Go ahead, take it. The lemons are from Capri. That Mediterranean sun makes them extra good. " His deep, gentle voice assures me there is nothing to fear. I know better. Logic dictates that nice guys don't just walk up to total strangers with a glass of lemonade.

"I made it myself. All fresh ingredients, not like that powdered stuff they sell at the concession stand. The cup is recycled paper. Better for the earth." A fleeting sadness shadows his face before the corners of his mouth turn up again.

Don't take anything from strangers, my mother's voice echoes from the past. *Don't take anything from strangers*, I've told my children for years.

"Don't be afraid," he says, soft brown eyes affirming his words. And I am not.

I take the cup. The perfect mix of lemons, water, and sugar flows down my throat. Sweet, tangy, utterly delicious. It clears the fuzziness from my brain, which can now function enough to wonder why a stranger is offering lemonade. The best that's ever graced my lips. Then it hits me. What if he's *selling* this?

"I can't pay for this," I say a bit too late.

"It's a gift." Dark eyes twinkle. "No payment required."

I thank him, wondering what in the world I look like after soaking in saltwater and falling asleep on the beach? I run my fingers through sand-gritty hair.

"Mind if I share your shade?" He gestures to a patch of cool sand a couple of feet from where I'm sitting. "It's the best spot here."

His gentle demeanor overshadows my desire to tell him I want to be alone with my endless tangle of thoughts. Best to offer him the spot with a smile, and find another sanctuary for myself further down the beach.

"Actually, you can have it." I turn toward him, my smile forming all on it's own. Natural. "I was just leaving." Still leaning against the palm's trunk, I swipe sand from my grainy cheek, then my calves. He plops down cross-legged a few feet in front of me. I wince as my over baked feet anchor into the sand in an effort to push myself up. Sinking back down, I examine flamingo pink blisters—my reward for hours of walking shoeless in the sun. One thing is sure, I will not be returning to Rosa's by the same mode of transportation that got me here. Despite the fact it is the only mode I have.

"Pretty view, don't you think?" He stares at the water, unaware of my predicament.

"Uh-huh." Sorry, Beach Man, it's the best this fragment of my former self can do. Please sit quietly and ignore me. But no, he turns completely around, facing me full on. Forsaking all that I've learned about manners over the past thirty-eight years, I stare like a star-struck adolescent, though the reason eludes me. He is certainly no Hugh Jackman in the looks or body department. He would never make top twenty of any rag magazine's hottest men list. Yet…he is beautiful. Soft hair, kind, confident, eyes. His face an alluring combination of tender and masculine. My hand, the very same hand that could not reach out to comfort my son, wants to touch his cheek. Warmth permeates my heart. Why are these feelings washing over me? If I leave now, I will never know.

He sits unfazed by the gaping stranger before him. "Decide to stay awhile?"

"Uh-huh."

"I see." He fixes his eyes on mine, thoughtfully contemplating my dimwitted answer before turning his gaze to the water. "Beautiful, isn't it?"

"Yes."

Sparkling water caresses the shore, then slips back again, hypnotic in its beauty and rhythm. Time melts away. We stare at the water, the sea birds, people playing on the beach. I am part of the salty waves and island breeze, the warm grains beneath me and the endless atmosphere above. He turns to face me again. A question forms on my lips.

I point to his shirt. "Do you believe that?"

He looks down at the words 'life is good' with its silly stick man. "Do *you*?"

Normally it bugs me when someone answers a question with a question, but he seems to sincerely want to know what I think. "No. I used to think it was pretty good. Not anymore."

"Because something shipwrecked your world." No question mark punctuates the statement.

"How did you know?" This island is starting to feel a bit Twilight Zone-ish, like everyone possesses a sixth sense.

"Stands to reason. Something joyful happens, people believe life is good. When the bottom drops out, vice versa." He fingers the sand, watching the grains cascade from his palm, turns his gaze back to me. "Yes, I believe life is good. A gift from our Creator. Abundant in miracles, for those who choose to see them. Brimming with opportunities for each of us to shine like lighthouse beams." Distress shadows his face. "But people often make choices that dull those beams, or never even bother to shine them at all. So my answer is…life is good. Whether it's good for an *individual,* well now, that depends."

"On?"

"What you believe, where you turn for guidance. Choices."

"Sometimes things just happen. No choice involved."

He sprinkles sand on my hand, smiling as I brush it off. "The choice lies in how you respond. More importantly, what you do before responding."

"What do *you* do?"

"I pray. I figure, if God can make the heavens and Earth, tornados and volcanoes. Babies. Chocolate…can't forget that. And if He loves us unconditionally like the Bible says, then I want to tap into that. Know what I mean?" His smile outshines the Florida sun. Never have I been so enraptured by a face. A voice. If I listen to him speak until sundown, it will not be long enough.

"Prayers don't always fix things." I wait, anxious to hear his response.

Ocean-blue eyes gaze into mine, beyond that red hot "K." I cannot unlock my eyes from his. Wouldn't if I could. In the silence, I feel him exploring the valleys and caverns of my heart. Seeking the dark, cold place from which that statement came.

"Josie." He sighs my name, the sound of it visibly hurting him in some incomprehensible way. "I don't believe you're speaking from experience."

When did I tell him my name?

"Preacher mentioned you to me. We are long-time friends."

But…I didn't ask him out loud.

He pats my hand again, his weathered palm warm as the sun-baked sand. The name thing becomes utterly insignificant as I await his next words.

"The One who created you wants to hear from you. Wants to guide you toward good choices, a brighter future. Hope."

It sounds so simple. Even kind of…beautiful, with a hint of disconcerting. If God really listens, all He's heard from me is anger. Why should I shift gears? A prayer isn't going to bring Carmie back. But what if…what if something changed? What if that something helped

Ana? Or got me home? I pluck a fallen palm frond from the sand and tie it in knots, contemplating my answer.

"It's just a conversation," he says, gentle words falling like silent snow. "A private communication between you and someone who loves you, someone who understands anger and pain. And broken hearts."

"My heart's fine."

He grimaces. "Please don't lie." The sadness shadowing his beautiful face shames my soul. What this stranger thinks of me shouldn't matter. He's no one to me—just a guy on the beach getting way too personal. Too deep. No, nothing he says should matter at all.

But it does. Because some primal desire inside me, buried beneath granite slabs of guilt and grief, wants to believe there is hope.

I toss the knotted frond onto the sand and sigh. "Okay."

"Great." I am rewarded again with the smile. "Now one more thing. A favor, if you're willing. Go to Preacher's church, Sunday after this one. I've been helping him with the sermon. You'll like it."

"You help Preacher?"

"Always. He'd really like you to come."

Guilt constricts my heart. Rosa says Preacher works hard on those sermons, making sure every word reflects God's true message. He asked so politely the other day—nothing pushy, just letting me know I'm welcome to attend. "I'll think about it."

He squeezes my hand. Releases it. "I know."

"Why the Sunday *after* this one?"

"It will be particularly good. Anyway, you won't be ready this Sunday."

"How do you—"

"Have we been walking on coals?" He cuts me off...on purpose. Concerned eyes fix on my blistered feet.

My eyes follow his gaze to toes that can't even wiggle without cracking like sun-dried tomatoes. "Something like that."

"Looks painful."

Compassion weaves through his words. It is something I do not deserve and definitely don't want. Or do I? "Not really."

He sighs. "Another lie." He reaches into his backpack, withdrawing the thermos once again. "Let's rinse them off and see how badly you've managed to maim yourself."

Lemonade on my feet? Images of black ants crawling between sticky-sweet toes send a shiver up my spine. "No, thanks."

"It's special water. It will feel good. Trust me." Without waiting for a reply, he drizzles the cool water over my feet, rinsing away the sand, transporting my feet from Death Valley to a shady, green forest. I forget that I'm miles from my new refuge, sitting on a beach where someone I've known for fifteen minutes is pouring water over my feet. Only it feels better than water, more like aloe vera gel. I want to soak my feet in it from now 'til Tuesday.

"Mmm. That feels amazing."

"There are far more amazing things in this world, Josie Caruso. In time, you will experience them. This is not amazing, but I'm glad you feel better."

His gaze quiets my spirit. Leaning back against the tree, I breathe in the island scent of saltwater and coconut oil. Palm trees swish melodically in the warm breeze. An egret swoops to shore, its snowy feathers gleaming in the sunlight. Logic tells me my world is still a war zone. But my mind floats in a sea of tranquility, drifting in the silence between us.

"Close your eyes and relax. I have to make a call." He returns the thermos to his backpack and pulls out a cell.

I am perched under a palm tree in the Florida Keys, conversing with a long-haired stranger about matters of the heart, and it all feels as natural as breathing. My eyes close at his suggestion and I lean against the palm trunk, thinking about that prayer and wondering what I'll say. Wondering if it will make a difference.

"May I please get a pick-up at Sunnyside?" His hypnotic voice distracts me from my thoughts. "Yes, that's fine. Would you please send Hector Santiago?" With a "thank you," he clicks off the phone. "Think you can make it to the parking lot? Your cab will be here shortly. Hector will take you back."

"I can't pay for a cab."

"Gotcha covered." He sets his hand, palm up, on the sand. A lime green lizard scurries onto it and stops. He strokes its back with a fingertip.

"You can't pay with a lizard."

He bellows a laugh so hardy it sends the lizard scampering up the tree's patchy trunk. "I've always loved your sense of humor." My mouth opens to question the "always," but the master of cutting me off does it again. "I was actually planning to pay in cash."

"No. It's very thoughtful of you, but I can't accept it. You don't even know me."

"Sure I do."

"And I don't want you spending money on me."

"Believe me, money is no big deal. Really. People have made it so, but it shouldn't be. In a perfect world, we wouldn't even need it, right? Anyway, you'll be helping someone." He fishes around inside the backpack. "My cabbie friend, Hector, has a sick daughter. No health insurance. He takes extra shifts to cover her high-priced medicine. Today's been slow and he could really use a fare. Please, Josie. For Hector."

What do I say to that? I nod. "Thank you."

"My pleasure."

His hand reappears from the backpack holding a hundred dollar bill, like it was just lying in wait. "This is for the ride."

Does he realize it's not a twenty? "Umm…wow. A bit much, don't you think? I doubt he'll have change."

"Don't want any."

Words elude me. I've helped people with my time and money, but this gesture…the sincerity of it…it's like he's paying the cabbie with a chunk of his own heart. "You're a good friend. I hope Hector knows that."

"He does. We've traveled many roads together. Lost touch during his early twenties, but he found me again. We've been tight ever since."

Again his hand disappears into the backpack, this time emerging with a twin to the hundred. "Please give him this tip when he drops you off." He presses it into my palm as my brain contemplates the possibility that a local bank got robbed this morning.

No sooner does the thought enter my head than I hear his soft chuckle. So weird.

"How do you know I won't keep this?"

He smiles, patting my hand once more. "It's not even a remote possibility."

Now *there's* a trusting soul. I wonder how often he gets ripped off. "Why are you doing this?" blurts out of my mouth.

"People need to love one another, take care of each other. It's important, Josie. It could change the world."

There he goes again, using my name like we're long-time friends.

"I should probably start making my way over there." Fisting the sand, I begin to shift. "It may take the whole ten minutes for me to go that short distance."

He stands, effortlessly, which I can't help envy. "I will carry you."

That is so not going to happen. "No, I'll be fine. You've done so much already."

"Please, I'd like to do this."

"Thanks, really, but I can walk by myself."

He shakes his head, like I just gave the wrong answer in math class. "That's not true, Josie. Walking alone will only hurt you more. It's time you figured that out. Let me grasp your arm. Lean on me." He doesn't wait for an answer, just holds out his hand. "Come on, you're going to need help getting up. That's the hardest part."

I grab his hand. Warm, strong. He pulls me up like a father lifting a toddler. The heat must be getting to me. Nearly limp with tranquility, I force myself to let go, though holding on feels so natural, so right. But it isn't. Imagine Rob, seeing me hand in hand with a stranger. Rob, whom I left behind despite promises to stay for better or for worse. But worse was never supposed to be like this. "Worse" was supposed to mean things like losing a job, a broken leg, a leaky roof.

The hot sand sears my tender feet. I stand on my own, knowing he is waiting for me to lean on him. Not sure yet if that's a good idea.

The cab driver does not recognize the beach man. I see it in his eyes, but ask anyway to make sure I'm not crazy. He hands the hundred back to me when I pay him. "No, señora. Too big. No change." Confusion clouds his eyes when I say I don't need change. After reassurances, he tucks it in his pocket, whispers "*Dios mío*" and crosses himself. I reach into my pocket for the tip, my pulse kicking up a notch in anticipation of giving it to him. It is the first trace of excitement I've felt since that night. When I produce the second bill, Hector's eyebrows nearly arch off his face.

He shakes his head, waving one hand. "Too much, too much."

"It's not from me. A friend asked me to give you this."

"Who is this friend? Why he give?"

How do I explain someone and something I don't understand?

"I don't know him. Please take it. He really wants you to have it, and so do I." It's easy enough to see he is a proud man, determined to earn his own money. But this is a gift—a gift that he desperately needs to help his daughter. And still he hesitates. This is going to take a little more effort on my part. I reach forward and press the bill into his hand.

Eyes shiny, he cups my hand in his. Part of me wants to pull away. But another part, struggling to surface through the anguish, wants that man's joy to blossom in my heart.

"*Es un milagro.*" He whispers the words as he gazes at the money, then locks eyes with me. "A miracle." He does not let go. I realize he is waiting for confirmation.

"Yes." I nod. He does not release his grip until I repeat it, nodding again. I slip off the back seat with a "muchas gracias" and watch the cab until it turns out of the driveway.

Thanks to Rosa, bandages and thrift store gym shoes protect my battered feet as I walk the trampled path to the barn. It is after hours, my favorite time. All the visitors have left the shelter, though a few still linger on the beach. I breathe in the heavy sea air, rewinding the cab scenario, trying to make sense of something that is inexplicable. Why did Beach Man pretend to know the cabdriver? It is just one of many questions ricocheting around my brain like a pinball. Why did I feel so peaceful in his presence? I haven't felt comfortable around anyone since that horrible night.

Sudden movement in the parking lot benches my thoughts. A leg disappears into a blue rental car. The door slams, and the car zips away before I can see the driver's face. Must be in a hurry. I watch the car without knowing why it has captured my attention. The red glow of brake lights surprises me. It stops halfway down the drive. I stare like I've never seen a car before, unable to look away. Cemented to the sea grass. The brake lights flicker off and it continues onto Highway One. Crazy, like everything else that has happened here, with people and beasts coming and going. One thing is certain: it couldn't possibly have been anyone I know.

Something deep inside cries out, as has happened nonstop since... Carmelita. I try to shake anxious thoughts from my head. Continuing to the barn, I push open the tall double doors and head into my sanctuary.

In the dim mustiness, the young horse balances on reedy legs inside his stall. Head hung low, but standing. Rarely does he go more than an hour without a visitor to ensure his water pail is full and his courageous heart still beats. Melissa slipped out the door moments ago. It is just he and I.

"Hey, buddy." My words float, whispery. His soft whinny nearly bursts my aching heart. In seconds, I am at his emaciated side, stroking the sleek neck hidden beneath a straggly mane. The kids are aching to wash and brush him, soon as Dr. Mike gives the thumbs up.

"How ya doin' today?" He nuzzles his response. A velvet nose, soft as Clover, brushes my arm. "Did you enjoy your pasture romp?" It was actually more of a stagger, but he looked happy out there...considering. "You're looking better. I guess in your case anything beyond almost dead qualifies as better."

Lizards scuttle across the wooden rail, stopping to rest in a patch of sunlight. That's what we need, Lightning and I. A bright, warm, glowing patch of sunlight. Something to gently melt away the pain. The memories. Maybe Melissa and Connor will be Lightning's rays of sun.

"Those kids are going to love away your past and make you healthy and strong." I brush the forelock from his deep russet eyes. "A credit to your name." He nudges my arm again. "Now don't you go getting too attached, okay? Melissa and I are both leaving soon. Best to set your sights on Connor."

Lightning's warm breath feathers the hair on my bare arm. I whisper the question that's been asked since the dawn of man.

"Why us?"

The only response is the dull sound of a leather sandal stepping on the wooden barn floor. Lightning's eyes widen. I jerk my hand away with a gasp. Ears forward, head up, he stares over my shoulder.

"So tell me, why do you talk to this horse?" The voice comes from behind a high stack of hay. Preacher steps out, a dented tin pail dangling from his hand. We gaze at each other as my temporarily unguarded heart hastens to rebuild its walls.

"You were spying?"

"Not intentionally, señora. I generally leave the spying to Connor, who unfortunately does it well and often. You started talking before I had a chance to make my presence known. You have been so quiet with us, Josie. I thought it might help to listen, get to know who you are."

"Oh."

"So my question remains. Why do you talk to this horse and not to us?"

A small gray bird flutters around the rafters, searching for a way out.

"I don't know."

Preacher opens the barn door, but the bird zips up to the hayloft window and thumps against the glass three times before retreating to the rafters. I long to fly. Escape. But of course, cannot.

"Hmm. I am thinking. A horse, he is not judgmental like people? Am I right?"

"I guess." I run my fingers over the silky outside of Lightning's ears. Movement above catches my eye. The bird finally discovers the open door and heads for freedom. How I envy it.

"And a horse, he will not ask you questions that perhaps you do not want to answer."

"Okay, yeah."

Preacher sets down his pail, sits on a bundled hay bale. "But a horse, he cannot guide you. He cannot provide advice or compassion, wisdom or strength. So when you are done talking, nothing has changed."

"And nothing will." Lightning walks toward his water bucket, leaving me to face Preacher alone.

"Josie, if I may ask, do you believe in God?"

Here we go. I can't prevent the sigh that slips out like a slow air leak in a tire. "Yeah, I guess."

"But?"

This man has given me shelter and food without pressing me to say anything about anything. It's only right to engage in this conversation, if such a thing would please him. I owe him that much. And yet…the beach conversation was enough for one day. Another one might send me over the edge.

"Here's the thing." My fingers wrap around the railing. "I just don't want to discuss this. I'm sorry. You deserve more than that." Who knew I had room for more guilt? But there it is, heaping itself comfortably on top of the pile.

"No, no, it is not a problem. We won't discuss it, if you will just finish your thought. You believe in him, *but…*"

"I'm not a big fan. Sorry."

"Ah. I see. No need to apologize. Not to me, anyway. How about the devil? He is a fair topic of discussion?"

"Red face, pointy horns, nasty. That one?"

"On the contrary. Beautiful, charming, intelligent. So very enchanting." He sets down his bucket and bends to pet Lucy, who's nudging him with her nubby little horns.

"Apparently, we watch different movies."

"Josie, if the devil were as you say, who would listen to him?"

"I don't know. Vampires, werewolves?" Lucy bleats as if distressed by the mention of monsters. Mama goat saunters over and offers a comforting bleat.

Preacher gestures, his palms up, sermon style. "But they are myth, and Satan is horrifically real."

"I never really gave him much thought."

"Starvation, war, greed, slavery. He infiltrates like a poisonous fog. He convinces people that his lies are truth."

"I don't know, Preacher. I've got God's mighty foot squashing me into the ground, so there's been precious little time to contemplate the other guy."

"The greatest trick the devil ever played was convincing people he doesn't exist."

"Interesting line."

"Stolen line. My favorite from *The Usual Suspects*. And sadly, it is also true. Here is another line for you: 'In this world you will have trouble. But take heart! I have overcome the world.'"

"Stolen again?"

"Borrowed from Jesus. We can borrow lines from the Bible. God encourages that."

Lightning returns, water dripping from his lips, then tosses his head. Drops splatter my T-shirt. I welcome the comic relief, but it is far too short-lived. "So what's this all about, Preacher? Your message eludes me."

He stands up and joins me at the horse enclosure, scratching Lightning gently behind the ears, but keeping his gaze on me. Eyes deepen. "The devil lies, Josie. And there is no one better at it than he. It is something I felt you needed to know, because he is lying to you."

"You're saying *the devil* is lying to *me*, Josie Caruso. And what exactly is the devil lying to me about?"

"Ah, *that* is the question. I will leave you and Lightning alone to ponder it."

Chapter 13

Preacher

I return the phone to the safety of its cradle, having just ended my conversation with a battered soul. Ana was always the happy one, with a smile just looking for a reason to burst forth. Oh, how her laughter always made others laugh, too. Sweet Ana, so excited when her precious Carmie was born.

It's a girl, Manny! I have another little princessa! Savanna is so excited to be a big sister. Oh, Manny, when can you come visit? You and Rosa just have to see her. She's an angel.

We talk nearly every day now, her pain seeping through the telephone into my heart. In the midst of her despair, she asks about Josie. Is she all right? Is she eating? Does she talk about coming home? Sometimes her concern is replaced with anger, sometimes hurt, but one thing remains constant—Ana wants her safe. How many times have I promised not to let Josie leave this place? If it makes Ana happy, I will promise every day. But I fear this promise has led me to continue my deception. Perhaps some deceptions are acceptable. Does a desire to protect justify deception, or am I justifying sin? If I tell Josie I am Ana's brother and she runs off, I have broken my promise not only to Ana, but also to Josie's husband. The man has called me three times since surprising me with a visit. My conviction wanes. It is wrong not to reveal my identity to Josie. I must find a way to tell her who I am, while assuring her this is a healing place.

Ah, Lord, Your broken animals, they are easy to fix. Good food, medicine, lots of love. This combination nearly always ends in happiness. But we humans are a complicated mess. We entangle ourselves in pursuits and beliefs that do not come from You. I look at Your broken Josie, knowing You want me to help her, not knowing how. Worse, remembering she was driving the car. I try not to reveal my judgmental heart to the world, but You see it all.

My office chair will no longer do. I slide off, my bare knees thumping on the carpet.

Oh, God, You have placed many in my path. Never have I felt so torn. Guide me, tell me. Make it loud and clear so it will crash through my muddled-up soul. Rain down Your strength and wisdom on me in torrents. Help me reach her with the message You want her to hear.

I seldom notice the ticking of my abalone wall clock, but now it fills the room like a mariachi band. How can I hear the whisper of the Holy Spirit with all that noise? I move back into my chair, face in hands, letting exhaustion sweep through my body. Still half a day to go, and already I feel like sinking into that bed with Rosa curled up next to me, breathing in the lilac scent of her hair, her skin.

A thump calls my attention to the window where a tuft of red hair emerges just above the outside pane.

Mi amiguito. I open the door to find him crouched beneath the window. Connor looks at me with no apology.

"You done?" He stands up, grinning that missing-tooth grin.

"With?"

"I seen you prayin', so I figured I'd just keep peeking till you were done. Dad said not to bother you when you're prayin.'"

"Yes, I am done. Thank you for not interrupting, though I prefer to be *completely* alone when I am having a private conversation with the Lord. *Entiendes?*"

"Yeah, I get it. Sorry." With the tip of his gym shoe, he scuffs lines in the sandy dirt. "So, who was the guy in the blue car? Was he from Illinois like Josie? He had a Chicago Cubs shirt."

I was hoping no one would see him, but the boy misses nothing.

"Just a visitor." My heart quickens as I imagine him telling Josie about the Illinois visitor. Trying to prevent it will only bring a deluge of questions. She doesn't need to know her husband was here. Not yet. Best to distract him. "Does your father know you were coming here after school?"

"Yeah, it's okay. Rosa called yesterday to see if I wanted to meet Rocky. Someone on the rescue squad found him yesterday off Summerland Key." Connor reaches into his blue jeans pocket and pulls out a package of lime green gum, the kind that comes in fat little squares. Removing two pieces, he hands one to me. "Try it. It's got the juicy stuff in the middle."

I accept, not sure "juicy stuff" sounds particularly appealing. "So, this Rocky...Green Sea Turtle or Loggerhead?"

Connor tosses his piece in the air, opening his mouth like a baby bird. The gum finds its target. "Ain't neither one. Hawksbill. Boat propeller got him." Connor shoves his gum wrapper into his front pocket, already bulging with who-knows-what.

I pop the gum into my mouth and bite down. Sweet, sticky liquid squirts onto my tongue, mixing with the sugary gum. Hopefully, Ben is keeping up with Connor's dental check-ups. The boy has enough to handle without cavities, too. But despite having more challenges than any boy should, he stands before me with bright eyes, a good mind... and such a heart.

"Rosa said we could see him today." A green bubble pops all over his lips. "You comin'?"

"Would not miss it."

Conner's eyes twinkle as he prepares to tell me the next part of his plan. "I was thinkin', maybe after the Turtle Hospital, we could go to the Hurricane. You know, for chicken wings. Fried cheesecake, too."

"When you *think*, it always empties my pockets." I pull out the inside of my shorts pocket for dramatic effect.

A leathery lizard scuttles by just inches from Connor's gym shoe. He dives for it but misses...as always. "Shoot!" Connor's brow scrunches with the seriousness of a grown man.

Little does the boy know how much we enjoy taking him to dinner, watching his eyes widen as a plate of food and a milkshake are set before him. I cannot make it too easy, though. No, no, that would take away all the fun. His face lights up with a new way to justify the outing.

"I got an A on my spelling test today."

"Well, that might be something worth celebrating." Running up from the beach, Frisco woofs in agreement.

"Yes!" A victory smile covers half of Connor's face as he shoots his fist into the air. "Hey, Preacher, you think Josie would want to come?"

"She barely eats anything, *amigo*. I do not think she would be interested."

"Not to the Hurricane!" He is appalled that I would make such a connection. "To the Turtle Hospital."

"*Ay yi yi*, Connor. You must warn me when we are switching topics." Frisco flops onto his side for a belly rub, and I'm happy to comply. "It is difficult to say what Josie would like to do. You may ask her, though."

"She's kinda weird, huh? I mean, not bad weird, just weird. Nice, though. I ain't saying anything bad about her, right?" As quickly as he appeared, Frisco lopes back to the beach, content with his human encounter.

"It is all right for you to ask. Perhaps this Josie has a problem, you know? And she doesn't want to share her problem, so she stays very quiet like our Lightning. He doesn't run around or make much sound because he is healing, no?"

"You think somebody starved *her*, too? She's kinda skinny."

I turn my face away so he does not see the smile. Heart-rending topic, to be sure. Still, his naiveté, despite what he's gone through, makes me want to chuckle. "No, I think Josie is thin because she is not eating, and she is not eating for the same reason she is so quiet."

"The secret problem?"

"Sí."

"I'll find out what it is." Suddenly he is a boy on a mission, ready to engage his sleuthing skills. "I'll listen in when she talks to Lightning. She does that, you know, when she thinks nobody's there. Don't worry, she won't see me."

I have full confidence in his ability to accomplish the mission. Still…

"Oh no, no. Listen to me, Mr. James Bond. You let Josie figure this out for herself. Give her privacy. When she is ready to talk, she will talk. Entiendes?"

"Yeah, I get it. Come on; let's go ask her. Maybe seeing the hurt turtles will make her problem seem like not so bad."

I couldn't love him more if he were mine.

The four of us drive to the Turtle Hospital in Rosa's car, despite the protests of one eight-year-old who loves riding in the back of my pickup. That freckle-faced Dennis the Menace actually got Josie to come. She sits silent as the turtles we are going to visit. Undaunted, Connor provides an ongoing recitation of the hospital's current inhabitants, their ailments, the doctors.

"Sometimes they have bubble butt." Laughter explodes, preventing him from further explanation. His words do not convey a lack of sympathy. The child simply cannot say bubble butt without erupting in giggles. Josie offers a tight-lipped smile as Connor winds down. "It's when the turtle gets hit by a boat's hull. They get a big lumpy thing on their shell." Having exhausted all his sea turtle knowledge, he moves on to the doctors, providing names, descriptions, and commentary on their personalities.

"And my favorite is Lucille, 'cause she's always real happy and nice."

The boy speaks the truth, but I know the real reason for Lucille's prominent position on Connor's pedestal. "And she always gives you a candy, no?"

"Yeah, but I'd like her anyways. Lucille is Black, with glasses and super short hair. She's the operator on the shark attack turtles, right, Rosa?"

"Oh, yes. She is an excellent surgeon." Rosa reaches over and places her hand on my leg as we drive past resorts and souvenir shops. Rainbow-colored wind chimes dangle from the gutters of Mermaid's Gifts and Treasures. With a glint in her eye, Rosa points to The Honeycomb, her favorite candy store. I love the child inside the woman. I nod my understanding. We will stop on the way back.

"So now you know all the doctors." Connor leans back, crossing his arms, clearly pleased with a job well done.

Will Josie acknowledge his lengthy dissertation? Please, señora, give the boy a little something. Josie nods her thanks in my rear view mirror. Just when I think that is all our Connor will get, the corners of her mouth turn up. "Sounds great," she says. "Can't wait to get there."

I turn into the Turtle Hospital parking lot, my car's interior radiating light from Connor's triumphant smile.

Lucille slips Connor a peanut butter cup as she tells us Rocky's prognosis is good, though he will be a three-finned turtle from this point forward. No internal tumors is the good news of the day. In the other room, her assistants are prepping the unconscious patient for the first of two surgeries. Rosa tells Lucille she will hold a fundraiser to help pay for his treatment. She whips a notepad out of her purse to jot down ideas.

Back in the car, she appears preoccupied. I let her be, knowing her mind is whirling with ways to raise money.

"Turtle Brownies day!" She claps her hands together. "It is just the thing. I have a wonderful recipe from Nancie." She shifts to turn toward Josie in the back seat. "Nancie McDermott and I go way back, before she was a famous cookbook author. Her recipes are wonderful!"

"You're friends with Nancie McDermott?" An unexpected note of excitement, ever so subtle, infuses Josie's words. "I have three of her cookbooks."

I smile, knowing Rosa will call Nancie as soon as we get home to tell her our somber guest actually spoke to us when Rosa mentioned her name.

Rosa turns to face forward again. "We will make her Turtle Mocha Brownies and sell them next Saturday at the gift shop. I'll call Sam at the newspaper as soon as we get home, and he'll write it up. It doesn't hurt to have a reporter on the Rescue Squad. Think we can sell one hundred? That would be a good start."

She does not see what I see in the rear view mirror. Horror whitens Connor's face, brown eyes wide as teacup saucers. When the reason sinks in, I swallow my laughter and open my mouth to explain. Too late.

"No! Rosa! Noooo!" Near hysteria catapults Connor's pitch and volume. He leans forward, straining against his seat belt to wrap trembling fingers around the top of Rosa's seat. "You wouldn't! You can't!"

Enthusiasm plunges from Rosa's face, taking her brilliant smile down with it. "What? What did I say?" She turns expectant eyes on me, but comprehends the boy's crisis before I can answer. "Oh, my goodness," she laughs, then stops abruptly, knowing Connor is nearly traumatized. "Querida, turtle brownies are made with chocolate, caramel, and nuts. They're named after those chocolate candies with the pecan feet. Remember? We bought some during Pirates in Paradise."

Connor sits back, the fire fading from his eyes. "No turtle meat? You promise?"

"I give my word. You think the president of the Turtle Rescue Squad would eat sea turtles, hmm?"

A sigh escapes the boy as the momentary distress diminishes. "Well you said *turtle* brownies." Color returns to his face in abundance.

Josie is AWOL. Melissa's search of her room, the barn, and the beach did not produce a sign of her. She must have snuck away while it was still dark, because I have been up since five-thirty and heard no one leave. That is her answer. She will not be coming to our little trailer park church today. Understanding the need for free will does nothing to diminish the disappointment it often produces.

I grab the last of the food boxes to load onto the truck, knowing the task of packing is far from over. Three folding tables and stacks of chairs rest on the sea grass. How I miss our young Owen. Chores are far more pleasurable, and easier on these old bones, when he is here to share the load. But I would rather lift a hundred tables myself than take one precious moment away from Owen's honeymoon. Quiet Owen…

SUSAN MIURA

married to a free-spirited girl who laughs like a bubbling brook and endears herself to everyone she meets. The notion makes me smile, and the smile elicits the realization that, here alone, I've dwelt on a happy thought. Not Carmelita.

For once…not Carmelita.

My shoulders strain beneath the weight of several chairs as I heft them into the pickup. Rosa will surely need to rub ointment on my back muscles tonight. The thought of her lovely hands caressing my back almost makes the task worthwhile.

Mike's car barrels down the driveway, looking as though it will surely collide with my pickup. He honks like a teenager. Yes, Mike, I see you.

He hits the brakes before yelling through the open window. "Hey, aren't you too old to be lifting that stuff?"

"And who's going to help me? Rosa in her wheelchair or our pregnant Melissa?"

"Personally, I think you should make the kid do it." He jumps out, striding over to help me rearrange boxes to make more space.

"The *kid* is with his father this morning. They are meeting us at the trailer park to help unload. Now…to what do I owe the honor on a Sunday morning?"

"Owen. You owe it to Owen. He actually called from Idaho. Made me promise not to let you kill yourself before service. As for me, I was afraid that without you in the picture, Rosa might get all sad and forget to invite me for Thanksgiving." He grabs four chairs and stacks them in the truck.

I'm right behind him with another four. "On the bright side, the other guests might get some turkey." I check my watch. "What about your mass at St. Vincent's? Won't you be late?"

"I got forty-five minutes to get you loaded, pick up Kasie, and get our butts in church. No problem."

We each grab an end of the folding table and lift.

Mike slides it toward the back to make room for more. "So what's your topic today at the not-Catholic church?"

"Non-de-nom-i-na-tion-al." I say it as though teaching a child a

130

new word, even though Mike knows it well. "That is a big word for you, no? The topic is loving across racial and cultural divides."

"Owen ought to be doing that one. He's the expert on loving across racial divides." Mike belly laughs at his own joke. "In fact, he's probably fully engaged in that right now!"

That man could make a corpse laugh. I cannot help joining in. "Yes, our blond *Americano* and his beautiful Cuban wife. Such a striking pair they make, no? That sweetheart Elena, she will be good for him. But…you *loco* veterinarian, that is *not* what I meant!"

"I know, I know. It's a good topic. Break a leg…or whatever one says to a pastor before church."

I shake my head, my heart lighter than it has been for weeks. God has blessed me with a good friend—a friend whose face tells me we are moving on to a more serious topic.

"Hey, you still have Josie's husband calling you everyday?"

"Si. Not only calling, he came."

"What? When?"

Such a nice man, that Rob. But so confused, hurt. Being around him would only add to her layers of pain. I envision the heartache in his eyes as I label boxes with a marker. "The other day. Josie was gone. He said he had to talk to her, bring her home. I begged him to give her more time and space. She is so fragile, Michael, but there is a whisper of healing. I sense it. Returning home now might shatter her all over again."

"Aw, man, that's gotta be hard." Mike points to a couple of food boxes I forgot to put with the rest. I nod and he stacks them with the others. "For him *and* for you. So she never saw him?"

"Almost. She arrived as he was leaving. It was close, but I do not believe she saw. Josie never said anything."

"She know, yet, about you being Ana's brother?"

"No. The time has not been not right. Soon, though." A scan of the grounds tells me everything is ready. I close the back of the truck and turn to face my friend.

"I don't know, Preach. She may not be happy when she finds out you've been hiding that."

"Sí. I am well aware, but my reasons have been valid. At least, I hope that is true. The woman is on shaky ground. I have promised her husband and Ana that I would do everything in my power to keep her safe. Sometimes I feel she is just one step away from…I do not know, crashing. I have been wary of saying anything that might push her away."

"Yeah, I get it. Still…be careful. If she finds out, we're talkin' head-on."

Above me, a small gray puff stands out against an otherwise clear blue island sky. "I have considered this as well. It is time to tell her."

Help me be the sunlight, Lord. Not the cloud. I am not so sure which one I have been for Josie.

The sign at Grandma Nettie's Breakfast Hutch declares Thursday's morning special is *huevos rancheros*. Visions of fried eggs atop warm tortillas, bathing in green chili, elicit a quiet growl from my stomach. This morning's toast is little more than a memory, but the huevos will have to wait. There are far more important matters at hand.

Ben sits quietly in the seat beside me, his body filling the cab of my pickup. He was doing so well, but the minute trouble appeared, he hit that bottle. This addiction to alcohol, it is not something I fully understand, despite all the alcoholics I have counseled. Why turn to something that temporarily makes you *feel* better, when God can actually *make* your life better? Permanently. It is crazy. Ben loves his son, he wants to be a good father, but every time he heads down that straight and narrow path, he stumbles onto a rocky one. And hidden behind those rocks is Naomi. Always Naomi. When that girl broke his heart, she shattered it to its core. Then again, she had a good teacher.

Ben yawns, eyes squinting in the morning light.

"Work late last night, Benny?"

"Yeah. Closed at two, went home beat. But man, I just couldn't fall asleep. All those crazy thoughts about that bi—my ex, just kept runnin' round in my head. Last time I checked the clock, it was almost four." He scratches his head, yawning again.

"Well, let us see what my friend Charlie has to say. He is a good man; a good lawyer, too. If there is a way to straighten this out, he will find it."

Ben shakes his head, rubs his grizzled chin. How good he would look with a shave, a haircut. Clear eyes.

"I don't know, Preacher. She's the mom, you know? Moms always seem to get the kids. If they had arrested me at your place last week, I would've lost him for sure. I'm such an idiot. Every time I think I'm gettin' it right, wham! I mess up again. I don't even know how to thank you anymore. And that Josie. I can't believe she came through for me. I thought for sure it was over when they asked her about pressin' charges."

"She did well. The question is, what do we do with her?"

"What do ya mean?"

Sometimes my voice betrays me. I did not realize I said it out loud until Ben responded. Indeed, what do I mean? "Oh, you know, she does not speak much."

"Yep, she's a quiet one. Must be holdin' somethin' in, I guess. Maybe she got raped or somethin'. Or had a dad like Naomi's." His pause reveals the soft spot for her, buried beneath a mountain of anger. "Guess we all got our problems. Thing is, I don't want to make my problem Connor's, you know? He's a great kid. Deserves better than two loser parents. But of the two, I'm the better deal for him. Ha! How sad is that? And I can't let her get him, Preacher. Have you seen her arms? They're a friggin' road map!"

A motorcycle with a young man and his scantily clad girlfriend cuts me off. I hit the brakes, barely missing them. Ben's word is on the tip of my tongue with a few choice nouns to follow, but I fight the temptation and win. I have to.

"Anyway, she's got track marks from here till Tuesday. Now she's sayin' she's off the stuff for good. Clean as a whistle. Yeah, right. Even if it's true, Connor hardly knows her. I mean, come on. She cruises up here on her Harley every year for his birthday to show motherly love?"

"You need to calm down, Benny. Pray about this. Pray from your heart." The sun is blazing into my eyes this morning, as though bent on blinding me. My hand feels around in my CD compartment and touches smooth plastic—my extra dark sunglasses for days just as these. "Your Naomi, she is running silent and angry and deep."

"No way you made that up."

"Barry Manilow. 'Read 'em and Weep.'"

"Never heard of it."

"You were a child when that came out." I switch to my Men in Black sunglasses. "How about this one? With faith the size of a mustard seed, you can say to a mountain, move from here to there, and it will move."

"Yeah, I know that—it's one of your Bible verses. It's a good one and all, I just don't know if it applies to me. Naomi's a pretty big mountain." He gazes out the window as we pass Key Lime Liquors. "You really think you can take care of this? For the boy, I mean. We can't let his life get more messed up than it is already."

"I will do my best, Benny." Will that be good enough? Will "my best" protect Connor from his mother's demons?

We cruise past Midnight Sun Tattoos as a young woman is entering. Long black hair, just like Naomi's. How I hope her tattoos are purely for adornment, rather than a futile attempt at masking a wounded heart. "The way I see this, you have a lot on your side. How long has Naomi been gone now? Two years?"

"Three. Two years ago was...you know, the accident. And she'd already been gone a year by then."

"The time, she is flying so fast. But you are right. Connor was only five when she left. Not even in school yet." Just like Carmie.

Guess what, Uncle Manny. I'm gonna be five now! I wish you weren't so far away so you could come to my birthday party. Mommy bought me a yellow dress. Can't you take a plane, Uncle Manny? Please?

I rub my eyes.

"You can't rub the sleep out, Preacher. Trust me, I've tried."

Nor can I rub out the pain. "I have been up for three hours, Ben. I went for a swim, ate breakfast, called my son, and helped the kids feed the animals."

"Show-off." He pulls two sticks of gum from his front pocket and offers one to me. I can't help but smile and shake my head at this super-sized version of Connor. Ben is too preoccupied with unwrapping his gum to notice. "How far is this place, anyway?"

"Just over the next bridge, Atlantic side."

Three men stand along the bridge's railing, casting out lines. Ai, how I long to be among them. There is nothing like the warm sun on your face, fingers wrapped around a pole, the tug of something wild on the other end. Years ago, dinner depended solely on what that "something" might be. Those men might need good black fin tuna or mackerel to feed their families. Or not. Maybe it is just a relaxing day of fishing and friends. A day like that is truly a gift.

I got one! I got one!

Calm down, Carmie, or you'll lose him. Reel him in like this.

We'll put him back, right, Uncle Manny? I don't want him to die. His family will be sad.

Ben turns to face me. "So what do you think?"

"I am sorry, Ben, my mind, she drifts sometimes." I try to blot out the Carmie smile. Those eyes. "What did you say?"

Ben and I stand in the parking lot, recapping the meeting with Charlie, waiting for the air conditioning to make the car fit for humans. The scent of peppermint drifts my way as Ben happily chews his gum, analyzing the various scenarios explained by my lawyer friend.

"So, it's all good, right? Naomi pretty much doesn't have a chance, right? Ain't that what Charlie was saying?" Ben leans against the car, his gaze seeming to drift across the street to young ladies in tank tops and shorts that barely cover their bottoms.

"It would appear so. But remember, he did not promise anything because he does not have all the facts yet. He is a lawyer, not a miracle worker. We do not know what her lawyer has planned."

Ben's brows crease at my answer, his attention now one hundred percent back on our conversation.

"So you sayin' I should be worried?"

I sigh. He wants what I cannot give. "I am saying you should be cautiously optimistic, amigo. It sounds like the law favors you keeping Connor. Given the circumstances, Charlie cannot imagine any judge letting Naomi take him. So the odds are in your favor, but you see, that is not a guarantee."

"Then I'll focus on the odds being in my favor. That don't happen too often."

True enough. But my lumbering friend does not realize his penchant for alcohol is what often weights the wrong side of the scale.

Chapter 14

Josie

"Ugh!" My bare foot lands splat in the middle of a rotting fish. Putrid sliminess oozes over my skin, between my toes. Disgust gives way to pain as a bone shard pierces my pinky toe. I jerk away, remnants of fish guts coating me from heel to bloody toe. The rancid odor wafts upward, swirling around my head, into my nose, crawling into my stomach where it flops around like something half-alive. My half-digested muffin may soon reappear and join the fish.

I limp toward the water using one foot and one heel.

"Mommy, that lady walks funny." The little girl points so vigorously other beachcombers stop to look. Perfect. I freeze in place with my fish foot in mid-air.

"Shhh, Kaitlyn. That's not nice." Her mom points a finger at her. "And don't point."

Obediently putting her arm down, Kaitlyn clothespins her nose. "She smells funny too."

"Kaitlyn!"

"Sorry." Her hand remains in place.

It's okay, kid, you're right. It's stinky and gross.

The embarrassed mom grabs her daughter's hand and strides down the beach. I continue into the cool Atlantic, where saltwater flows over scales and rancid bits of flesh. My foot is washed clean, but the pain remains. I scout out a place to sit. No boulders, logs, or abandoned beach chairs are in limping distance. I plop onto the sand to examine my injury.

Careful not to break the fragile fish bone, I tweezer the protruding tip with my thumbnail and forefinger, ever so slowly easing it out. How can something so small send waves of pain coursing through my entire foot?

Sudden motion catches my eye from up the beach.

"Josie!" A silhouette waves to me from the direction of the sun. Beneath the shade of my hand, my eyes focus on familiar features. Melissa. The doctor appointment. How could I have forgotten? At home it would have been in bold letters on the calendar I check each morning and again before I go to bed.

But I am not at home. And I am not the Josie that would have been the encouraging, comforting companion Melissa needs today.

Honey blond hair wisps into Melissa's face as she approaches my spot on the sand. Her happy-to-see-you smile only adds to the guilt of knowing I am about to bow out on my commitment. Being with her will do more harm than good. There she is, carrying a precious new baby inside her womb. Inside her heart. While the remnants of mine hold only guilt.

Melissa sits down next to me, scooping up a handful of warm sand, letting it sift through her fingers. "I'm so glad you stopped here. If you'd have kept walking, I might not have found you in time."

"I'm so sorry, Melissa. I completely forgot. No excuses."

"It's okay. Connor pointed me in the right direction, in case you're wondering. Normally he'd be in school, but there's some parent-teacher conference thing."

"Connor?"

"Yeah, his eyes and ears are everywhere. It's kind of creepy, but cute, too, because he doesn't mean any harm. He's just kinda lost, you know? Mom's a wacko in Key West. Benny's okay most of the time, but you never know when he's going to flip out, like that whole drama at the barn. To be honest, that's the first time I saw him like that. Heard about things, though."

I nod with an "Mmmm." Tell her, Josie. Tell her now. She'll be better off going to the doctor by herself.

Melissa scoops another handful of sand, swirling the grains to make a pattern as they fall. Amber eyes study her beach art. "Josie...I know you don't really want to come with me."

"It's not that I don't *want* to..."

"And I know there's something hurting you inside, so I feel real bad that I even need to bother you with this. But the thing is..."

She scooches up her legs, hugging knees as her gaze switches to the gulls diving for their breakfast. "The thing is...I've been bleeding the last couple of days. Just spotting, but I don't know what that means. I didn't realize till now how much I love this baby."

My heart cringes at the thought of anything hurting this sweet country girl or her baby. She may be young, and unmarried, but she'll be a wonderful mother. With her family standing beside her, she'll do fine. If only the baby is okay.

She sniffs, wipes her nose on her arm, takes a breath. "I mean, now I know how I really feel, and it might be too late." Tears trickle from her face and splatter her sand creation. "So I'm glad you're coming with me. You don't have to talk or anything. I just want someone there in case...well, just in case."

Another of my plans gone awry.

I look at Melissa, envisioning the old Josie hugging her tight, assuring her everything will be okay, stroking her hair with promises that I'd be there for her. Can I do for her what I couldn't do for my son? Can I wrap my arms around this sad, frightened girl? She places her hand on the sand next to mine.

I reach over and squeeze it. "Let's go."

The hand squeeze on the beach is all the encouragement Melissa needs to lay everything before me. We are friends, my silence notwithstanding. She drives the ancient Caddy down Highway One into Marathon, a familiar route for her since coming to Cielo Azul.

"Mom and Dad like David all right. I mean, he's polite and all, and he's doing good in college. He wants to be a high school math teacher, so they figure he's pretty smart. But when I told them about the baby, man, oh, man, they just went crazy, you know? Mom was crying; Dad was yelling. Ugh. I told them don't worry 'cause I'm not keeping it anyways. I had an appointment at this family-planning place and…"

"An abortion clinic?" Please say no.

"Yeah, that. I wanted my mom to come with me 'cause I was nervous. Found out real quick *that* wasn't happening. She went from tears to pure insanity when I asked her. Now I get it, but back then, it just seemed like a quick, simple way to settle everything. I mean, I had just started my first week at college, you know?"

I nod, unable to imagine anything that would make me abort a baby. But I left my children, didn't I? Left them without so much as a kiss goodbye.

"The next few days were a nightmare." Turquoise water shimmers along both sides of the Seven-Mile Bridge as Melissa continues the tale that landed her here. "I didn't expect David to freak out when I told him I wanted to, you know, to get rid of it. But he was all, 'are you crazy? That's our baby in there!' So it was another angry lecture about not killing something God created. That night my Dad blew up…again. I just couldn't take it anymore. My appointment was supposed to be the next day, but I ran away instead." Melissa reaches into the cup holder for her lip balm, flips off the lid, and coats her lips. "How about you, Josie?" Her tone, her mannerisms hint she would like to quit focusing on herself. I know the feeling. "How did you end up at the shelter?"

"I was heading for Key West."

"Key West? Me, too. Funny how we both ended up here. I never even heard of Cielo Azul. My tire exploded just as I neared Preacher's place. I hit this chunk of metal and boom! Freaked me out. I swerved into the mile marker, almost hit his fence. They said it was a miracle I came away with just scratches." As Melissa talks, my brain can't stop replaying "just as I hit Preacher's place." It echoes for reasons I can't explain, making me feel uncomfortable in my own skin.

"The police brought me to Rosa, figuring I could calm down, call home," she continues. "Didn't want to call, though. Preacher and Rosa invited me to stay. I figured, what the heck, might as well. That's when

I realized my backpack was gone. Ditto my money."

"All of it?"

"Four hundred bucks. I still had some in my purse. Spent some staying overnight in Key Largo. That's where someone stole my backpack. Must have happened at the Waffle House."

A power surge quickens my pulse. "In Key Largo?"

"Yeah. There was this old guy who kept staring at me. I mean, he must have been around since Moses. When I told the waitress I was going to Key West, he shouted out something weird and kept repeating it. It was like he didn't want me going there. I hit the road in a hurry 'cause the guy creeped me out. Someone got my nice little treasure."

Chills prickle my spine. I have to know. "Melissa, did he say 'the sky is far enough?'"

A long silence is my answer. "Yeah." She turns to me, brow wrinkled. "How did you know?"

"He said it to me, too."

"Weird."

The engine's hum fills the space between us as we drive past palms, restaurants, and dive shops. The Crazy Conch souvenir shop, with its seashell mobiles and luminescent streamers, marks the corner where we turn off Highway One. Melissa doesn't speak until we pull into a parking space at Middle Keys Medical Center. "Did you know Cielo Azul means blue sky?"

"Yes."

We park under a shade palm. I get out and look at the cielo azul above, wondering if an unseen hand had kept us from going too far.

Melissa lies on the examining table, bare tummy exposed and slathered with gel. A stoic nurse slides the scanner across her belly, peering at a monitor. I try not to stare, focusing instead on a wall poster depicting a pregnant woman's anatomy. It is useless. My eyes keep going back to that nurse, searching her face for a glimmer of hope. Her expression never once betrays her findings. Come on, lady. Give us something here. I force myself to breathe, inhaling a lungful of tension-filled air, exhaling with a sigh. Melissa turns to me, eyes glassy. "Josie," she whispers, "will you pray for my baby?"

Pray? If she knew what I'd done, she would never ask. I can't deny her this…or anything else right now. But where do I start?

It's just a conversation. A private communication between you and someone who loves you, who understands anger and pain. And broken hearts.

I nod. "Sure." I draw in a breath, knowing I face a moment of truth. Knowing I'm about to ask the Creator of the universe for a miracle, even though He never heard a peep from me until a month ago, and not a very pretty peep at that. Fury. Blame. Demands. How can I expect Him to listen, acknowledge, and bestow? I don't even know where to start, but for Melissa…

I close my eyes, fold my hands. I want her to physically see that I'm praying. That was the easy part. Now for the rest.

Lord, please listen to this prayer…for Melissa's sake. She is one of Yours; a real sweetheart. She kept her baby because of You, so please make it healthy. Please…for Melissa, for her child, for the boy somewhere in Michigan who loves them both, make everything be all right. Amen.

My eyes moisten beneath my lids. They open to the sight of the nurse setting the scanner back in its cradle.

"I'll be right back." Her words shatter the silence of the sterile room. She grabs her clipboard and strides out, leaving us to suffocate beneath a blanket of apprehension.

"This can't be good." A tear slides sideways from the corner of Melissa's eye, soaking into her hair. She reaches out her hand. My cue.

I grasp it…and hold on tight.

Please. I am begging You. My heart splits open and the words burst forth, silently shooting up to Heaven. *Do what You want with me, just protect this girl and her baby.*

He hears me, I am certain. I feel Him listening, like I did when Connor prayed in the barn. And there is no other explanation than that.

Chapter 15

Preacher

Meeting with Charlie seemed to calm Big Ben. I, too, stepped lighter as we left the office. Charlie has been in the lawyer business a long time. If the situation did not strongly favor Ben keeping custody of Connor, he would have said so. Ben is, by far, the better parent. But I have to agree with what Ben said in the car. Connor did not fare well in this arena.

"So you're saying it looks good for Ben?" Mike selects three coffee mugs from the cabinet and sets them on the table for Rosa to fill. "The scumbag mother isn't going to get Connor?"

I wince at his words. Dark, tortured eyes emerge in my mind, dissipating like a wisp of smoke. "Charlie could not promise, but it would appear Naomi has a minimal chance of succeeding."

"Good. Last thing he needs is a crazy junky in his life."

This cannot continue. He needs to know, needs to soften his judgment. "Michael, please do not be so hard on her. That girl's tattoos cover her father's sins. He was particularly fond of using lit cigars as punishment when she would not cooperate with…with his sick desires."

"Cooperate? You mean—"

"Yes." I cut him off, sparing myself from the words. But even unspoken, their ugliness surfaces like the black killer oil that poisoned our lovely Gulf years ago. "He was shot and killed when she was fifteen. And may God forgive me, it should have happened sooner."

"Manuel! Such words for a pastor!" Rosa chastises me only because it is expected. Inside her heart, I know she agrees.

"Oh, man, I didn't know." Disgust and anger harden Michael's face. No doubt he is also disappointed that I never divulged this information. He does not quite understand that our friendship does not preclude my role as pastor. My head and heart near the bursting point with other people's secrets…and some of my own. "I guess that explains the drugs," he adds.

"Sí. She turned to drugs to fight her demons. A bad choice, no? When she decided she was not fit to be a mother, she left. Took off one night and moved in with friends in Key West. That is when Ben started hitting the bottle."

"Yeah, that part I knew." Mike wraps both hands around his mug of hot coffee as if it were forty degrees outside instead of seventy-three. He lifts it to his face, breathing in the cinnamon-scented steam. That man. Same routine every time. He just loves Rosa's coffee, and she loves it that he does.

"Mmmm." His eyes twinkle at my wife. "It brings peace to my soul, Rosa."

She glows. "If that's all it took, I would make it for the world."

"And then the whole world would fall madly in love with you." He winks.

A soft pink blushes her face, reminding me of the eighteen-year-old girl I fell in love with.

"If you are quite done flirting with my lovely wife, Mr. Veterinarian, you could tell us how our Lightning is doing. And what about Lily? Those pups should be here soon, no?"

His mischievous grin takes ten years off his face. He looks like a college boy planning a prank. "Whatsa matter, old man? Afraid she might leave you for something better?"

"That could happen, of course, but as there is nothing better in the room, I am safe for now."

"Touché! One point for the senior citizen." He reaches for three of Rosa's chocolate walnut cookies. Two make it to his napkin, the third disappears, washed down with a gulp of coffee. "Lily's temperature is down to one hundred and she's dripping milk. Doing great, though.

She could deliver tonight, possibly morning, so be ready."

"Oh, no, not tonight!" Rosa's concern is no surprise. I know exactly what her next words will be. "Tonight we are going out for our anniversary. Oh, Manuel, I don't think we can go. Should we make it next Saturday instead?"

Always something. Always. I care about Lily, truly I do, but we need a little time for us. "No. Melissa and Josie will be here to check on Lily. They can call us if anything happens. Tonight we celebrate forty-three years of marriage, and nothing is going to stop us." I try to smile away the firmness of my words, lest I sound like more of a dictator than the romantic husband I am attempting to be.

Rosa nods. "You are right. This is our night for celebration. So, Michael, what about our Lightning? How fares he?"

"Your dedicated crew is doing wonders with that horse. He's up eight pounds, steady on his feet. He's more trusting than a horse in his condition should be. But… he's not out of the woods yet. He's still skin and bones, extremely weak. Somebody really did a number on him."

My heart cringes at his words. I shake my head, wondering what pleasure can possibly come from torturing an animal. And then I think about the children we have seen on mission trips over the years. India, Taiwan, Africa. Young ones oppressed and abused, suffering at the hands of evil. It is no wonder someone can hurt a horse if they can commit horrific acts on a child.

"You all right there, Rosa?" Mike says. "You're getting a bit glassy-eyed on me."

Ah, my wife, she is thinking these things as well.

"Can you imagine if everyone just loved each other and our fellow creatures?" Rosa gazes out the window at the great blue heron swooping toward the beach. "What a different world this would be."

"I wish I could imagine it, but truth is, I really can't." Mike's cell vibrates and he checks the caller ID, then places it back in his jeans pocket. "Our trip to India last year gave me a new set of eyes. People living in cracked sewer pipes. Kids forced to clean toilets with their hands. Made me sick."

His eyes reflect the painful visions that haunt me daily. Children who should be sitting in a classroom, playing on swings, laughing, experiencing the world with wide-eyed wonder. But that is not the world for the Dalits, India's "Slumdogs." Untouchables. Not so untouchable that they can't be sex slaves, but certainly too untouchable to teach…or feed…or care about. Poor Mike, he really didn't know what he was in for when he boarded that plane with us in December. We tried to warn him, but words and photos do not prepare you for toddlers with protruding ribs, ten-year old prostitutes, maimed teenagers begging for food.

"Michael." Rosa squeezes his hand. "It always comes back to that trip, doesn't it?"

"Something about that place just won't leave my head. Those kids on the street, the pain in their eyes. That's a whole new level of heartbreak. Who has the right to say all the descendents of this family are going to have the best of everything, while that family must live in garbage and be used as slaves? All that food and medicine we brought over, it was nothing really. A drop in an endless sea."

He does not understand. "It was not nothing to the people who received it, Michael. Remember the smiles? Remember little Kapi wearing his new T-shirt, grinning while he ate his food? That young mother crying with joy because we had antibiotics for her toddler? They will not forget."

"I know. Still…it wasn't enough to change anything."

Rosa looks at me. We know well the frustration of feeling like we cannot do enough for those in need. I can tell she is struggling to find the right words of encouragement for our disheartened friend. She pats his hand again. "It is not easy to be one of God's warriors. Once you really see what's going on in our world, you're never the same. And that is good. Difficult, but good, because now you are one more person making a difference. And I will tell you something else." She leans forward, intensity in her eyes. "I believe the Holy Spirit is whispering in your ear."

Mike looks at Rosa like she just grew antennas. This is not a concept familiar to him.

"The Holy Spirit, huh? Hmmm. Not sure I'm the type, but just for kicks, what do you think He's saying?"

"Oh, Michael, that is between you and Him. Just make sure you listen."

I anticipate a funny retort, perhaps a snicker, but Mike's face softens. Eyes grow contemplative as he offers Rosa a scarcely visible nod.

"All right, señor," I say. "Now it's time for me to whisper in your ear. Put your veterinarian hat back on and tell me more about our stick figure of a horse."

He leans back in his chair, relaxing as he re-enters his comfort zone. "I'd say it's fifty-fifty at this point. Just keep him on the same regimen. You don't need to mash the hay anymore. Whatever else you're all doing, just keep doing it."

He opens his mouth to say more, but stops as the back door opens and Melissa walks in. Wet, puffy eyes gaze directly into mine, but it is Rosa who speaks first.

"Querida! What happened? Come, sit down and tell me."

Melissa smiles through her tears. "Everything's fine. Everything is wonderful and fine and I have a perfect baby girl growing inside me! And if it wasn't for you guys..."

Pure joy warms my face, swells my heart. That tiny baby girl was almost a statistic, and now she will be a daughter, loved and cherished. God is good. Mike leaps out of his chair, laughing a "congratulations" and nearly hugging the baby right out of that girl.

"My turn," Rosa says, extending her arms to Melissa. Well I know how much she wants to jump up, too. Through her teary smile, I see the frustration of being stuck in that chair. "Oh, *mi cara*, I prayed for you all morning." She can hardly get the words out as she and Melissa go into full-fledged crazy emotional women mode. "I am so happy."

Mike and I look at each other, sharing an eye roll while trapped in the middle of a chick-flick moment. It is then I realize Josie is standing in the doorway, keeping herself separated from the love fest.

"Thank you for going, Josie. I am so glad you were..." A hint of a smile, the first I'd seen, is accompanied by a tear trickling down her face. "There is a box of tissues on the counter. You might want to grab one before these two use them all up."

She swipes away her tear and turns to go. "I have some in my room." And poof, she disappears. Perhaps I should go after her, talk to her. Why is this so difficult? I can picture knocking on her door. She answers it…and there the image ends. Perhaps it is time I tell her who I am. My stomach tightens as a Carmelita memory floats into my head.

What do you think heaven is like, Uncle Manny?

I think it is more beautiful and wonderful than we can even imagine. It is a place full of love, where nothing bad ever happens and we can live with God forever.

Do you think there's white ponies and beautiful flowers like the ones in Mrs. Caruso's garden?

I do.

Wow. I want to go there.

You will, Carmie. Someday you will. But not too soon, all right?

Whether the memories of these conversations are a curse or blessing, I do not know.

Melissa and Rosa recover enough to start laughing at themselves. "Now, young lady, take a seat and tell us everything," Rosa says.

"Oh no you don't." I hold a chair out for our young mother-to-be. "I need to leave for a moment. Hold your story. Mike can tell you about his little adventure with a ninety-pound Akita while I'm gone."

Mike gulps the rest of his coffee. "Yeah, you gotta hear this one."

He launches in and I hear Melissa giggle even before I reach Josie's room. Two knocks open the door. Sad eyes peer at me.

"Are you all right, señora?"

"Fine. Really."

"Would you like to talk?"

Josie shakes her head, then, to my surprise, reaches up and gives my arm a gentle squeeze. "But I want you to know how grateful I am to you and Rosa. This place…it's just what I needed. A place where no one knows me, or anything about me. I just want to be anonymous for a while and figure things out. I hope you understand."

My well-intentioned words dissolve like sugar in coffee. How can I follow that with "I am Ana's brother?" And yet, the deception eats at my heart. Tomorrow, perhaps. I will tell her tomorrow.

"Whatever you wish, Josie. You are welcome to stay here as long as you please."

Back in the kitchen, Michael is finishing his story, embellishing as only Michael can do.

"And there I was, lying on the examining room floor with this dog's butt on my head."

Laughter radiates through the kitchen as I join the joyful threesome and wrap an arm around Melissa. "Now, I believe you have a story to tell us.

Mike glances at the wall clock. "Yeah, but tell us quick, because I have to leave in five minutes to pick up the honeymooners."

"Ay, they are returning today? How could I forget?" I know exactly how I forgot. This brain of mine is overflowing with too many things to remember. It will be good to have Owen back.

Melissa sips her milk and sets two cookies on her napkin. As she relates her story, elation lights her face...and dazzles the kitchen. She tells us of the nurse robotically sliding the wand across her stomach, then leaving the room without a word. The minutes dragged on for eternity as she and Josie held hands. So...Josie had stepped up. A good sign. It is so hard to know what is going on inside that broken soul. Melissa said she tried to prepare for the worst, tried to pray, tried to stay calm, but nothing worked.

"And then...the miracle. The nurse returned to that sterile room with the news I wanted—needed—to hear. The baby is doing great! She's right on schedule. Did I tell you she was sucking her thumb? And her tiny heart is beating loud and clear! I heard it, you guys! I listened through the stethoscope. It was amazing! Josie heard it, too."

"Josie, too?" And what did that do to her, I wonder. This dispirited woman, knowing she forever stopped one little heart from beating. What would it feel like to hear the sound of one just entering the world? The vision fills my head and envelops my heart.

You should meet Mrs. Caruso, Uncle Manny. She's my friend. She has the best bunny in the world. We make cookies together sometimes and I

*help her plant flowers. Mrs. Caruso bought my Barbie a real fancy dress
with sparkles! You just gotta meet her someday.*

Ana's words echo in my head. "Josie loved her, Manny. This has to
be killing her. My feelings for Josie are all mixed up right now. There's
just too much pain in me. But God sent her to the right person. You
can help her, I know it."

Can I?

Chapter 16

Josie

I hadn't wanted to listen. I'd done my part, going with her, holding her hand. But when she said, "You've got to hear this, Josie," the black hole in me swelled to cut off my breath.

"Oh, my gosh, it's incredible!" streamed from Melissa.

Before I could decline, the nurse put the stethoscope in place. The sound of life flowed into me like a love song straight from heaven. Thump-thump, thump-thump. Sweet perfection. The music of angels. I could have sat and listened for hours to the sound of life in its purest form. Beautiful, untainted, already loved beyond measure. A miracle in the making, and I was privileged enough to bear witness. I closed my eyes, wanting that wonderful rhythm imprinted on my brain. Everything else disappeared, and just for the moment, all was right with the world.

Gratitude filled my heart, overflowed, and spilled from my eyes. God heard me. He answered. Even though I'd been so angry, said all those things to Him. It could be nothing more than a coincidence—perhaps Melissa would have been fine either way—but there was a feeling. Something that could not be seen or touched.

But there it was.

The anniversary couple is ready for their night out. Rosa glows in a pretty peach dress and fancy hair comb. Preacher walks somewhat stiffly in his suit and tie, but the man cleans up well. It's not hard to see the twenty-year-old guy she fell in love with, despite her parents' protests.

"Happy anniversary!" Melissa hugs them both. "You'll be turning heads wherever you go!"

"Forty-three years is certainly something to celebrate these days, no? I guess it is reason enough to wear this monkey suit."

Rosa waves him off. "Oh, Manuel, stop. You look dashing. Doesn't he, ladies?"

I smile and nod. Melissa answers with an enthusiastic "totally!"

"Okay, okay, I think we better go so we are not late for our reservation. I just want to make sure I haven't forgotten anything." Preacher holds out his hand, ticking off tasks using his fingers. "The animals are fed, the barn is locked, Lily has a nice clean blanket for birthing. Tomorrow's sermon is as done as it is going to get. The two of you will check on Lily every hour and call me if anything is happening, right?"

"Right," we answer in unison.

"Good. And Connor is staying with a sitter while Ben is at work."

Rosa's brow crinkles at his words. "I'm still not comfortable with that. He could have stayed here with Josie and Melissa."

"We talked about this, *mi vida*. He is with a friend of Ben's. He will be fine."

"There's something about it that bothers me. I can't help it."

"Ay, yi, yi, woman. You worry too much. Please, let us have an evening to celebrate *us* and not worry about anything." He takes both her hands, kissing the top of each. "Just us tonight. Me and you."

Rosa's face softens as she rewards her husband with a smile. Preacher wins.

Melissa grins at them. "Where you guys going?"

"The Key Colony Inn, a lovely place in Key Colony Beach. Mostly French and Italian food. Fresh seafood too, but we get enough of that. Tonight my taste buds are set for steak *au poivre*."

"Mmm. I don't even know what that is and I love it anyway."

After they leave, Melissa turns to me with the dreamy-eyed look of someone who's just watched a classic romance movie. "I love when he calls her *mi vida*. It means *my life*, you know. Isn't that sweet?"

"Yeah." She's still looking at me, waiting for more than one syllable. "Yeah, it really is."

Later, with Melissa reading in her room and the anniversary couple out on the town, a hush blankets the peaceful seaside house. No drama, no little red-headed spy, no television, or guests in the kitchen. Silence enough to think a whole train of thoughts without getting derailed. And my train aches to head north. Tonight's topic of inner-thought discussion: what do I need to do in order to get on board?

Heading home is easy to imagine, but anything beyond that is a smoke gray screen on my mental monitor. I lay on the couch, southern stars flickering through the big bay window. Saturday night. Mitch would be arguing with Rob about how late he could stay out with his buddies. Ashley might be having a sleepover, or snuggling next to Rob as they watch the newest Disney flick. There had been less Sponge Bob this past year as she made her way toward puberty and drama queen status. Kind of an important time to have a mom in the picture.

I reenter the weary arguments. What is best for my family? Do they understand it was better this way—better than living in the shadow of my disgrace? My dysfunction?

What would I say to Ana?

The phone rings, crashing through the tranquil darkness to send me jumping out of my skin. I grab it on the second ring.

"I need Preacher!" Connor's panic streaks through the line.

"What's up, Connor? He's not here."

"Dad got shot! Gus did it!"

My stomach tightens. Who—who's Gus?"

"M—Mom's boyfriend. Dad's bleeding real bad."

I squeeze my eyes shut, knowing there is no time for a foggy mental state. "I'll call an ambulance and be right there."

"No, you can't! He'll get in big trouble. I'm not supposed to be here." Muffled words emerge from the other end. "What, Dad? Okay, here."

"Get the boy, Josie." Pain seeps through each of Ben's labored words.

"Hurry. They'll take him away if he's at the bar. Please."

"I'm on it. Put Connor on."

"Josie, do you understand?" Ben's booming voice has been reduced to a graveled whisper. "You *can't* call 911 till you get here. You can't tell a soul about this. Promise."

"Ben, please—"

"Promise!"

"Okay, okay. I *promise*." What am I saying? This is crazy. "Put Connor on."

Seconds pass as the phone switches hands. My own hand trembles. I try to force my heart to slow, my mind to focus.

"Josie, you comin'?" Fear trills Connor's voice.

"How do I get there?" I whip open the end table drawer. There sits a pen and pad, just like in a hotel room. I'm ready for directions.

"It's on Highway One."

Naturally. What isn't? "Which way?"

"Don't know. It's just on Highway One!" He's shrieking. This is way too much for an eight-year-old…and most adults I know.

"It's okay, buddy. I'll find it. Benny's Beach Bar, right?"

"Yeah, hurry! My Dad's gonna die! Look for a sign with a palm tree."

That pretty much describes everything in Cielo Azul, but I'll find it. God knows, there is no other option. "On my way."

I click off the phone. No wonder Rosa has this list of numbers on the table. I grab the keys from the nightstand and knock on Melissa's door, knowing she will insist on coming. That can't happen. Who knows if that maniac is still around, or what danger lies ahead tonight? My calm façade is Academy Award material. "Hey, Mel. I'm going for a short drive." I fight a quivering voice. "I'll be back shortly, okay?"

"Want some company?"

"No, just have some things to figure out. Need to think. Maybe I'll call home." That'll stop her.

"Oh, that's good, Josie. You should do that."

I GPS the address on my phone and fly past the dive center, followed shortly by Blue Waters Trailer Park on the left. An SUV driver glares at me as I pass. Yes, I'm speeding. There are more important things than speed limits at the moment. Over on the Gulf side is a quaint seaside motel next to a church with a lit-up sign: "Will the Road You're On Get You to My Place? God." The road I'm on better just get me to Benny's… and fast. Come on, neon palm tree, where are you?

A curve in the road unveils the glowing green sign. Benny's Beach Bar, home of the boozin' dad. Focus on your job, Josie. Get the boy. I screech into the parking lot Batman style and park along the curb. Lights from the billboard announce tonight's band, "Tequila Sunrise." Their Jimmy Buffet sound-alike music blares through the parking lot.

"Free and easy, no cares in the world
Just give me a mojito and a tan island girl
Caribbean music on a sunset beach
Yeah, it's just another perfect night in the Keys."

Yes, another perfect night in the Keys. Who could ask for more? I push through the door to a mixed-up world of tourists and locals singing and laughing. It's easy to tell the difference, even after a few weeks. Weathered skin and sun-bleached hair denote the locals, who drink shots and beers. Tattoos abound. Tourist ladies don sundresses or trendy T-shirts, drinking colorful umbrella-clad margaritas and hurricanes in frosty glasses.

Nowhere in the sea of people do I see that redheaded boy. My eyes scan the scene, taking in every corner, searching beneath the bar, inspecting tables where customers snack on conch fritters and barbequed shrimp. Pure instinct kicks in. The kitchen. Busy bartenders don't bother looking up from their pouring and mixing as I slink underneath the counter and dart into the back room. A sweaty fry cook glances up from a sizzling basket of something battered and indistinguishable. Muscles bulge from the short sleeves of his stained T-shirt. Eyes glare. I am unfamiliar, therefore I am the enemy.

"Who are you?" He shakes the square metal basket. Tiny drops of hot oil spatter the ground around him. All that's missing is a cigarette dangling from his lips.

"Where's Connor?" The firmness in my voice surprises me, but there's no time to be intimidated by this man who could pummel me with one hand.

"He ain't here. Kids ain't allowed in bars." He hisses in a voice graveled by whiskey and cigarettes. "Who are you?"

"Connor's babysitter. I know he's here. It's okay. Ben called for me to pick him up."

"Why should I believe you?" He squints his eyes to intensify his look of hatred and mistrust. Yes, Cookie, I get it.

"Please. I swear, I'm a friend."

"Thought you were the babysitter."

Wow, you're good. "I'm both. I live with Preacher and Rosa. You know them?" Please know them.

He grunts. "Yeah, that don't mean nothin'." The man's loyalty is admirable…and extremely annoying. I consider telling him that Ben's been shot, but Ben made me promise not to tell a soul.

"Listen, just between you and me, the people from Children and Family Services might be coming by tonight to see if Connor is here. If I don't get him out quick, Ben could lose him." Who knows? It could be true.

"You better be tellin' the truth, lady. Anything happens to Benny or that kid, I'll come find you myself, got it?" He points an oily spatula at me like it's a dagger.

I believe him with all my heart.

"Out back," he says, jerking his head toward a dilapidated screen door. "Ben was talkin' to some dude out there."

Outside again, warm sea air brushes my face. A carrot-top head pops up from behind a huge pile of conch shells.

"Psst, Josie. Over here."

Muted light from a half-moon is enough to illuminate Ben…and the blood pooling beneath him. It oozes from his left side, just above his hip, where a mammoth hand does little to stem the flow.

"I'm here, Ben."

Groan.

I grab the cell from Connor's hand and dial 911 for the second time in three weeks. In twenty years of living in Riverbank, I never dialed those three numbers.

"Sheriff's Department. What's your emergency?"

"A man's been shot behind Benny's Beach Bar. He's out back. By a pile of shells. He's lost a lot of blood." I click off and kneel next to Ben. Before I can say a word, he grabs my arm with a bloody hand, pulls me toward him.

"Get him out." Wild eyes shout what the man can only whisper.

Distant sirens trail his labored words. I grab Connor's hand and dash to our beloved rust bucket, heading north on Highway One as an ambulance and police car streak past in the opposite direction. Blaring sirens and crazily flashing lights seem to settle Connor, who's been fidgeting and looking back, as if to see his dad. The calvary to the rescue. If only I could see it that way.

Lights and sirens. Thick fog stealing my vision like a thief in the night. Crimson-stained angel wings. The road blurs as I try to grasp the wheel with sweaty hands. Screams fill my head, but they don't emerge. That face, lifeless, eyes forever closed, haunts my thoughts and sends my heart racing. I killed her. I did it. A thunk sounds as I sideswipe the side mirror of a parked car. It jars me from dreadful images back to the present.

The boy. I must take care of the boy. I pull to the side and park. Grasping the top of the steering wheel, I inhale deep breaths, willing my heart to find a normal pace. From the back seat comes a sniff as Connor leans forward. "He'll be okay now, right?"

I swallow hard, afraid to promise anything.

"Right, Josie?"

He deserves a better rescuer than me. "Yeah."

"You did real good, Josie. Thanks."

Oh, God.

Another squad car flashes past, leaving horrific memories in its wake.

Can you tell us what happened, ma'am? How fast were you going? Do you know the victim? Do you need to sit down, Mrs. Caruso? Hey, Vince, help me here. She's fainting.

"Can we go to the hospital? Find Dad?" Connor swipes his cheek and fumbles around for the tissue box Preacher keeps in the back.

"What? Oh, the hospital. Let's go back first. Call Preacher."

"You all right? You sound funny, Josie."

Couldn't be better. It's just another perfect night in the Keys. "I'm okay."

White light blazes into my rear view, causing me to squint. I turn my head, only to get blinded by headlights. A car door slams, followed by heavy footsteps heading in our direction. Everything inside me tenses as a warning blares through my head. "Something's coming, Josie," it says, "and it ain't good." I barely have time to hit the lock switch before a tattooed mammoth blocks my driver side window.

"Hey you in there!" His voice bellows through the window, assuring me he could huff and puff and blow my car down. "Give me the boy now and you won't get hurt."

Over my dead body. My spine stiffens. White knuckles form a death grip on the steering wheel. Images of Carmelita disappear, along with the fog inside my head. My heart pounds out adrenaline, sending it racing through my veins like liquid dynamite. I don't know why this is happening or who these people are, but one thing is certain: they are *not* getting Connor.

A tri-colored skull leers at me from hardened muscles. Vulgar words spew from drunken lips. I wish I were stronger or braver...or armed with an M16. My head jerks sideways as someone raps on Connor's window. The light of a storefront sign illuminates more tattoos, some sort of spider and a black rose winding around a skinny arm. Greasy strands of black hair partly cover a girl's face, making it tough to tell her age. Heavy black eyeliner rings vampire eyes that flick from Connor to me.

"It's my mom," he whispers.

Nice.

"Open up, Connor. I just want to talk to you." Her saccharine voice is reason enough to keep these doors locked and hit the road. The leather get-up and monster boyfriend are just frosting on the toxic cake. "I love you, sweetie. I have a present for you in the truck."

"Don't open that door," I whisper.

"I won't. Let's go."

Skull Man nearly smashes my window with his fist. Having succeeded in getting my attention, he whips out a gun and points it directly at my head.

"Open up *now!*" he screams.

Oh, God. Not like this. There are things to figure out. That need to be said. Help us. For Connor. For my kids. Please.

Getting out of this car will be instant death for me, and who-knows-what for Connor. My hands seem to work with no cooperation from my brain. I put the car in drive, peeling out like a NASCAR racer, waiting for a bullet to rip into my head. Instead, the woman screams, "Don't shoot. You might hit my kid!"

The car's lights appear in my rear view. Find cops, Josie. Think clearly.

"Where's the police station?" Maybe Connor knows. Maybe, by the grace of God, it's next to his school or something. As I earlier prayed for Melissa's baby, I pray for Connor. For protection. My teeth chatter through each silent syllable. Words frozen like ice. Dry ice.

"Somewhere past Dr. Mike's place. We went there once on a field trip." He machine-guns the words. "You turn on a street where there's a pink hotel, or maybe green. Or maybe it was a restaurant."

Time for a new plan. There's plenty of cops at Benny's bar. I donut the gravel in the empty lot of a pancake house and beeline south. Skull Man does the same, only faster. But it gives me a chance to see that he's driving a black muscle car with a jacked-up rear end.

"Where are we going?"

"Back to the bar. We need the police." Those headlights spotlight us, blaring in my rear-view. I'm already going twenty over. Can't risk going any faster with Connor back there.

"We can't!" Connor screams. "Dad'll get in trouble. I'm not supposed to be there."

"You have to trust me, Connor."

Bam!

Freddy Kruger and the Bride of Frankenstein smack into us. I jerk. My belt cinches my middle. Connor screams again. I crank up the speed. Please don't let anyone be crossing the road. Not tonight. "We've gotta get away." Everything inside me is shrieking, but I speak as though we are strolling on the beach. It is what he needs. "The police at the bar will help. Gus won't follow us there. Even if he does, the police will protect us." I reach for his thin arm, desperate to connect. "Now lie down on the seat so no one can see you. We don't actually have to talk to the police, just be near them."

"Kinda like tricking them, right?"

"You got it."

Connor lies down, his seatbelt stretched across the seat. "Josie?"

"Yes?"

"That's the most you ever talked to me."

Call it nerves gone wild. Call it crazy. In the midst of being pursued down a dark road by gun-toting Gus and hell's version of mother-of-the-year, I laugh.

"Josie?"

"Yeah?"

"My mom said she loved me, but if she really did, she wouldn't have left me, right?"

My insides implode, yet the answer has been lying in wait. Forever. Or maybe just since I drove past that flowery cross without looking back. "You're wrong. I think she left you *because* she loves you. She probably knew she couldn't be a good mom. At least, not right now."

Really? We're having this discussion *now*?

A calico cat runs across the street. My foot hits the brake. What is it about me and cats? It streaks across the other lane and disappears between a swimsuit shop and a Cuban deli.

"That's just stupid."

From the mouths of babes.

We zip past the trailer park for the third time tonight. Within seconds, that beloved neon palm tree looms ahead, along with the far more comforting sight of red and blue strobes. I knew they'd stay to question people. I knew it. I swing in and slow down, approaching a police car as if I'm going to park right next to it. The black car continues south on Highway One. Those high-riding taillights get smaller and smaller, then disappear into the night.

Thank you.

Chapter 17

Preacher

Don Farmer hunches down in the back row of our outdoor church. Navy blue shorts and a white polo shirt put him in the best-dressed category for this crowd, except for the girls in sundresses. Arms folded, he stares at the sea grass, glances toward me, down again. Torment shadows his face. His position at the bank, his status, the fancy boat...they all mean nothing without Laura and the kids.

It started by accident. That is what he told me last week. He was online when a window popped up. Curiosity clicked the mouse...and there they were: naked bodies, sumptuous curves. He looked briefly, then closed out, disgusted. Until the next night, and the next, as one site led to another. Images permeated his mind. Close-ups, videos, things his wife would never do. He'd come home from work and hit the computer. "Work" he'd tell Laura.

And then the storm. Arguments, threats of divorce, promises to get help. Only Don didn't get help, he just got better at deception. Last week she left his suitcases on the porch and changed the locks. Don stayed with a friend that night and was waiting in my driveway when I went out to give the animals their breakfast.

Three rows ahead of Don sits Loni, holding her little girl's hand. That waitress job at Shrimp-n-Stuff isn't nearly enough to cover a single mom's expenses. She hasn't gotten caught yet with forging those checks at Don's bank. It's just a matter of time, though. Please let me

161

see her talking to Don after the service. Then I will know my argument convinced and convicted her.

Further down, Vince sits hand-in-hand with his wife, Samantha. On his twenty-first birthday, Vince lay in a hospital bed. Doc said he probably wouldn't make twenty-two, but that was six years ago. He gently pats Samantha's belly and waves me over with a smile. "Hey, Preacher, you ready for two new mini members of the fold?"

"Please, my friends, I delivered six puppies at three o'clock this morning. There is little left of me. Hold onto those babies. I promise to preach fast."

"Wow," Samantha says. "You must be *delirious* to make a promise like that!"

And so I am.

Vince stands up, lowering his voice. "How's Benny doing? I heard about last night."

If only God's word would travel as fast as this island's grapevine. "He lost much blood before the surgery. Doc says he will pull through. We are visiting him after service."

"Hey, Preacher!" James Johnson's voice booms over the crowd.

I wave to James, turning back to Vince and Samantha. "Nice to see both of you. Remember, no babies for an hour."

I cut through the row and head up front, where James the Giant threatens to crush a folding chair beneath the weight of his muscles. He stands, wraps me in a bear hug capable of cracking several ribs.

"How's my favorite holy man this week?" Before I can speak, he continues. "Hey, wanna go fishing? We haven't been in months. I hear the lings are biting like ants on a honey bun. And you don't get better eatin' than that." He smiles, white teeth contrasting dramatically with his ebony face.

Months? Nearly a year. Not James' fault. The man offers every week. Why is a day of rest the hardest of all the Lord's commandments? Always there is something to do. Someone who needs me. Broken animals, broken people, lost souls, sermons to write.

"Sí, this is true," I answer. "They are *muy delicioso*. But so much is happening lately, *amigo*, it is hard to get away. Soon though, James. Perhaps after Thanksgiving. For now, maybe there is someone else who might like fishing."

James' smile fades. The switch from jovial to melancholy twangs my heart with guilt. His high spirits are so contagious, but now I find the same is true when they crash from that height.

"You think he would? I mean, he's only met me once. Do five-year-olds fish?" He slaps a hand to his forehead. "See? This is what I was trying to tell you. I don't know nothing about kids. Other dads get to figure it out as they go along."

"Some fathers do not find out they have children until those children are adults. Some never do. Missing five years is not so bad in comparison."

"Yeah, I know. Still…it was just plain wrong. She should have told me. I would have done right by her. Now I don't even know what I'm supposed to do."

Time is growing short. This is not a conversation to be rushed. "You and God will do this together. Come by the coffee table after service. We will talk."

"Manuel!" Rosa calls to me from her front row seat. "It is nearly eleven." Seated in an adjacent chair, Josie glances behind her, whispers something to Rosa. Melissa leans in to hear, not one to be left out of anything.

Soon Melissa's seat will be occupied by someone else, someone God is guiding toward me. Maybe at this moment. I will miss that girl. She reminds me and Rosa of Dulce, our baby, now with a family of her own. The old rhyme plays in my mind: "sugar and spice and everything nice." Si, that is what Melissa and Dulce are made of.

Thank you, Lord, for leading Melissa to us, for guiding her choice. Destroying that baby would have crushed her sugar-cookie heart.

It is a full house today. I walk past familiar faces, others I do not recognize. Saints and sinners, every one. Many regulars, a peppering of tourists. Some who come just for the post-sermon snacks. Rosa's idea, of course. She knew I was trying to feed the souls of people who also needed food for their bodies. Our congregation grew by almost a third.

Hector's family sits together, taking up most of a row. Lines around his eyes tell me he still works the extra shifts. His wife looks in need of rest as well. She gifts me with a dainty wave, arm wrapped around her youngest daughter. Pallid. Skinny. All four children sit politely waiting for service to start. Such a beautiful family. If only they were not suffocating beneath the weight of a bad economy.

Rosa takes Owen's place, announcing a pot-luck lunch, the teen group meeting, and registration for a Haiti mission trip. The sweet sound of guitar chords rides the air, a signal for all to stand and sing. Words and music fill my head, my heart, my soul, embracing me like a prayer.

Open the eyes of my heart, Lord. I want to see you.

I walk to the pulpit. Only a handful of the seventy-five folding chairs appear empty. Owen and Elena, on the last official day of their honeymoon, come rushing in and fill two more. I nod to them and open my Bible. Voices hush, eyes turn toward me, expectant, waiting.

Will I make today matter?

Bless this sermon, Lord. There are battle-scarred hearts out there, desperate for Your healing power, aching to be loved, crying out for Your mercy. There are empty souls who have found their way here without even knowing why. For all of them I pray. Breathe Your message into my words. Amen.

I welcome the group, commenting on the beautiful day, thanking God for the gentle breeze that gives us comfortable conditions. I ask if anyone saw yesterday's Buccaneer's game. Groans emit from the crowd. Time to dive in.

"A few months ago, I crossed the Bermuda Triangle to visit a poverty-stricken area of Puerto Rico. Now, we have all heard the stories of planes and boats disappearing in this mysterious place. Some people blame aliens or the devil. Scientists say magnetic force fields or methane gas bubbles. But the triangle is just one of many mysteries in our world. Perhaps if asked what is the greatest mystery, you men would say…"

A handful of voices bellow "Women!" The congregation laughs.

"Of course the women would say…"

"Men!" Despite the predictability, they laugh again. Even Rosa, and she helped me write it. Not Josie. She remains expressionless, waiting for this to end. Here as a courtesy.

"Do you want to know the *real* mystery of this world? The number one question people want answered?" I pause, letting them ponder. Tension builds. And here we go. "If God is good, why does He let bad things happen?"

Josie's lips part. A light flickers in her eyes.

"Why is there starvation, slavery, deadly hurricanes? What about fatal diseases and freak accidents? How does a loving, all-powerful God allow these tragedies?"

People nod. A few turn and whisper.

"Here today are people who received that dreaded phone call in the middle of the night, the divorce papers they never saw coming, the alarming medical report, the miscarriage. These and worse happen all over our world. Why?" Attentive faces stare at me, waiting. Even the younger ones, who sometimes daydream or look off toward the woods, hoping to see a little Key deer. "A powerful question, is it not?"

Okay, Jesus, it's me and You. Please be here in this place. Bless these words. Touch these souls.

"Remember this today. Write it if you have to. God is not the author of evil. He created us to be in a relationship with Him. He loves us *unconditionally*. Do not underestimate the meaning of that word."

Rosa encourages me with a smile. I explain the depth of that love, the sacrifice, the path to salvation open to anyone who will take it.

"So then, *where* is God when we are crying out in pain? When our hearts are breaking? When terror grips us like a cobra's fangs?"

Josie sees me glance her way, quickly looks down. What comes next better be good. Something tells me I will only get one shot at this.

"He is right here, offering His strength, drawing you closer, making good come from the bad, beautiful from the ugly." She needs to know, they *all* need to know, there is no depth beyond God's grasp. There is no "hopeless" when the Holy Spirit lives within you.

"The two questions we must ask ourselves when evil rears its head are what is the cause, and how will we respond. You may not always know the answer to the first, but the second is easy. Pray for guidance." Well I know that some will scoff at this, but who is better qualified to direct our paths than the One who created every living thing? I encourage them to tap into that power. That wisdom.

I explain that bad circumstances arise directly or indirectly from greed or malice, other times it is simply nature doing its thing. But the tougher answer, the one they won't want to hear, comes next. My hands clench the lectern. "Often we create *our own* downfall, seeking blame elsewhere. How many of our illnesses are caused by smoking, drinking, drugs, poor eating, or living a sedentary life? What about the toxic chemicals we pour into our planet? Sometimes parents set bad examples for their children, then blame God when they get in trouble."

Oh, how I hope they see the significance of what I say next. Free will—such a beautiful thing, but so very dangerous. A critical component in why bad things happen.

"You see, God did not create us to be puppets or robots. No, He gave us choices. Love Him or do not. Believe in the Son He sent to save us, or do not. Follow the ways of Jesus, or follow the ways of the world. When you choose the latter, you must be ready to accept the consequences of your choice."

I can guess their thoughts. Yes, that makes sense for *some* things, but how do you account for a freak accident that ends a life? Muscles tense as I prepare to tackle yet another unpopular segment of this sermon.

"Then there is the one we don't like to talk about, but the Bible is clear on this, my friends. Satan does exist. He focuses his efforts entirely on destroying our bodies, minds, and souls. Targets our most precious relationships. The Bible says this in First Peter: 'Be alert and of sober mind. Your enemy the devil prowls around like a roaring lion looking for someone to devour.'"

Volumes of books have been written on a topic I am trying to cover in forty minutes. How can I possibly say all that needs to be said? What was I thinking?

"Now how is that for an image, eh? But you see, the worst part is not always the bad thing that happens. No…that comes next. The devil whispers in your ear, tells you his lies, convinces you that God made it happen. God does not care, does not love you. Perhaps He does not exist at all. Satan has one goal, ladies and gentlemen, and it is this: to separate you from God."

The Holy Spirit spreads through my soul until it is a fire inside me. *Please, God, let the sparks ignite this gathering.*

"My friends, you *can* survive the death of a loved one, a pink slip at work, a home destroyed by a hurricane, but you *cannot* overcome separation from God!"

I have their eyes and ears. God, I pray, their hearts as well. Now for the finale.

"Jesus said, 'The thief comes only to steal and kill and and destroy; I have come that they may have life, and have it to the full.' My friends, make God-honoring choices, wear His protective armor. Turn to Him for strength and guidance when life knocks you to your knees. *And when it doesn't.* Choose life…in all its fullness."

We close with a song, followed by a prayer. People exchange hellos, hit the snack table. Rosa beams at me, silently assuring me this was a good one. Her Sea Turtle Rescue friends engage her in conversation as I move toward Josie. Handshakes and pats on the back line my way.

"Excellent sermon today, Preacher."

"Great job, Preacher."

"Very powerful, I listened to every word."

"Hey Preach, that was like…awesome!" This from a member of the teen group.

I humbly thank each one, grateful for their kind words. Josie is still seated, hands folded in her lap. I take the seat next to her, vacated by Connor, who bolted for the sweet table before the last "amen" was fully spoken.

"So, señora, what did you think of your first visit to Living Word?"

"It was nice." She glances at me, then toward the parking lot.

Heat rises to my face. Nice? That is what she got from the Lord's message? Ice cream is nice, a day spent fishing is nice, a visit from a friend, perhaps. I poured my heart and soul into this message for her.

For everyone, of course, but I wanted to reach her, heal that heart, open her eyes. I felt the Spirit moving in me as I wrote it, again as I delivered it. I saw true emotion and understanding in the eyes of many.

Nice?

Father God, it is not praise I seek, but a simple sign that my efforts were not in vain. I tried. Truly I did. Her face tells me nothing. It is not my place to question You, but You know what is in my heart. This task of helping Josie, it is not for me. I am neither worthy nor qualified to face it.

My congregation mills about. Some wave in my direction. My people, my flock. I would row to Cuba on storm-tossed seas to bring back one who wandered. But I am not the right shepherd for this Josie.

The devil lies, Manuel. And there is no one better at it than he. It is something I felt you needed to know, because he is lying to you.

I ponder the familiar words, but my work here is done for today. "I promised to meet someone. Please tell Rosa I will be a few minutes."

Josie nods, her face a blank slate. "Okay."

My eyes sweep the crowd and rest on Rosa talking to Hector and the rest of the Santiago family. She will surely fill me in on their conversation later over coffee. It will be a short but welcome respite on this busy Sunday. My day of rest. I turn to go, hoping my deflated ego does not affect my conversation with James.

"Wait."

Was that for me? I turn back to Josie, her eyes shiny now, lips tight as a fortress, barricading the words she wants to say.

"Yes?"

She stares at the ground. A tear slides down her cheek, falling to the grass below. I glance toward James and he waves me over. Ah, such timing.

"Josie, tell me what I can do."

More drops hit the sandy dirt beneath us.

She shakes her head. "I don't know."

I wait, sure there is more.

"There are things you don't know about me, and things I don't understand."

"Let me help you understand. As for what I do not know, you can tell me when it feels right, or not tell me at all. I will not push."

Because I already know.

She sniffs, nods, brushes her cheek with the back of her hand.

"Hey, Preacher!" James' megaphone voice booms over the crowd. "You comin'?"

Maybe cloning is not such a bad idea. Three of me would make life much easier.

"Un momento, James. I am coming."

"You go," Josie says. "I'm fine. Really."

"Oh, no, you are finally talking to me, señora. I do have to keep my promise to James, but we will talk back at the house, yes? First we visit Ben. When we return, we can go to my office. Do we have a plan?" I hate to walk away, fearing she will flee like a skittish Key deer and never come back.

Josie nods, the hint of a smile emerging through her tears. "Go. He's waiting for you."

I give her arm a gentle squeeze. She allows it without stiffening. Maybe I just caught her off guard. Or maybe I'm not the wrong man for this job after all.

James waves his arm as though guiding an airplane toward a hangar. Yes, yes, I am coming. I wave back, then stop in mid-stride, frozen. My spine shivers. What is it? My eyes take in the small crowd, two boys chasing each other, Hector's family at the snack table, cars heading out to the street. James' eyes crinkle with confusion as to why I've stopped. Beyond him, amidst a clump of skinny pines, a young woman leans against a motorcycle. Haunted eyes lock onto mine, half-hidden by long black hair. Tattoos artfully cover wounds that have never healed.

Oh, Lord, she has been running far too long in the wrong direction. If only I had known her when it was happening. I try to break the grip of her gaze, but fail in that effort. I signal James to wait one more minute…and turn toward Naomi.

A sigh escapes me, taking all my energy with it. So many plates are spinning already. I fear one more may send them all crashing to the ground.

Chapter 18

Josie

Ben looks good. Real good in fact, for someone who was half-dead just fifteen hours ago. Bloody memories from last night race through my head. Thankfully, Rosa and Preacher were home when we finally got back. I needed them.

Clear plastic tubing links Ben to an IV. The nurse said the morphine drip will be used for a day or two to ease the pain. Next to him, Connor sits on the edge of the bed, his hand protectively on his father's arm. We stay for half an hour, until the medicine kicks in and Ben's eyes begin to droop.

"All right, everyone, let us give Benny some time to sleep." Rosa picks up her purse and sweater.

"No."

Eyebrows bow as she turns toward Connor. "Excuse me?"

"I want to stay, Rosa. Please. Dad needs me." He rubs his father's arm, draws closer.

Ben grunts in an attempt to respond, but the morphine wins. He sinks into a drug-induced sleep. Preacher sits on the bed, facing Connor, his back toward us.

"You are right, amigo. Your father does indeed need you. Without you there last night, he might not have made it."

He's so good at this. And truly, Ben does need that boy. Connor's a daily reminder to him that there's good in the world. Love. A reason for fighting off the bottle.

"I know."

"Right now he needs you to let him sleep so he can heal. Let's give him some peace and quiet. I will bring you back after dinner. Rosa has pork chops and those crescent rolls you like to eat with honey butter."

"And we still have some turtle brownies left from the fundraiser." Rosa's mention of the brownies softens the defiance in Connor's eyes.

"Well…I don't know."

"When we come back, we will pick up Owen," Preacher says. "I know he would like to join us. Perhaps he will tell us all about his trip."

"Owen? Really?" Connor jumps off the bed. "You promise?"

Preacher holds up a finger, then fishes his cell out of his pocket. A quick conversation confirms the plan. "Sí, now I can promise. Owen will come."

Connor smiles, kisses his Dad on the head, and leads us out of the sterile confines. We pass the room next to Ben's where a family is gathered around an older woman—maybe their grandma. I glimpse inside and see her smile weakly at them, despite whatever challenges she's facing. She needs them like Ben needs Connor…like I need my family.

But do they need me? If Rob had been the one to kill Carmie—if he were all messed up the way I am now—I would still want him home. I would want him to need me. It is a perspective I hadn't considered until now. Like a seed of hope, the thought nestles into my soul, awaiting the nourishment it needs to blossom and grow.

Those breaded pork chops head into the oven, with forty-five minutes to go before they join the salad, rolls, and asparagus being prepared in the kitchen. If I'm going to keep my word, these feet better head to Preacher's office now. Instead, I grab a stack of plates and set them on the table. Rosa and Melissa talk, allowing me to work in silence as I set napkins and silverware around plates.

"So then David said we have a lot to talk about. He thinks we should do it in person. I said, 'yeah, I know,' and then he said he hasn't stopped missing me for one minute since I left. Do you guys think he really meant it? He's not just being nice because of the baby?"

Rosa plops the crescent rolls down onto a cookie sheet, curving each one into a doughy half moon. "I believe he truly meant it, Melissa. What do you think, Josie?"

They're so sweet to include me, but speaking is still such a struggle. I manage a "yes," with an encouraging half-smile, hoping it's enough.

"By the way," she continues, "I have invited Hector's family to be our Thanksgiving guests. It will be wonderful to have them, and will help take my mind off my son and daughter being away this year." Rosa looks at the oak wall clock, then turns to me. "Weren't you and Manny going to talk?"

With the phone to his ear, Preacher motions me to sit. "Someone just came in, so it might be better to continue this conversation later." A pause, then, "Yes. Maybe I'll have something more to share with you when we talk tonight."

Awkward. He should have just let me wait outside. Nice office, though. Warm. Filled with photos of family, friends, what appears to be mission trips. Three crosses grace the walls, as unique as they are beautiful. One is crystal, with a blue dove that glimmers at its center. Intricate carvings make the ebony cross look as though it were formed from twisted rope. The third is my favorite: two pieces of bamboo fastened with leather strips. Simple. Earthy. Unexplainably powerful. What is it about a cross? My eyes can't look away. I imagine Him there, bleeding, forgiving. Preacher's words from the sermon come back to me. "Choose life…in all its fullness."

What I am doing is not life. It is existence, and barely that.

Preacher holds up a finger to indicate he will only be a moment. "No, señor, I still do not think that is a good idea. Not yet."

Hmm. Must be someone from church. I wonder what isn't a "good idea." I gaze at the wooden shelves, many lacking purpose. Collecting dust with nothing to hold. Odd. He speaks again, stuck in place with a landline phone. "I know. It is equally difficult on this end. My prayers are with you and your family every day." Silence for a moment. "You have my word."

He sure handles a lot of problems. What is that person dealing with? Is it worse than a mom and wife who left because she couldn't be either anymore?

The receiver clicks in place. Tired eyes focus on mine. He was up all night. First Ben at the hospital, then helping Lily give birth. Long night for all of us. He smiles softly, folding his hands on his desk.

"I am glad you came. I was not sure you would."

"Me, either."

"Did I ever thank you for helping with the puppies this morning?"

"No need. I was glad to help."

"Can you believe we have an albino? Dr. Mike says he has never heard of an albino Newfoundland before. It might be worth a lot of money, and I know many in our congregation who could use some of that."

Most people I know would already be making travel plans, remodeling. Not Preacher. Somebody's situation will improve because a white puppy came into this world.

"I was happy you chose to attend service today."

"Thanks." Is that even the right response? Expectant eyes look into mine, waiting for the conversation to commence. I pick up a paper clip from his desk. Stretch it out. Rebend.

Preacher clears his throat. Here we go. "You said there are things I don't know. Would you like to tell me?"

It's now or never, Josie. There must be a reason you are sitting in this office with this man. You came here for something. Whatever it is, it's bound to involve speaking.

"Josie? Would you rather not have this conversation right now? It is up to you."

Really? Because I don't feel that I actually have control over anything these days. "I really appreciate all you and Rosa have done for me."

He folds his hands, leans forward. "We are happy to have you here.

174

But you are not happy. That much is clear. We would both like to help with whatever is troubling you."

If only. "I know. It's just…that's impossible. There's no other way to say it. Simply impossible."

"Impossible is just a word, Josie. To some of us, it means nothing. Two years ago, after the accident, doctors told Rosa she would never walk again. Fire lit those lovely brown eyes. 'No,' she said. 'I will walk.' They said, 'impossible.' Little by little, she is proving them wrong, no? Each month, a tiny bit stronger, a tiny bit more time on her feet. It is a long, hard battle, but she will win."

"This is different."

"You must remember you are talking to a man of faith. I think anything is possible if God is in on it."

This was probably a bad idea. Look at him, so hopeful. Thinking he can fix me. I am far beyond being fixed by kindness and prayers. He needs to know. "I did something horrible. It was an accident, but that doesn't change the outcome. It cannot be undone…even if God is in on it."

"Perhaps not undone. But can it be overcome? Can there be healing, forgiveness, a renewed spirit?"

I gaze at the ebony cross on the wall behind him and take refuge in the intricate carvings. I am running away again. Mentally, but still running. This must stop. "You are a good man, Preacher. You have helped a lot of people through all kinds of things, but this one may be over your head." He nods for me to continue. I draw a breath, conscious of the nausea overtaking my stomach. "I killed a child. A little girl." The words burn on my lips. It is the first time they have been uttered. Painful images sweep into my head, blurring thoughts, vision. He's saying something. It's muted by drums pounding in my ears. I force out the rest. "Her name was Carmelita. She ran in front of my car. There was fog. So much fog. I couldn't see anything." What made me think I could say it out loud? I stand up, Gumby knees threatening to collapse.

"It was an accident, Josie." He shakes his head, strained words telling me this conversation challenges him. "An accident. Please, sit. You are white as a ghost. We will talk about this. Is that not what you came here for?"

My legs become marmalade. I collapse into my chair, asking myself what I came here for. His chair scrapes the floor. Strong arms wrap around me. He is on his knees, talking softly in Spanish, stroking my hair like I am a frightened child. Coaxing more words from my battered soul.

"I left my family. My children, my husband. That's not who I am, who I used to be. I would do anything for them. Die for them. But this is what I had to do instead. Dying would have been easier."

"No, Josie. Shhh. You have been blessed with much love in your life. Sometimes love can be painful. Sometimes life brings us to our knees. But always, God is there. Loving you. Holding you up. If you want Him to. He is a gentleman, never forcing Himself on someone. God led you here for a reason, querida. He is not done with you yet. In fact, I believe He is just beginning."

Not done with me yet? That's what I'm afraid of. "I listened to you today, I really did. But I don't know if God can make a difference with something this…permanent. This big."

He gently pulls my hands from my face, holding them in both of his. "Josie, have you ever asked?"

Had I? I think back on all the words I've silently shouted up to heaven since that horrible night. And telling the Beach Man "prayers don't always fix things."

I don't believe you're speaking from experience.

"Have you prayed for strength? Have you asked God to pull you up out of your despair? To help you heal your relationship with your family? The child's family?"

I shake my head. Could divine intervention heal Ana? Or prevent her from glaring at me with the same hatred that filled Roxy's eyes and led to years of loneliness?

"Maybe this would be a good time to start," he says.

In that silent examining room with Melissa, I felt something unexplainable. But I was praying for *her*—a sweet, loving, pregnant Christian girl. This time would be different. I would be seeking healing from the same God who let it happen, who could have pushed her out of the way with a blink. No! I grab the edge of his desk and breathe deep, willing myself not to faint. He stands next to me, holding my arm. The haziness filling my head begins to dissipate. Strength returns to my legs. Enough to get me into the veil of darkness blanketing the beach.

The golden orb rises silently from the sea, washing the sky in watercolor streaks of lavender and pink. Three pelicans coast toward the sandbar to join their friends. Pink birds, beaks flattened at the ends, voice their displeasure with the pelicans' intrusion. Within seconds, however, everyone settles down, and the pinks again search for tiny sea creatures in the shallows. Ashley would love this. As for me, after that disastrous meeting with Preacher last night, my sleep-deprived body would love just one thing.

The rich aroma reaches me just half a heartbeat before the word. "Coffee?"

I am too baffled by Beach Man's presence to respond.

"Go ahead, you'll like it. Real Wisconsin cream, none of that powdered stuff." His lovely smile greets me like a blessing as he holds out the steaming cup. "The beans are from Reunion Island."

How did Beach Man appear without my noticing? And with coffee, no less? I shake my head, wondering if he is a vision born of too little sleep and too much heartache. He remains. "Where?"

"Reunion. Small volcanic island near Madagascar. Quite beautiful. Good, rich soil." A familiar thermos leans against his backpack in the sand.

The first sip is delightful beyond belief. The perfect hint of sweetness. "Mmm. Thank you. You're not having any?"

"No, I prefer water or fresh juice. A glass of wine on occasion."

"But you had the coffee in your—"

His laughter interrupts me. "Look, Josie." He points toward the horizon. "See the dolphins? There are three of them. Watch and you'll see them jump."

One by one they leap, tossing a fish as the sun rises behind them.

Palms swish and a warm morning breeze blows the hair back from my face. Curiosity intrudes on the lovely moment. His presence. The perfect coffee. Just like the lemonade.

"How did you know I'd be here?"

"I was just walking. Morning is such a pleasant time to walk, don't you agree?"

"But how...."

"Gorgeous view, isn't it?" He points to the group of pretty pink birds with unusual bills. "Love those spoonbills. All birds, actually. In fact, all critters. Love 'em all."

He talks as if we are old friends. Yeah, we'd already met, but usually it takes awhile before people are that relaxed around each other. The coffee seeps through my body, deliciously wakening my senses. My mind comes to life, recalling the question. "That cab driver, Hector, didn't know you. Don't get me wrong, he was ecstatic. Grateful beyond measure. But he didn't know you."

"He knows me. He just didn't recognize me."

"Why?"

"I didn't want him to."

As if that makes any sense at all. This has got to be the weirdest, nicest man I've ever met.

He pulls another thermos from his backpack and pours juice. Pineapple, from the scent of it. We sip, watching as a group of exotic white birds swoop down on the now crowded sandbar.

He empties his cup, setting it down next to the thermos. "So...what did you think of Preacher's sermon?"

Darn! I forgot to ask Preacher if someone helped him write the sermon. "It was good. Powerful, even. He was really into it."

"I was more interested in hearing whether you were into it."

"Right. Well, it did answer some questions. And it made me think about things." Please let that be good enough. Don't make me say it resonated in every corner of my heart, made me want to leap off that fence. Made me want to...dare I think it? Believe that I was loved unconditionally. Forgiven. Able to become a new creation.

"Such as?"

Much as I'm eternally grateful for the coffee, I'm not willing to pay the price demanded by this man. "Look, you are a really nice person. I appreciate this coffee and that lemonade the other day and the cab ride. But you don't really know me. The truth is…"

His eyes intensify, deepening from sky blue to sapphire. "I do know you, Josephine. And I know what the truth is. You are hurt, angry, confused. You are not thinking clearly. You are grieving over something horrible that happened in your life, but you should know…"

"I never told you that, not any of it."

"I'm very good at reading people. The pain in your heart is reflected in your eyes, your body language. It shadows you with every step. As far as what the truth is…you heard it in Preacher's sermon. That is the only truth you need to know."

The morning sun hovers well above the water now, brightening the world as it gains altitude. I empty my cup, wishing there was more. He refills it without saying a word. A large gull waddles toward us seeking a handout.

"No, no, no," he admonishes, like a loving father setting his child straight. He points to the ocean. The gull turns, takes to the air, its wide wings flapping over the water.

"Everyone wants the wrong things." He sips. I wait, wondering if I imagined that bird just obeyed him. "That water is teeming with good healthy fish. He wants popcorn and chips. Same thing with people, don't you think?"

We're not talking about food, I'm sure of it. "People don't always know what they need. Lines blur between the whole need/want thing. Sometimes what you need isn't what's best for the people you love. Then what?"

No answer. He waits, as if expecting me to say it.

"I left my family." I focus on the birds, aware of him staring at me.

"They miss you."

"I know."

"Families need each other." He puts his palm on my cheek. Warmth radiates through my face, my neck, my entire body. His words seep into me, echoing through my mind and heart. "They were created to stick together. Help each other. You should give your family a chance to do that."

Are you okay, Mom?

We'll get through this, Jo, me and you.

Come home, Mom.

I sigh, wondering if I'll ever again know what's best for my family. For Ana. For me. Maybe he's right.

"*I am* right."

It's been hours since Beach Man left me with more thoughts than my brain can hold. But more than that, more resolve than I've felt in weeks. I thought my presence was nothing but a black storm cloud, sucking the joy out of everyone who walked beneath it. And maybe that was true...but that can change. I can change it, though I may need a little help along the way. Like a miracle. And my family.

Are they doing all right? The answer far exceeds the significance of my inner chaos. I need to call. It's been three days since I've had that connection. Feels like three hundred years. Stomach muscles wince, readying for pain. Love shouldn't hurt this much.

I pick up my cell and scroll down to "home." Monday morning. I close my eyes, imagine buttering toast, pouring juice, sending off backpacked kids with hugs.

Have a great day. Love you.

Love you, Mom.

Be careful.

I hit send. Everyone should be gone with the possible exception of Aunt Theresa. Just a quick message, that's all.

Two rings give way to one breathless word. "Mom?"

My answer fails in its attempt to squeeze past the monolith blocking my throat.

"Mom? It's me. Ashley."

Like I could ever, for one split second, forget that voice. "Hi, sweetheart."

"Are you okay?"

My baby girl. I left her without warning. She still wants to know if I'm okay. "Uh-huh. Are you?"

"Yeah. I miss you, though. A lot."

My heart shrivels and burns like a marshmallow dropped in a campfire. "Me, too, honey."

"When are you coming home?"

Oh, God, please help me.

"I don't know. It's complicated."

"Why? All you have to do is drive back and be here. It's simple. Dad says if you say the word, we'd come and get you in a heartbeat. Just like that, Mom. In a heartbeat."

My throat tightens. I struggle to speak. "He said that?"

"Yeah, but I'm not supposed to ask you, because you need time to get better. So don't tell him, okay?"

"Okay." Her soft breath whooshes through fifteen hundred miles of air, so how can I feel it on my cheek?

"If you come home, we could help you get better."

I suck down a breath of air and wonder how I will survive this conversation. "You know, I'm starting to think so, too. Let's talk about you now. No school today?"

"Parent-teacher conferences."

"Oh." And I'm not there to see your science project and your grades and hear the teacher gush over how sweet and smart you are.

"Me and Dad are going at one o'clock."

"He stayed home?"

"Yeah, because Aunt Theresa had to do something. She's here a lot since you left. She makes us dinner and does laundry and stuff."

My stuff. The stuff a real mom does. Can I do it again?

"That's good. Are you and Mitch eating good, staying healthy?"

"Yeah, but a lot of things are different now. Dad cooks once in a while." She lowers to a whisper. "Sometimes he burns stuff or makes it wrong, but he's really trying."

Rob takes over the grill one night each summer and makes his own toast in the morning. Bobby Flay he isn't. "Dad cooking…that is different."

"And we go to church now, Mom. Aunt Theresa asked Dad if she could take us. We wanted him to go too because we felt kinda weird. When we get there, Mitch goes to the teen group and I go to the fourth and fifth grade group. Dad and Aunt Theresa go to big church. And guess what? Elizabeth and Luis from my school go there, too."

Images of Rob swirl in my head. Attending a school conference, cooking, going to church. He was always a good dad, but now he's… involved. Part of things. He's influencing. Can I resume that very same thing?

"How is it?"

"I like it. I'm going to see if Kaylie can come with us this Sunday. I've been telling her all about it. How come we never went, Mom?"

"We go on Easter and Christmas, honey. Every year, remember?"

"Yeah, but it's different on regular weekends. Not so crowded, you know? And the youth pastor is really cool. I understand more stuff about God now."

"I'm glad, honey." And I mean it. Something about Ashley going to church and liking it breathes life into my charred marshmallow heart. "Does Mitch like it too?"

"Uh-huh. He brought Savanna last week, even though she has her own church."

Yes. Another breath of life. Warm as the sea breeze to my soul. "So they're friends again?"

"Oh, yeah. They always walk home together and everything, just like before the…you know. Mrs. Gutierrez brings dinner over on Sunday nights and Aunt Theresa brings dinner over to their house on Wednesdays."

"You're kidding." I don't even know the world she's living in. But I want to. I'm glad for my babies. My man.

"It's real nice, don't you think? It's like what Jesus says about taking care of each other. Oh, Mom! I almost forgot! Mrs. Gutierrez had her baby last week—Juanito. He's so cute, Mom. You should see him."

Ana's baby. I would have been there, visiting her in the hospital with an armload of presents and flowers, making dinners for her family. Touching that perfect baby cheek.

"You there, Mom?"

"Yeah. Sounds like everything is going great."

"It's not great without you here. I miss you sooo much."

A door slams shut in the background and the sound of heavy footsteps tells me it's either Mitch or Rob.

"Dad, it's Mom! It's Mom!"

The footsteps get louder, followed by a muffled exchange, then "No! Please, please, please. I want to talk to her some more!" Her words trill with panic. I squeeze my cell, nearly crushing it.

"Say goodbye, Ash." Kind, but firm. He's always been good at that when the situation calls for it. "I need to talk to her."

"I have to go. But will you promise to think about coming home soon? Please?"

"Honey, it's…I'm thinking about it. I am. Just remember I love you, Ashley, and tell Mitch I love him, too. And I'm sorry…about leaving you, about everything. Tell him that for me, okay?"

Silence, then a sniffle. "Okay. I love you, too."

The last word is three octaves higher than her normal voice. Rapid footsteps in the background. She is running to her room, where she will bury her face in her purple striped pillow and soak the whole middle section. And I won't be there to stroke her hair and make it all better.

Teeth clench as I prepare to face the unknown. After three days of unanswered messages, what will Rob say?

"Josie?"

"Hi." His name settles in my throat, declaring me unworthy to say it out loud.

"Did you get my messages?"

Messages? No, my phone was dead. It fell into the ocean. A seagull ate it. I have been wrong. So wrong.

"Yeah. I did." Here it comes.

"You okay?"

I almost laugh. My husband is asking his crazy, runaway wife if she's okay.

"If I was okay, there wouldn't be fifteen hundred miles between us. And I wish there wasn't even one, Rob."

"There doesn't have to be, Jo. There's a flight at two. Time enough to taxi you to the airport, then it's just three-and-a-half hours to O'Hare. You could be home by dinner."

Dinner. Me in the kitchen, making pot roast. Ashley sitting at the table, brow furrowed as she concentrates on math. Mitch playing video games, promising to do his homework later. Such a lovely picture. I want it to be my reality. I am so close, and yet…

"How is Ana?"

"Please, honey. Don't change the subject. Come home where you belong. See for yourself."

"I love you, Rob. Miss you. All of you. I'm trying to get home, but I need a little more time."

"Really? You're trying?"

"Clicking my ruby slippers like crazy. I think I'm almost there."

Cielo Azul is a tropical paradise. A good place to quiet the voices inside. The ocean soothes my soul. The sand warms my feet and the people warm my heart. But Dorothy was right.

There's no place like home.

Chapter 19

Josie

A pale turkey, stuffed with dressing, limp legs tied together, rests in a roasting pan awaiting its three-hour stint in the oven. Before the day is out, it will feed the current residents of Rosa's Haven, along with Dr. Mike, Ben, Connor, and Hector's family, *abuelos* and all. Rosa is making a squash-and-pepper recipe handed down by her grandmother, while Melissa takes on the green bean casserole. Beneath the cover of a large Dutch oven lies the Azteca soup I helped Preacher make yesterday. The combination of garlic, tomatoes, celery, and peppers spiced the air for the rest of the evening. Mike and Ben are rounding out the feast with pies.

And what will Thanksgiving be like at the Caruso home this year? They'll likely be at Aunt Theresa's house with all the cousins. Wish I could mail them my sweet potato pie and homemade cannolis. Liar. Wish I was there, peeling those stupid sweet potatoes. Watching the kids dip cannoli ends in crushed pistachios. Making everyone say three things for which they are grateful. Are there happy Thanksgivings in my future? In Ana's?

"Josie, dear, are you all right?" Rosa's words jar me to the present.

"Yes." I empty my coffee with one last gulp. "I'm going to clean the stalls. I'll be back in time to help in the kitchen."

"The stalls can wait a day—they were cleaned after dinner last night." She picks up a potato from the pile in front of her and begins to peel.

185

"Oh." But the stalls are my reason to escape, to be alone. They provide a mindless task that calms me for reasons I can't explain. Without my time alone, how can I face this day of people laughing, talking, feasting? How can I face a celebration with images of home firmly planted in my mind?

Preacher looks at my face and turns to his wife. "You know, it might be good if she just gave them a light cleaning. That way it will not get too smelly in there."

"Manuel, it is Thanksgiving Day! What are you say—?" She looks up from her peeling, exchanges a glance with her husband. "Oh, well, it probably would be a good idea. You know best when it comes to the animals. Thank you, Josie, if you're sure you don't mind."

"Not at all." My hand releases its death grip on the coffee mug. I wash it, grab a carrot from the fridge, and exit as they discuss plans for the day. A cool north breeze blows hair in my face, pushing me toward the barn. At least the sturdy barn walls will keep out the wind.

Faint yips greet my ears as I enter. They mix with the now-familiar melody of munches and snorts, stomps and peeps. My nose takes in the scent of wood, hay, and a crazy combination of fur and feathers. But it is the light from above that makes me catch my breath. Rays of gold stream through the hayloft windows, softly illuminating the barn like a centuries-old cathedral somewhere in Italy. It is almost enough to make me fall to my knees.

No other humans intrude on this unlikely sanctuary today. The floor beneath my feet is padded with hay, but squeaks as my foot lands on Lily's ducky toy. I heed Dr. Mike's warning, giving the new mom her space and watching from a distance. She picks up her big black head to acknowledge me, then sets it back on the blanket-covered hay. Her five-day old pups blindly crawl over each other, one standing out like a full moon in the night sky. He snuggles next to his mama, safe and sound with a milk-filled tummy, oblivious to the rumors that he is a warm and fuzzy little gold mine.

I stop to scratch the head of our newest resident, an adorable pot-bellied pig, on my way to the bunny hutch. Sunny awaits, knowing it is time for a few minutes in my arms. She hops over to greet me, ears nearly touching the floor. Maybe Clover would like one of her own kind, especially since we're gone so much. Everyone needs a partner.

I think about mine. The way he makes me laugh, listens with his heart, knows me better than any friend. Loves me anyway. I squeeze my eyes, imagine sitting on the couch with his arm around me. When I open them, Lightning whinnies his displeasure with my delay.

"Hold on, I'm coming." I stroke Sunny and close my eyes again, trying for one precious moment to imagine I'm in my living room holding Clover as we all watch the Macy's Parade. I ache to smell turkey in the oven—*my* turkey with *my* stuffing. But no virtual transportation takes place, not even for a second. They are there and I am here.

My lop-eared friend bounces away as I head for Lightning, who stands without leaning, head up, ears perked, eyes bright and clear. To an outsider, his protruding bones would be heartbreaking, but we Rosa's Haven refugees know differently. We see the metamorphosis. Whether it's the TLC, the food and vitamins, the fresh air...I don't know. Maybe it's pure miracle.

That velvet nose nudges my arm and finds the carrot protruding from my jeans pocket.

"Taste good?"

His eyes sparkle a "yes."

"You're looking great, fella."

Munch, munch, munch.

I open the storage room and take out a rake and shovel. Might as well start cleaning. I shovel the manure and dirty hay into a wheelbarrow, set it off to the side, grab some fresh bales. Working like an automaton, my mind drifts to the conversation with Rob. Can't believe he went to a parent-teacher conference, but that pales in comparison to his taking a lower position at work. Mr. Climb the Ladder, whatever it takes? I try to envision him coming home each day at five, no business trips, sitting with me at soccer games, band recitals. Maybe going on dates again. I strain to see him sitting at the dinner table. The picture is hazy.

But the harder I try, the clearer it gets.

Preacher opens first the door, then his arms, as the Santiago family walks in to warm hugs and warmer smiles. Hector carries a casserole dish, his wife Marisol right behind him with a colorful tote bag filled with wrapped packages. The abuelos follow, children bringing up the rear. Their youngest daughter is paler than the rest. Definitely in need of a big, fat Thanksgiving dinner. Sad eyes scan the room, but brighten in recognition as they land on Connor. Preacher covers the introductions, then suggests Connor take the kids to see the puppies. He doesn't have to ask twice.

Hector politely asks if he may say something. After Preacher nods, he shyly steps forward. "I thank Preacher and Rosa for invite us to this Thanksgiving. *Mi esposa*, Marisol, she make tamales for meal." He hands the casserole dish over to Preacher.

"Oh, ho! Homemade tamales!" Preacher grins and pats his chest. "The way to my heart. Muchas gracias, señora."

Marisol smiles. "*De nada.*"

"She also bring gift for women." Hector motions to Marisol, who reaches into her tote bag and distributes the brightly wrapped packages to me, Rosa, and Melissa.

"*Abramos,*" she says, making an open book motion with her hands.

Rosa goes first, tearing open the green tissue to reveal a pendant of frosted green glass mounted on a silver disc. The combination is beautiful. Rosa holds her necklace up for all to see as it dangles from a thin silver chain.

"Is seaglass," Hector explains. "Glass go in ocean many year. Broken bottles, jars, these things. Then ocean, she whoosh and whoosh." At this his arms imitate ocean waves. "Then the glass, she get smooth. The ocean, she bring smooth glass to beach."

Melissa's package is the largest. She gently opens the pink tissue and squeals happily at the lovely driftwood frame inside. Frosted pink glass pebbles of different shapes, sizes, and shades decorate the wood, with a milky white sand dollar secured to each corner. Marisol pats Melissa's tummy, points to the frame.

"Yes, I will put my baby girl's picture in there. It's perfect!" Hormones and happiness spill from her eyes as she hugs Marisol. "Go, on, Josie. Open yours."

I unwrap mine to discover an amber frosted glass pendant bordered by a small striped shell on either side. It dangles from a thin leather cord.

"It's beautiful," I say to Marisol's beaming face. "I've never seen anything like it." Rosa translates for me, adding her own accolades while Melissa keeps repeating "I love this, it's awesome!"

Marisol and Rosa briefly converse before Rosa's eyebrows arch with an *"Es verdad?"*

Preacher had taken the tamales to the kitchen, returning just in time to hear the excited pitch in Rosa's voice. "Is what true?"

"Marisol made this lovely jewelry herself. These are all handmade, Manny. Can you believe it?"

"She made these?" Melissa asks. "No way! Seriously?"

Hector nods vigorously. "Sí, sí, she make. She do many years. She find seaglass and shells on beach. She buy jewelry at garage sale, then use parts—the chain, the hooks—to make her art. See frame?" He points to Melissa's gift. "I make from wood on beach. Marisol use seaglass to make beautiful."

I'd seen seaglass jewelry at some craft fairs back home, but none as lovely as this. And that baby frame! The gift shop customers would love this stuff. So would Ashley. She'd want something purple, of course. Always purple.

Deep breathes. Ashley is fine. They're all fine. They want me back. But does Ana? One thing's for sure, the answers won't come here to Cielo Azul. I've got to find them for myself.

"Josie? Are you all right?"

"Yes. Really. I was just thinking how much my Ashley would love one of these necklaces. Could you ask Marisol if I could buy one from her? A purple one?"

"Si." Rosa grins. "I will." She turns to Marisol.

The idea comes from a shining star, beaming into my head, bursting with light. I grab Rosa's arm before she speaks. "Wait. Wouldn't Marisol's stuff sell great in the gift shop?"

The light is contagious. It illuminates Rosa's face. She smiles, laughs, hugs me. "Josie Caruso, you are a genius."

Spanish words bounce back and forth between the two women. The light brightens Marisol's eyes, which dart to me as the word Josie pops up in the conversation. Marisol's hands fly to her face. Eyes tear. Another hug. More than I've experienced in many weeks. More than I've allowed.

"Gracias, Josie." Marisol squeezes me tighter. "Muchas gracias." She releases me, launching into a rapid-fire conversation in Spanish with her husband.

Rosa wheels into the kitchen, asking me to join her.

"God blessed us with this good idea to help Marisol," Rosa whispers. "Don't you think?"

Actually, no, I hadn't thought of it that way.

But maybe so.

Melissa and I grab up everyone's empty soup bowls as Preacher, Ben and Mike bring out the main course dishes. Rosa expertly slices the turkey, despite lacking leverage from her position in the wheelchair. Clanging dishes and silverware fill the next few minutes, as turkey, tamales, and vegetables are passed around. My plate is a cornucopia of colors and cultures by the time the noise settles down. A forkful of Rosa's squash and peppers mixture is halfway to my mouth when Ben repeatedly clinks his fork to his glass as though signaling a bride and groom to kiss.

"Sorry to interrupt, folks, but I have an announcement. By the first of the year, Ben's Beach Bar will no longer exist."

I guess getting shot made the man do some thinking.

Several people are talking at once, asking, "why?" and, "what happened?"

"Here's the deal. Some of you may know I have, let's say, issues with drinking. So owning a bar probably isn't the best idea for me. Some of you also know I got shot last week, which made me consider a few changes for the future."

Hector translates for Marisol, who lets out a small gasp and covers her mouth.

"I need to be here for Connor, you know? So me and Freddie, my cook, got together the other day and started goin' over some ideas, lookin' stuff up on the Internet and all that. He has a degree in business and he's pretty tired of bein' a cook."

The grease-covered thug who threatened me with his spatula has a business degree?

"So we gave it some thought, decided to open a laser tag place so teens have somethin' better to do than drink beer on the beach. Part of it will be a juice bar with music and video games. Between birthday parties during the day and the older kids comin' at night, we should do okay. Freddie checked it out and there's nothin' like that in the Middle Keys, so we just might be onto somethin' here."

Laser tag. Mitch would love it. I can almost hear the laughter that echoed through the room at his last birthday party. Twelve boys reliving and reenacting just-played rounds of laser tag as they scarfed down pizza and cake. My Mitchell laughing—what a beautiful sound. Yes, Ben. Laser tag is perfect.

The clapping starts with Preacher. By the third time he smacks his hands together, we all join in. Ben's glow warms the room, and something deep inside me as well. My heart swells with pride for a man I hardly know—a man I attacked less than a month ago. Preacher goes on and on about what a great idea this is, overflowing with suggestions for Benny's new venture. Rosa, Melissa, and Marisol brainstorm a variety of creative names, like Cosmic Storm or Star Quest, before asking Benny if he'd thought of one.

"Yeah. Laser Tag."

And therein lies the difference between men and women. I smile to myself, knowing it's exactly what my Rob would have picked.

Chapter 20

Josie

A sliver of molten gold gleams where ocean meets sky. Just off the sandbar, white birds dip apricot beaks into the dark ripples. Newcomers. I would remember if I had ever seen beaks that long. Distant trills accompany the occasional swish of palm fronds to form a sweet morning melody. I dip my toes into miniature waves playing tag with the shore, and feel a little like Eve.

Guess what, Mrs. Caruso. When we were in Florida, I saw the sun come up out of the ocean.

I've seen that, too. Wasn't it beautiful?

Oh, yes. The most beautifulist thing ever.

I close my eyes.

God, help me. I am begging You. Lift me out of this trench. Get me home. Please.

The universe sends me saltwater kisses on a breeze likely born off the African coast. It blows the hair back from my face, which is warmed by the rays of the rising sun. I extend my arms out to my sides, palms up, just because it feels right.

He is here.

I feel You. Peace flows through me like a river, its gentle current pooling into my heart until it spills out, flooding my soul.

And I, you.

There is still so much I don't understand.

Be still and know that I am God.

But I still have fears about returning home, facing Ana.

Do not be terrified; do not be discouraged. I'll be with you wherever you go.

You really love me?

Always. Unconditionally.

I open my eyes and catch a movement down the beach. A man walks away from me along the shore, his backpack dangling from one shoulder. He is little more than a silhouette, but there is no doubt he is wearing worn leather sandals and a familiar T-shirt. He turns around, walking backwards for a minute to wave, then continues on his way. On the sand near my feet, two footprints face me, then trail off in the direction of my Beach Man.

There is something surreal about these sunrise walks—something that makes me feel like the horror of that foggy night does not have to define me forever. That there is a love beyond measure that could give me hope, bring me back to mornings beneath my powder blue comforter with Rob warming the mattress beside me.

The golden orb rises higher, brightening the earth as it announces the start of a new day. And here am I, facing a choice as big as the ocean.

But I am not alone.

"Josie, please hand me those scissors. This young lady would like to wear her new hat and we cannot have the tag hanging, right?" Mrs. Cohen, queen of the gift shop, smiles at the little green-eyed beauty as she places a starfish baseball cap on her head. The child offers a thank you, sans two front teeth, before walking away with her daddy. The gift shop is buzzing today.

Mrs. Cohen tosses the tag into the garbage, adds another hat to the rack. "You know, dear, there's something different about you today. I can't put my finger on it."

I smile at her, happy I've had the chance to work with this sweet woman.

"Ah, that's it! You have a lovely smile, Josie. It has not graced your face until today."

Do I? "Thank you."

"Whatever the reason for it, I'm glad it's there."

"Me, too." There is a glimmer inside me. Small, but just enough to push away the darkness and promise brighter days ahead. My grief is not gone, but waves of hope are washing over my despair.

"Thank goodness we got Marisol's sea glass on the shelves in time for these Christmas shoppers. Rosa tells me this was your idea."

"No, not really."

Mrs. Cohen doesn't look convinced. "Well, it was a darn good one. We needed something new in here. That sea glass was just the thing. In fact, a few more new ideas wouldn't hurt a bit." She points discreetly at two teenage girls gazing at the necklaces. "Look at how they love her gorgeous things."

Before the shop opened, I'd cleared shelves, displaying the shimmery sea glass against midnight blue velvet. Irresistible. Visible from the entry, it beckoned customers like the sea from which it emerged.

"Let me see." Mrs. Cohen brushes a gray tendril from her face before opening the cash register. She retrieves a small notepad and flips it open. "Three necklaces, a frame, two trinket boxes in the first half hour. And I gave up writing it down after that." She glances at a display of palm tree and seashell clocks. "Oh, my, that was over three hours ago! This day is simply flying."

The sea glass shelf is once again in need of more items. I enter the back room and find Marisol dabbing her eyes with a tissue. If only I knew more Spanish. She smiles at me. Oh…happy tears. I get it.

I pick up a wooden trinket box edged in green and blue sea glass. The lid is adorned with delicate spiral shells in a creative design. Ashley would love it. I search my memory for something to say to Marisol.

Mommy fixed my hair special today, Mrs. Caruso. Look at my curly pony tails!

Oh, Carmie, they are very pretty!

You mean 'muy bonita.' That's how you say 'very pretty.'

"Muy bonita." I hold up the box, hoping I'm saying it right.

"Gracias, Josie." She hugs me. "Muchas gracias *por todo*."

Later, during a lull, I catch up with Rosa and ask her the meaning of por todo.

"It means 'for everything.'"

Marisol isn't the only one reaping a good harvest today. According to Connor, two of the curly feathered chickens, the pot-bellied pig, and a black rabbit have been adopted. All in all, a good day for man and beast alike at Rosa's Haven. Perhaps this sea glass will help buy medicine for Hector and Marisol's daughter. I imagine her healthy, eyes bright, laughing.

Believe me, money is no big deal. In a perfect world, we wouldn't even need it, right?

Rosa straightens pretty greeting cards on a metal rack, takes a deep breath, pushes herself up. Her face tightens into a grimace as she stretches for the cards on the top shelf. I nearly knock over a plant stand as I run to help her.

"No, Josie." She waves me away. "This is good for me. Hard, but good. It is only a month or so that I've been able to stand for a couple of minutes at a time." Her eyes shine, causing mine to blur slightly. "It is a miracle. But I must continue to work hard to get back to normal. And I will, querida."

"You're amazing."

A sad smile graces her lips. "Not behind the scenes. I cry, I hurt, I get angry at God. I try to hide that part of me from the world, but my Manny sees it. That man, he is a saint. Drives me loco sometimes." She laughs, brown eyes crinkling at the edges. "But still a saint."

I have a saint that drives me loco sometimes too. He tells me I'm beautiful, even when I'm not, and keeps my car filled with gas, though I never ask him to. And sometimes he brings home flowers "just because." But he's gone way too much. Or he used to be. Seems like that might be changing, if what he said is true. He doesn't deserve this new life. Scrambling to work, taking care of the kids without the one who promised "'til death do us part." Well, I am not dead. Just far, far away.

And that can be fixed.

Rosa sits back down, unable to hide the momentary scowl as she strains her weakened muscles. "What is it, Josie? Tell me."

"Nothing. Just thinking."

"You miss them so much, it's killing you."

Deep breaths. "I do."

"What are you going to do about it?"

The simplicity of her question nearly makes me laugh. But instead, I stay silent, letting an answer take seed and push through all the muddled thoughts that have darkened my mind since that horrible night. Could the answer be as simple as the question?

"So?" She taps her foot. "I am waiting."

"I think." Dare I finish the sentence? "I think I need to get back home."

Rosa's grin lights our little corner of the gift shop. "I think you are right, Mrs. Josie Caruso." She reaches for my hand and squeezes it. I squeeze back, feeling those inner walls melting from the warmth of her hand. "Now go. Take some time for yourself. You have been working all day. We'll be closing in an hour and there's three of us here to close up."

"No, you go. I'll stay. You could use some rest."

She shakes her head, eyes determined. "I've got a woman coming in half an hour to talk to me about one of Lily's puppies. Mrs. Cohen won't go because she doesn't trust anybody to close up...even me!" More bubbling brook laughter. I start to speak, but she interrupts. "Don't say Marisol, because she has to wait for Hector to return. Now, go, go." She shoos me toward the door.

A fresh sea breeze blows away thoughts of retiring to my room. After a day in the gift shop, I crave the outdoors in a way I never have before. I walk past the fence where Lucy's budding horns got stuck a month ago and continue north for the first time. A shop ahead draws me in with a kaleidoscope of color. Silken banners of pink, turquoise, and lime green decorated with tropical fish, dolphins, and palm trees flutter from the eaves. Five happy manatee mailboxes guard the store like comical sentries. Who knows? Ideas for Rosa's gift shop might float about this happy little place.

Behind the front counter, a middle-aged woman smiles at me, but hooded eyes harbor a bitterness that contradicts the upturned lips. She sets down a box filled with shell necklaces and greets me.

"Hi. Welcome to the Treasure Trove. I'm Gail. Feel free to look around."

I nod and smile. Something about Gail both intrigues and unsettles me, causing me to stare just a moment longer than the standard "hello" glance.

"Can I help you find something in particular?"

Her troubled eyes do not see the vacancy signs on my pockets. "Just looking. Thanks."

A large copper crescent moon glimmering on a far wall draws me to the back of the store. The perfect excuse for preventing further conversation. Variants of color catch the sun's rays from the storefront window, glimmering the copper's browns, oranges, and golds. Smaller moons and a few stars occupy the wall space around it, allowing an admirer options for size and price. Rosa would love this, but she would want suns as well as moons. At the edge of my peripheral vision, Gail arranges the shell necklaces on a revolving column. She stops to look my way.

"All of our items are created by locals. Lots of talent here in the Keys."

Your picture is so beautiful, Carmie. You are truly a talented artist.

I know. I'm going to be a famous painter when I grow up. And you can have my paintings for free, because you're my friend.

"Yes, I agree." Blown glass egrets, watercolor seascapes, everything bursting with color and creativity. I can imagine the hand-painted tropical fish securing a spot on my basement wall, those lovely brass wind chimes dancing to their self-made music.

"You on vacation?" She folds her hands on the counter. The smile doesn't soften the hardness in those eyes.

Good question. What is this exactly? "Yeah, kinda."

"Where you stayin'?"

If I could think of one single hotel around here, I would blurt it out, but my mind is an empty screen. "Rosa's Haven."

Eyes narrow for half a second. Subtle, but enough for me to catch it.

"I see. One of Preacher's *guests.*"

Why the emphasis? "Yes."

"And I'll bet you're working in that gift shop and cleaning up smelly animal pens."

Red flags shoot up in my brain. "Actually, I offered. They've been great to me. I enjoy helping out."

Do I enjoy it? I definitely don't dislike it. The barn calms me, the work satisfies this driving desire to stay busy. As for the gift shop, the old me would have thrilled to work in such a delightful place, especially with a sweetheart like Mrs. Cohen. Still...enjoy. It's a strong word for someone away from her family, albeit a self-inflicted wound.

"Well, that's mighty nice for them. More free labor. Happens all the time over there. You never see anyone working *here* for free."

"It's more of a trade-off, really." I mentally smack myself for justifying my living arrangements with this woman.

"And I suppose they're plying you with all that God talk too? Hmph. Lottta good it's done the missus. All that faith and she still gets hit by a drunk. Now look at her. Pathetic. Stuck in a wheelchair the rest of her life."

I could write a book exalting Rosa. "Pathetic" wouldn't be on a single page. I tighten my lips. "She's actually doing very well. Her legs are getting stronger. She can stand now. Yesterday she took a step."

Why am I talking to this total stranger more than I've talked to Rosa and Preacher?

"Taking a step after two years ain't exactly what I'd call progress. No, she'll never be the same."

"I don't know about the same, but Rosa is the least pathetic person I know. She contributes more to this world from her wheelchair than anyone I know with functioning legs." I turn and head toward the door.

"Well, you can believe what you want, honey." Gail needs to let me know she's standing her ground. "Seems to me God don't do much for his fan club. I'm just sayin'. Lookit that guy out there." She points across the street to a man sitting on the sidewalk. Next to him, a small cardboard box reads "Please give." He holds a crumpled blanket on his lap, stares vacantly down the street. "Homeless Joe. Been there a few weeks now. Says stuff to the people passing by. Stuff like, 'have a blessed day,' or, 'God bless you.' Don't do him no good, neither."

Just being near her makes me want to shower off the ugliness she exudes. "You ever give him any food?"

"What?" she snorts. "And have him keep coming around for handouts? No, thank you."

"You ever talk to him?"

She looks at me like I just suggested she swim in boiling oil. "Why on earth would I do that?"

Oh, I don't know. Because he's a human being. Because he needs help. Because we should take care of each other, like Rosa inviting Hector's family to Thanksgiving. Aunt Theresa filling in for an absentee Mom. Preacher taking Connor and Melissa into his home. And me.

Beach Man pouring healing water over a stranger's feet.

People need to love one another, take care of each other. It's very important, Josie. It could change the world.

"Right. Well, don't worry about him marring your view any longer. I'll tell Rosa and Preacher about him. He'll have a meal and pillow for his head by the time you close up. That's what God does for his fan club."

"Yeah, and they'll have more slave labor too."

So not worth a response. I close the door, longing to slam it and shatter all her pretty things. Lucky for her, I wouldn't do that to the artists.

Out on the sidewalk I gaze at the homeless man across the street. Head down, eyes closed. Must be sleeping. Before I can turn away, his head jerks up. Weary eyes lock onto mine.

"Jesus loves you," he says.

I walk across the street, certain I'm about to disappoint him. It feels rude to stand over him. I scoot down, offer up a smile.

"Hi. I'm Josie." I extend my hand.

He stares at it. Have I crossed an invisible line? Is this inappropriate? Unwanted? He eases his hand off his cardboard "homeless" sign.

"Luke." Gritty fingers clasp my outstretched hand. A smile spreads across his face, blossoming into a yellow-toothed grin.

"Pleasure to meet you, Luke. I have nothing to offer you, though. I'm sorry."

"Got me a smile and a handshake. Haven't had neither since don't know when. Jesus loves you, Josie." He holds tight to my hand.

"I think you're right."

"Sure of it."

Please, Lord. Help this man.

The voice fills my head like a soft tropical breeze. Silent, gentle, firm. *I Am.*

Preacher supports Rosa's arm as she slides into the pickup and sets a bulging paper lunch bag on her lap "just in case he won't come with us." They head north, having already contacted a friend who runs a homeless shelter in Islamorada.

"I do not know how long this will take," Preacher says. "We will see what happens. You are sure you do not mind holding down the fort?"

"I got it, Preacher. We'll all be fine."

Rosa rolls down her window. "Be careful of those ostriches, Josie dear. Don't get too close."

"I won't."

"They're unpredictable, you know."

No more so than everything else in life. And maybe that's a good thing.

Chapter 21

Josie

Rosa informs me it is Christmas decorating day. We will have an early dinner of Thanksgiving leftovers before Mike and his girlfriend join us for tree trimming and decoration day dessert—Preacher's famous tres leche cake. He is already working in the kitchen as Rosa assigns tasks to me, Melissa, and Connor. The sweet cakey scent adds to the festive atmosphere, but outside, palm trees rustle and wind gusts rattle the windows. The coming storm sends chills up my spine, despite the warmth of a cozy living room.

The three of us haul cardboard boxes and plastic containers out of closets and storage areas, each with its contents neatly labeled. Rosa leads the way to the barn where we'll string lighted garland around pens and stalls.

"Nothing too low," she reminds us yet again. "You know that Lucy and her mama goat, they eat anything. And it has to be high enough so Diego and the ostriches can't get to it. Ah, those ostriches, they give me the willies. Thank goodness those people from the wild bird sanctuary are coming for them next month."

Between Connor's lack of height and Melissa's condition, the ladder work falls to me. No problem, though. With Rob's crazy schedule, I was usually the one who did the Christmas lights, anyway. Now that he's home more, he can do the lights this year while I decorate inside. My hand freezes in mid reach, leaving a strand of lights dangling as I replay that thought—the first I've had of me at home. Me wrapping the banister in garland, with Ashley attaching the bows and Mitch gathering his Star Wars ornaments for our tree trimming night. I devour the sweet image like warm Christmas cookies—the kind you just can't stop eating.

Two hours later, the barn glimmers with twinkling garland and a half-dozen straw wreaths, complete with red velvet bows. The fruit of our labor is beautiful to behold.

"This is so awesome, Rosa!" Melissa stands in front of the barn door, taking in the festive scene before us. "You should keep it like this all year."

"But then it wouldn't be so awesome," Rosa says. Her Melissa impersonation elicits giggles from each of us, especially Melissa.

We return the empty boxes to the storage room and spend the next hour feeding our furry and feathered friends. The burnt-tailed cat shadows my rounds. No one knows what happened to her. She was about four months old when she showed up, weak and ragged, infected and feverish. She leaps from hay to railings to floor, occasionally rubbing against my legs lest I forget she's there. Whatever tragedy befell her, it is long forgotten. At least, on the outside.

Am I healing in the same way?

Dusk blankets the island by the time we emerge from the barn. Only a few pale sun rays shoot up from the horizon, soon to be swallowed entirely by the sea. Sweet-scented warmth engulfs us as we reach the porch. Preacher's cake must be cooling on the counter by now, soaking up the combination of milks that give it its name. Maybe someday I'll try making it for Rob and the kids.

My appetite is returning. I don't get chocolate cravings or salivate over a cheesy sausage pizza, but I eat. And sometimes…I even enjoy it. Rosa warms up the turkey and gravy, tamales, and green bean casserole. When we are nearly done cleaning the kitchen, Mike and his girlfriend, Kasie, come over with a poinsettia plant nearly the size of Rhode Island.

"I figured it would help create the proper decorating ambiance." He turns to Preacher. "That's am-bi-ance, it means…"

"I know what it means, you loco vet. I'm just surprised you do."

Mike wraps an arm around Kasie's shoulder, pretends to whisper in her ear, though it is loud enough for all to hear. "That's just his way of saying he's happy to see me."

Kasie laughs. Not a giggle or a titter, a hearty laugh. She looks at Mike the way Rob looked at me when we were dating. The way Rob looked at me before the end of the world. I want to see that look again. Feel those arms around me. His lips on mine.

Preacher hangs up their windbreakers and invites them into the kitchen for cake.

"It's not that tres leche again, is it?" Mike winks at Kasie. "I mean, come on, we just had it last year."

"Oh, now, Michael," Rosa playfully smacks his arm. "It is your favorite, and you know it." She turns her attention to Kasie. "He asks for it almost every week."

"Such exaggeration. Only every other week. And now that what's-his-name is out of earshot, I can tell you this cake is amazing. Nobody makes it as good as Preacher."

"Preacher!" Melissa yells toward the kitchen. "Mike said you make the best—"

Mike cups his hand over Melissa's mouth. Melissa wriggles loose, breaks into a fit of laughter.

"Ewww, she licked me! Now I have gross traitor germs."

"You deserved it." Kasie smiles as she rebukes him.

The cake is unlike anything I've ever tasted. Creamy, sweet, and moist. Lathered in fresh whipped cream. If Mitch were here, he'd already be asking for seconds. That boy sure does love his sweets. My Mitchie. When that boy smiles, my heart turns to warm butterscotch pudding. That's what I want, more than a thousand tres leche cakes.

Rosa fills us in on the decorating plan as we enjoy our cake. Mike cuts a hearty second piece for himself, "just to be polite." Once the dishes are washed, we parade into the living room behind Rosa's wheelchair, waiting for the project manager to dole out assignments.

"Now, hold on a minute." Rosa's eyes sweep the room. "There is only one box of ornaments here. Where is the other? It is a red box. No, the red box broke last year when Connor tried to hide inside it."

Connor plays his part, looking at the ground, failing miserably at concealing a smile. "Sorry."

She places her hands on her hips, scrunches up her face, and glares at him. The result of those sweet brown eyes trying to look mean sets everyone laughing, including Rosa. "Maybe this year when we pack up, you'll accidentally get sealed in a box and stuffed in a closet." She ruffles his hair. "Let's see. I remember putting them in a plain brown box. I bet that is why they got left behind."

We search through the assortment of boxes that were emptied throughout the day. None are the missing ornaments box.

"All right, let's do this. Mike, you put that star on top. It is time for you to earn those two pieces of cake. Melissa and Connor can start on the garland. Manuel, would you please set up the little tree on the front porch?"

"Yes, mi vida." Preacher salutes her before grabbing his jacket and the tree box, then heads out to tackle his task.

Rosa turns to me. "As for you, Josie, would you be so kind as to get the other box of ornaments? It is not heavy. I'm quite sure it is still in Manny's office closet."

The abalone clock ticks away the seconds as I intrude on the silence of Preacher's office. I take a closer look at some of the photos I only glanced at last time. An eight by ten shows Preacher and Rosa standing under a canopy of flowers, him in a suit, her in a flowing ivory dress. White flowers form the number twenty-five atop the canopy. But it's not the pictures that draw me closer. It is the gaps I noticed last time. Wide spaces randomly appear between the photos. A thin layer of dust coats the shelves, but where there are gaps, the shelves are clear. Things have been removed. Recently. Like one of my favorite crime show detectives, I examine the dust patterns. At least seven photos are missing. I shake off a chill that comes from nowhere and head toward the closet.

Three boxes in various sizes are stacked on the floor. Might as well start at the top and work my way down. Good, no tape or strings. I pry apart the cardboard flaps, flipping them open to reveal the box's contents.

Inside is a drawing. Bright colors. Happy faces. A dark-haired girl holds hands with a man and woman. A blue donkey stands next to them. My heart careens toward arrest. Can't breathe. My hand has held that little artist's hand, combed her hair, tied her shoes. Numb fingers pluck the crayoned artwork from its resting place, revealing the photo beneath.

Her face stares up at me, smiling brightly. A glistening pink barrette holds back one side of her hair. My mouth opens, but no air comes in or out...until I scream.

And scream.

And scream.

I close my eyes to visions of fog, blood, flashing lights. A little coffin being lowered into the ground. Ana collapsing. Weeping. My arms wrap around Carmelita's framed face as I rock back and forth.

The door flies open, banging the wall behind it. Preacher bounds in, eyes wide, pained. I stare, frozen by his betrayal. Dark swirls of confusion envelop my head.

"Who are you?" I shriek the words through my sobs.

"Josie. I can explain."

"The devil lies, Preacher? Isn't that what you said? Are you the devil, then, with your pretense of kindness? Pretending not to know who I am, what I did?" Poison darts shoot from my mouth.

"No, please listen. I could not tell you. I feared you would run."

"Who is she to you? Tell me!"

"Carmelita was my niece. Ana is my sister. I wanted to tell you, I did truly. Please, let us talk. I can help you."

The words pound my skull. Preacher's niece? Carmelita? I grip my temples. No! He's lying. Lying. But my heart knows differently.

"Please, Josie. I beg you. Forgive me. Listen to what I have to say."

I place the picture back in the box. Cover my face with my hands. If it's true, Rosa knows, too. Everyone knows I'm the one. I did it. Ana and Rob must have known I was here even before cousin Tina came to see me.

"Josie, talk to me. Let me help you."

Hands fly away from my tear-streaked face. "Help me? How? Can you bring her back? I don't need any more of your help!" This is a nightmare. Everything I thought was real, true, all a charade. Why? My teeth clench. "Does Rob know who you are?"

"Sí. Rob came to bring you back. I convinced him to let you stay. Let you heal. It was not easy. You returned as he was leaving."

The man in the rental car. That day my heart had tried to whisper the truth. Rob came for me.

Preacher's eyes implore me to talk to him. Why is he still trying to pastor me?

"You sent my husband away?"

"You could barely speak. Wouldn't eat. God led you here for a reason. I wanted you to give Him a chance. He is the Great Healer, Josie. Only He could repair your shattered heart."

"Why do you care? Don't you get it? I killed *your* niece!"

He winces as the words smack his heart. "I know this." His words come softer. "Just as I know it was an accident. You loved her. You cannot let it kill both of you."

I was starting to think it wouldn't. A sliver of hope had appeared on my horizon. I'd been crawling toward it, slow and steady. Out of the murky depths down a lighted path that would lead me home. Now this. My grip slips, feet dangle over the familiar black pit. It calls to me in a velvet voice.

This is where you belong, Josie Caruso. Come. Accept your penance.

I look at her angelic face again. Touch the cheek. "Oh, Carmie. I'm so sorry."

"You are not the only one blaming yourself for this, Josie. Ana and Emilio—"

"No!" I scream it. "I don't want to hear anything you have to say! Leave me alone!" I rush past him, out the door, into the night. Preacher's voice carries down the beach as he calls my name. It only serves to push me harder, faster, into the darkness. I shout at the sea. It pounds an answer. Meaningless! It is all meaningless! With Preacher's voice ringing in my ears—more lies?—I sprint down the beach. Running. Running. I am so tired of running. And where, now, can I go?

Chapter 22

Josie

Cool water shivers my spine as it climbs toward my hips. Soon it will rise above my waist, signifying the drop-off—the Continental Shelf—the reason Preacher warns us to swim with a buddy. Ahead lies nothing but pure midnight and a sprinkling of stars. A broken shell pierces my next footstep and I freeze, awaiting the momentary pain. No matter. The shard will not cause agony that wraps around your soul, strangling, suffocating, diminishing the last rays of hope.

Hold on, hold on, the night breeze whispers, as the black water slaps against my knees.

Hazy memories of that other life's music swirl around me for a precious moment, then disappear, the notes forever silenced when the most evil of beings set everything in motion. With keen intelligence he schemed, flawlessly executing his diabolical strategy with one single-minded goal: my complete and total demise. On his command, the impenetrable darkness crept up from the depths of hell, obscuring the light and convincing me I'd never see it again.

The water rises to my thighs.

I know this much to be true: these cards were dealt me by the devil's own hand. My question: where was God's?

The pain from the broken shell subsides as I ease past the first set of white buoys, bobbing their silent warning. "Danger! Danger! Turn back!" Another step brings me closer to the shelf—a three-hundred foot plunge that could swallow me with one mighty gulp. But I won't take that plunge. No. I just want to stand there. On the edge. Feeling the saltwater wind on my face, the water flowing around me. Alone, where no voices can muddle my thoughts. Maybe out there, hidden by night, I will be able to think. Make sense out of senseless things, like a child dying at the age of five, or her killer being nurtured by the very people who are grieving.

What if Preacher was right? That there is hope, if I choose it. I could return to my family. Wrap my arms around my children. Feel Rob's warmth beside me in bed. Ana and I could sit on her porch, crying together over Carmie, and I would tell her I'm sorry. So sorry. Even if she never wanted to see me again, she would know our friendship had been one of the best things in my life. That I loved her daughter.

What if the feeling on the beach this morning, that oneness with God, could happen again? And again?

A soft light illuminates the black water to my right, then my left. It dances from side to side like a living thing. It is not lightning. There are no boats in view. I should look behind me, but fear of something otherworldly prevents me from moving.

"Josie, stop! Come back!"

I squeeze my eyes closed, try to shut out the sound of Preacher's voice. Can't I just be alone? Me and the ocean and my thoughts. He is ruining my plan. I turn to face him, momentarily blinded by his flashlight.

Breathy words come fast and labored. He must have run to the beach and through the shallows. "Please, Josie. I am begging you. Just talk to me."

"Go back, Preacher. Leave me alone." Something scaly brushes my leg. I jump, then continue on, muck and seaweed oozing between my toes. A siren sounds in the distance. It pierces my brain, releasing a toxic flow of memories. The beginning of the end.

No!

I am always with you.

I tread forward into the sea of darkness, Preacher's light continuing to set one small area aglow. The second set of buoys is just a short distance away, but the deeper I get, the slower I go. Black water creeps above my waist.

"This is dangerous!" He shouts. "A storm is coming. Currents can . change. Turn around!"

I twist toward him so my voice will carry. "I need some time alone. I'm a good swimmer. Go back."

"Everyone knows it was an accident." It is getting harder to catch his words over the increasing wind. "No one blames you. Not even Ana."

He'll say anything to make me stop. It's his job. He's good at it, though, I'll give him that. Other than that whole deception thing. Raucous splashing replaces Preacher's words. He is swimming, and darn fast by the sound of it. Hair whips into my face, sideways, forward. Nature moves like a bullet train around here.

I duck under the rope connecting the second set of buoys. Five more steps bring my feet to the edge of the underwater cliff. Heels rest on the ocean floor. My toes, however, dangle over nothing but water. Darkness below, darkness above. The stars that twinkled just moments ago have been extinguished by a cosmic candle snuffer. The moon, a pale orb veiled behind menacing storm clouds, faintly glows as a gust of wind sends chills racing up my wet arms.

Ana doesn't blame me? How I would love to believe that. Was leaving the wrong choice, even though it seemed right at the time? Is it really possible to move past that and become me again? Rosa didn't let her tragedy destroy her. That woman's faith is rock solid, even as she goes through life in that wheelchair.

But she didn't kill a child.

What now? Where do I go from here?

Another gust creates whitecaps that smack my chest while an invisible current tries to yank me back. The splashing behind me grows louder as Preacher nears. It must be tough going with that wind kicking up. There is no longer a hint of the moon's existence. Its light has been blanketed by the clouds. But it is there. Hidden, but there.

Preacher and Rosa believe God's power is mightier than my despair. If that's true, then there's hope. A shot at life. Not the same life, maybe, and definitely not a life without grief, but still…

"Josie, I am begging you to come back!"

Stubborn man. His breathless words struggle to overcome the increasing wind, even at this close distance. I watch him dive back in, disappearing beneath the black sea before emerging just a few feet away. The current now pummels my legs. He shouldn't be here. This is getting dangerous.

"Go back!" I shout. "I'm coming. I promise." Anything to get him to safety.

"I'll wait." He inches toward me, barely visible.

I stand facing him, my toes bouncing against the ocean floor as the water bobs me like a beach toy. "How did you know?"

"Connor. You broke the no-swimming-at-night-rule. He could not tell me fast enough."

Preacher moves closer, placing an arm around my shoulder. "Now please come back and we will talk. The ocean, she is getting angry. Carmelita is gone, Josie. That cannot change, but you can. You can heal."

"I know." I stare out at the darkness. "I know."

"The Lord did not create you only to destroy you. That wouldn't make sense. Think about it. Give him your pain. He will give you the strength you need."

I am so very tired of carrying this burden. So tired of the emptiness that was there even before the accident. I just didn't want to admit it, and had no idea how to fill it. But that was then.

Hot tears mingle with saltwater spray. Whitecaps smack the water around us. My arms wrap around his neck as torrents of despair and hopelessness flow out into the Atlantic. Instead of leaving a void, they are replaced with something else. Something light and warm. Peaceful and clarifying. And in the blackness of that wind-tossed sea, hope floods me like a lighthouse beam. I step back so I am face to face with Preacher. "Let's go back."

A sudden swell throws us off balance. I am grabbed by the muscular jaws of storm-surged water. Like prey in a gator's death grip, I sink and spin, tumbling over the shelf. Relentless currents pummel me into the side of the underwater cliff. My shoulder. My hip.

My head.

Lightning cracks inside my brain. Eyes open to a salty sting and pure blackness. My feet and arms work together like gas-powered pistons, but there is no point of reference. Disoriented, head throbbing, I kick frantically. Am I moving up? Down? A silent scream shudders my soul. I thrash…for my very life.

Cooler water signals a thermo cline. Down, then. I am going down. I shudder, my skin prickling like that night in the fog, a lifetime ago. Before that little goat led me to Preacher and Rosa. Before Connor's prayer in the barn. And out of the depths comes the miraculous heartbeat of Melissa's unborn child. A symphony of life, an answered prayer. Scenes flutter through my mind as my life unfolds. I feel Connor's arms around my waist after we escaped from crazy Gus. The healthy whinny of a scrawny horse echoes in my head. The whinny becomes the miraculous cries of my children as they entered this world, healthy and hungry, needing me, loving me. And my Rob. For better or for worse. The essence of his messages: he had meant it. *We can do this, Jo. Our love will see us through. Come back to me.*

There in the water's depths I clearly see what had been obscured by my own self-made veil. God's hand guiding me to Rosa's Haven, His ear hearing my cries, His heart holding mine. Patiently waiting, showing me His fingerprints in everything. He was there all the time, trying to pull me up while I refused. Shut Him out. Preacher was right, but I figured it out too late.

You are my child. I will never abandon you.

My hands push at the water, propelling me upward…or so I pray. What was I thinking? How did I get here? I can't hold my breath any longer. I need air.

I stop kicking, letting the salty Atlantic buoy me. Air. Desperate for air. I kick with my last ounce of strength, but make no progress. Has the water turned to quicksand? I want air. Oh God, please! My body jerks. Lungs burn, ready to burst.

Air, air air!

Tiny particles surround me, visible now by a light from above. That crazy man, he's still trying to save me. But it's too late. Way too much water fills the distance between my lungs and the oxygen they crave.

Help Preacher, Lord. And please...watch over my family. Give my children a new mom who will tenderly hold their hearts. Someone who loves You the way I love You now.

Through half-closed eyes I see the tiny ocean particles moving crazily in the turbulence from Preacher's kicks. He grabs my T-shirt, yanks me upward. I should help him. I try to kick, but my feet do not obey. Fog fills my head. Just before I disappear into the darkness, Carmie smiles at me, her sweet face radiant with joy.

And I don't need air anymore.

Chapter 23

Josie

Something beeps. Muted voices surround me. A strong hand holds mine. It is enough for now. Sounds and feelings drift in and out, as hazy fragments of memories swirl through my head. Toddler Mitch giggling in his dinosaur pool, little Ashley's sugarplum kisses on my cheek. Suddenly they've grown, faces illuminated by fireworks on the fourth of July. Fireworks become the light in Rob's eyes as he kisses me at the county fair, slips a gold band on my finger. A forever love.

In between fragments, I float. Is this heaven, then? I don't know, but it is a good place to stay. A place where nothing matters and all is well.

Darkness, light, shades of blue and gray. The blue becomes water washing up on a sandy shore. Sunlight shoves away the darkness and sparkles on aquamarine waves. I walk, but not alone. My companion puts his strong warm arm around my shoulder. I have felt the weight of that arm before, know what I will see when I turn to face him. Dark wavy hair, kind eyes, a tender smile. A face I long to touch. My strange Beach Man.

I breathe in the pure, primal scent of the earth, turn my face skyward, and feel warm rays kissing my face. "Is this heaven?"

His smile joyfully fills all my senses. "No, but you'll get there."

"Are you sure this is the right way?"

He laughs and hugs me. "Yes."

Warmth floods me. I am weightless. Don't ever let go. "How do you know?"

We resume walking along the water's edge. He gives my shoulder a gentle squeeze. "Trust me."

I do. No need for words. I know he knows. "You're kind of a mysterious guy."

"Yes."

"And full of surprises."

"That, too."

An eagle-sized bird swoops over us, wings whiter than falling snow. Emerald eyes. Beach Man extends his arm. The bird lights, its golden talons wrapping around its Master's wrist, golden beak shimmering in the sun. That beautiful white head cocks as it looks at me, letting me know I have nothing to fear. My fingers reach out to stroke brilliant feathers. Beach Man and I watch as the bird launches itself skyward, snowy wings majestically outstretched. It disappears around the bend of the shore.

I feel my smile nearly splitting my face. "I always wanted to do that. Pet a wild bird. Ever since I was little."

"Yes. That family vacation on Marco Island." He laughs. "The snowy egret strutting on the beach, always just out of reach."

I don't even question Him knowing. It seems so right. "You really care about me."

"So much, Josephine. So very much."

"I drowned, you know."

"Almost." He shakes his head. "Standing on the edge of the continental shelf in a storm was a bad choice. You can do better."

I laugh. "Yes. Let's hope so. But it wasn't almost. I really did drown."

"No. It's not your time yet. That's why Preacher was able to reach you. That's why I calmed those big waves while he was resuscitating you."

"Calmed the waves?"

He ignores the question. "And…that is why the paramedics got there so fast. God isn't done with you, Josie. Wait till you see what He has in store."

The statement does not frighten me. "Why am I here?"

"Your body needs rest. It needed to shut down, heal for a couple of days. Your doctor made the right decision by putting you in a coma. It won't be much longer now."

"So I'm alive?"

"Yes, Josephine." Eyes intensify, looking into mine. Into my soul. "You are truly alive."

I actually get that. But joyful as I am, there's something I have to know. "What about Carmelita?"

He smiles. "So happy. You can't imagine. Your heart breaks from the loss, and also for her family. But all will heal, Josephine. Look for the good that comes from the bad. There you will see God."

We stop. He slides his arm off my shoulder, takes my hand in his. We face each other and I see he is wearing a different T-shirt today. Whiter than the bird's feathers, imprinted with a golden Bible verse. Mark 5:34.

"What's that verse?"

"You know how to find it. Now close your eyes."

"Why?"

That beautiful smile again. "Trust me."

I do. The beach disappears. He gently squeezes my hand. Warm, wet drops trickle down my arm. Rain? But it was so sunny. The drops are quickly brushed away by soft fingertips.

"Please wake up, Mom."

Sniffled words strengthen my heartbeat.

"Mommy needs to sleep, honey." That voice. Deep. Familiar. A voice that has said, "I love you, Jo," more times than I can count.

Tender fingers wrap around my arm as sniffles become full-fledged sobs. "No, I want her back. Please, Mom, please wake up and come back to us."

Tears soak my arm. Fingers grasp tighter.

"It's okay, Ashley. She'll be okay, right, Dad?" The boy's voice cracks, betraying the confidence he tries to portray.

Mitch. Ashley. Rob.

Ashley's hand slides toward mine, gently squeezing. I squeeze back. "Dad!"

"What is it, Ash? What?"

She squeezes again, harder this time. I squeeze back.

It is time to leave the in-between place for good. I open my eyes to the most beautiful, amazing sight on earth, with one thought shouting joyfully in my head.

I am truly alive.

Chapter 24

Preacher

My wife's hot coffee warms my throat, glides through tired veins, and diminishes the morning cloudiness in this drowsy old head.

We are the only two awake in a house overflowing with people. Josie and her family fill the guesthouse, while Melissa and Connor take up their usual spots in the smaller bedrooms. Not for long, though. Melissa's father should be here by mid-afternoon; the Carusos will say their goodbyes day after tomorrow. Only this time, there will be no need to put up the sign. Our next guest is ready and waiting.

Oh Lord, if I can just get in a day of fishing, I would be so grateful. Just one day before facing what will surely be a monumental challenge, but one I happily embrace.

"What are you thinking, Manuel? You disappeared on me." Rosa stands at the counter. Stands. It will only be a minute or two, but that is a minute or two those doctors said would never happen. And she will do it throughout the day, every couple of hours, even though it hurts. She doesn't say, but I see it in those beautiful brown eyes.

"I am thinking, mi vida, that helping Melissa and Josie may seem like a walk in the park compared with our next task."

She nods. "Sí. But a worthy one, no?"

"As always." The toast pops and I plate a piece for each of us. "Do you know what I want, Señora Delgado?"

"A day of fishing."

"Of course. But something else even more."

"Even more?" She playfully slaps my hand. "Manuel! We have a house full of guests!"

I muffle my laugh so as not to wake the children, then kiss the hand that slapped mine. "Sí, I do want that even more, but I was talking about a road trip. We could visit Dulce and Alex. Perhaps spend a few days at that lodge on Table Rock Lake. The one Alex went to, remember? In the Ozarks? Me and you. All alone. We could even take a riverboat ride. What do you say?"

A dreamy look twinkles Rosa's eyes. "I say it sounds like a wonderful fantasy." She finishes buttering her toast, then starts on mine. I get the jams gifted to us from our friend Nancie. Damson plum for her, peach for me. How I love the comfort of our morning dance, but a little change might be nice as well.

"Don't I tell our congregation that husbands and wives need to make time for each other? We have not had a vacation in three years. Much as I love our mission trips, they are not vacations."

"Has it been that long?" I see her thoughts winding back to our week in Colorado, the cabin in Estes Park. "Oh, those mountains were so beautiful, so majestic. That was lovely, wasn't it, Manny? That night the band played outside, and we danced beneath the stars?"

"Wonderful, mi vida. Absolutely wonderful."

"We need to turn that fantasy into reality. I don't know how, but I do believe in miracles."

All heads turn in my direction as I walk through the barn doors and adjust my eyes to the dimness within. Diego stands erect as a bowling pin, buckteeth ready to start munching. The donkeys extend their heads past their enclosure, anxious for the same. Lucy bleats to make sure I don't forget her and mama goat, while Charro rubs against my legs. After all these years, the sight of my menagerie still makes me smile.

"Sí, animales, it is time for breakfast. Your young Melissa is sleeping in this morning, but she will visit you later to say goodbye." My own words catch in my throat. She is not my daughter, I must remember that. Her parents and I have had many conversations these past three months. Good people aching for their prodigal daughter to return. She made the decision I prayed she would make. That alone should fill my heart with glorious music. And yet...

I scoop oats into feed buckets for Lightning, Diego, and the donkeys, then toss them each a bale of hay. With a nod and a whinny, Lightning assures me he has crossed the threshold. Still too skinny, he stands sturdy, eating like a champ, mane and tail brushed clean, eyes bright. Soon he will be running through green pastures in a place very different than this one—a place where he can eat sweet apples right off the trees.

Over at the rabbit hutch, Sunny stands out among the rest, floppy ears framing her face in a way that endears her to Josie.

"And yet another goodbye is in order, no?" Sunny patiently allows me to stroke her soft fur, knowing that food will follow. She will be in good hands. I pray she and her large new friend get along well.

I close the heavy wooden doors to the sound of happy munching and immerse myself in island dawn. The eastern sky, she is streaked in shades of purple, like those tie-dyed T-shirts our Dulce used to make years ago. Soon the sun will slowly rise from the sea, but for now, the first glimmer of rays shimmers the horizon's edge. Gulls soar over the water, searching below the surface for a reason to dive. Large white egrets stand majestically in the shallows. The world is at peace. Morning's silence lacks the drama that will surely come as the sky brightens and the world wakes. I breathe in the absolute beauty of daybreak, its earthy scent fills my senses, drops me to my knees. Heaven, it would seem, must be very much like this.

Thank you, Father, Creator of the universe, for blessing me with this moment.

It is all I can say. I raise my hands skyward and soak in the love and mercy He rains down on me.

Mike's pickup is keeping company with mine. It is a common sight, but not so early on a Friday morning. The animal hospital will open in an hour, so what is this?

Our animals are healthy and Lily's pups are doing well. Perhaps he found a little beast in need of some TLC or a friend for our lonely llama.

Or something is wrong.

Mike pours coffee at the counter while Rosa transfers cinnamon rolls from a sealed container to a fancy plate. He wouldn't care if she tossed them onto a napkin, but that is my Rosa. Company is company.

"Sleeping in today, old man?"

Sleeping in? I have forgotten the meaning of the phrase. I grab an empty cup and he fills it for me.

"You are quite the comedian, Michael. I have already put in a full day's work and still have a full day to go. And you? It is nearly seven-thirty. What have you accomplished?"

"I'm showered and dressed."

Rosa wheels over to the table, the plate of rolls resting on her lap. "Here, you must try one of these. Cinnamon, butter, and ground almonds. Tell me what you think."

Mike takes a large bite, chewing slowly while Rosa waits for the verdict. "They're horrible." He reaches over and takes two more. "I'm just going to eat these so others don't have to suffer."

Laughter bubbles from Rosa, crinkles deepening at the corners of her beautiful eyes. "Oh, you. What am I going to do with you?"

"I don't know. Keep feeding me, and I'll follow you anywhere."

"Hey, hey. Get your own esposa. This one is all mine. And by the way, I hear you and a certain pretty nurse from your clinic were at Sandspur Beach, oiling each other up like buttered corn."

For once, mi amigo is silent. Smiling, but silent.

Rosa pats his hand. "You know, Michael, this is the first time we've seen you in love."

"Love, huh? You think so?" He shakes his head. "Nah, can't be. This would be a bad time to fall in love."

"Don't be silly," Rosa says. "What would make it bad? Kasie is a lovely girl. Just perfect for you."

His smile fades. His pause tells me there will be no quick-witted comeback. Whatever comes next will explain the early morning visit. My fingers tighten around my mug.

"I'm going to India for six months."

Rosa gasps. My coffee goes down the wrong way. Hot liquid burns my throat. Mike pats me on the back, which does nothing to help, but I appreciate the gesture.

"Relax." He says. "It's not forever."

Rosa nods. "I told you the Spirit was speaking to you about something."

"I just can't get it out of my head. Somebody has to do something about India."

While the statement speaks volumes, it echoes with a childlike simplicity that brings a smile to my face. Is he planning to fix India by himself? "And Africa, and Haiti, and so many other places."

He dunks a roll, up, down, three times. Always three.

"I know, I know. But India is the one I visited. Those faces keep haunting me."

My wife lays her hand on his arm. "That is exactly why Mother Theresa dedicated her life's work there. So tell us, what is your plan?"

Six months without my friend and my vet. "Yes, tell us. What about your practice, your patients?"

"It took some work, but everything fell into place. I met this Minnesota vet at that conference in Miami. Loves the Keys. Great guy. Good reputation. And get this, he works on farm animals, so he can take care of your little zoo here…at least most of it. I called yesterday morning. Told him to think about it. He said 'Mike, it's twenty degrees and snowing here. I'll be there by dinner!' Crazy guy. I told him that wasn't necessary. March first is the big day. Everything's all worked out."

He's only been on one mission trip. He has no idea what he is up against out there. "Are you aware of the danger? There are people who are against this movement. People who strongly believe the Dalits and the whole caste system should be left as is. They prevent Dalit children from learning English so they cannot progress, get a job."

"I know," he sighs. "It's a hopeless life. That's why I'm going."

"You may find yourself living in conditions you cannot tolerate."

Mike's blue eyes darken. He wraps both hands around his mug. "If a man hasn't discovered something that he will die for, he isn't fit to live."

"Martin Luther King?"

"Elvis."

He got me that time. "Ah, not bad, but I have a better one."

"Naturally." He wipes cinnamon glaze from his lips.

"If you spend yourselves in behalf of the hungry and satisfy the needs of the oppressed, then your light will rise in the darkness, and your night will become like the noonday sun."

"I'm guessing that wasn't Elvis."

"Isaiah. He was quite adamant about Christians helping those in need."

Rosa takes the empty cinnamon roll plate and fills it with fresh green grapes. She is convinced our friend's eating habits are going to earn him a heart attack, despite his healthy appearance. "Can you afford this?"

"Not really, but yeah. The guy who's taking my place will rent my house to cover part of the mortgage. I'll fill in the rest with my Africa fund."

I set down my cup. "The photo safari? You have been saving for years!"

"Yeah, well, Africa's not going anywhere."

Rosa's eyes pool with tears. "Oh, Michael. I'm so very proud of you." She squeezes his arm. "We will miss you."

He waits for me to say I will not miss him, good riddance, more food for me, et cetera. It's what we do, Michael and I. But the words, they will not come.

An overstuffed backpack leans against a suitcase by the front door. Two boxes, securely taped by my wife, are stacked next to them. Melissa is leaving with far more than she arrived with that day when her tire exploded. In a few hours, she will see just how much.

Rosa has been buzzing around her all morning with, "do you have this?" and, "don't forget that." It is a good thing Josie's family is still here for a couple of days. She will need the distraction.

Heavy tires on gravel tell me the time has come. Melissa and Rosa emerge from the barn as I step out of the house. I cannot see her expression, but know her eyes are wide, her mouth is open. She expected her father, but certainly not the horse trailer. He steps down from the truck, looking just the way he did three months ago when I talked him out of dragging her back home. Melissa runs into his open arms, sobbing like a baby and holding on tight. Not that her father has any intention of letting go. My throat tightens. I head for Rosa with long, fast strides, leaving father and daughter to have their moment.

My wife is losing the battle to swipe tears from her cheeks. I bend so we are face-to-face, but those deep brown eyes will not look into mine.

"This is the right thing, mi vida. There is no doubt."

"Preacher! Rosa! Come here and meet my dad. Oh, that's right, you already did. Well, come here, anyway." Melissa is a bouncing bundle of smiles and tears.

Her father gently places his hand on her belly and looks into her eyes. "How's my granddaughter doing?"

"Perfect, Dad. The doctor says just perfect. And I've been doing everything they say. Going to all my appointments, eating healthy. Even taking those monster-size vitamins."

"That's my girl." Another quick hug. No doubt there will be many more as they travel from here to northern Michigan. I extend my hand, and he clasps it with a firm, friendly handshake.

"Preacher, how in the world will I ever thank you and your wife for taking care of my baby girl?"

Melissa's cheeks go pink. "Dad!"

"What! You're still my baby. I don't care how old you get."

"Señor, it has been our pleasure. We will miss her very much. She is in our hearts forever."

Melissa steps away from her father to wrap her arms around my neck. Her tears moisten my shirt. "I don't know what I would have done without you."

"Ah, you would have found your way," I say, believing it is true, but thankful to have been part of the plan.

A bright smile breaks through her tears. "And now I want to know what's with the trailer. Did you bring Preacher one of our horses?"

"Not quite." He looks at me. "Go ahead, Preacher. You tell her."

"Your father had to bring the trailer. We couldn't let Lightning walk all the way to Michigan. He's not that strong yet."

Melissa's hand flies to her mouth. Eyes shimmer. "What? Are you kidding me?" She turns to Rosa. "Is he saying what I think?" Back to me. "You're giving me Lightning?"

"What am I going to do with a skinny horse when I've got all these other animals to care for? Your father kindly agreed to take him off my hands."

"Oh, my gosh! I can't believe it! This is awesome." Another hug, this one so tight I fear she will choke the breath out of me. I do not know if she can handle any more emotion, but more is coming.

"Is it time?" Her father must have read my mind. I nod, and Bob pulls a black cell out of his pocket and sends a one-word text. The back of the trailer opens.

And there stands David.

Melissa pales. She grabs her father's arm with both hands, hanging on as though he is the last stronghold before a waterfall. Hands in pockets, David walks toward uncertainty. Eyes lock. Neither one smiles. Melissa stands like an ice sculpture. What is happening inside that pretty little head?

I lean down to Rosa's ear. "What do you think?"

"Trust me, this will be good."

Rosa's words become Cupid's stardust, invisibly sprinkling over the young couple. Melting the frozen Melissa. She lets go of her father, bounding toward David, who breaks into a Texas-sized grin. I feel like we're watching a chick flick. Only the background music is missing. They kiss, she laughs, she cries, they kiss some more. Ay yi yi. Instead of Rosa's Haven, we should call this place House of Love. Of course, that could be horribly misconstrued on the Internet.

The next surprise can wait until after lunch.

We parade out to Bob's truck with full bellies and heavy hearts. We feasted on all of Melissa's favorites today, but it is not nearly enough to fill the emptiness in my heart. Rosa's, too.

Josie has taken her family to the beach, having already exchanged teary goodbyes with Melissa and Lightning. I suspect she left early so Rosa and I could have time with our young friend. Mike is on his way out, rushing back for a one o'clock appointment with a diabetic Dachshund.

"Thanks for coming, Dr. Mike." A single tear trails down Melissa's cheek. How can she possibly have any left? "I know you're really busy. It was so great you came to say goodbye."

"Say goodbye, my foot. I just came for the spanish chicken."

Rosa rolls her eyes, shaking her head at our resident comedian. "Oh, Michael, you didn't even know we were having chicken today."

"Fine. I just wanted to give last-minute instructions for Lightning. I don't want you Northerners messing up all my hard work. For all I know, you're going to feed him cherry pie, or whatever you people eat up there."

I fold my arms, turn dramatically toward my wife. "Now tell me, Rosa. Whose idea was it to give the horse to Melissa?"

"That would be Michael."

Mike cups his hand by the side of his mouth, pretending to whisper. "You two are going to ruin my bad reputation."

Bob laughs deep and loud. "I like this guy. Reminds me of my orchard manager. Now aren't you the one who's helping us with the plans for the dog, too?"

Melissa's eyes double in size. "What dog? Lily?" She turns to me, pressing her hands together, as though in prayer. "Please tell me its Lily. Michigan would be perfect. We have a creek she could swim in and lots of room to run. She could play with our other dogs. Oh, she'd love the winter and..."

"My goodness, *chica*, you don't have to convince us." I laugh through my words. "Yes, it is Lily. But she has to stay put and nurse her puppies. Next month, when Mike goes to his conference in Illinois, he will bring Lily. Your father will meet him there to get her."

"No way!" She wraps her arms around Mike's neck. "You're awesome, you know that?"

"Yes. Yes, I do."

A sudden vibration in my pocket startles me. Not a phone call now! I glance at it, planning to return it later, but the caller ID intrigues me. Why would the Waffle House be calling?

I hang up, baffled, wondering when my life became stranger than fiction. The Waffle House found Melissa's backpack stashed in the storage room behind a sack of flour. Inside was a wallet with $400. I return to my little group with good news.

An hour after watching the horse trailer turn onto Highway One, Rosa and I survey our work. Couch pillows rest neatly in their corners. The kitchen counter is free and clear of dishes. Melissa's room is empty. So empty. Only the scent of lavender soap suggests she was ever here at all. Silence can be a blessed thing, but today it leaves too much room for thought.

Chapter 25

Josie

Dawn's semi-darkness fills the space between butter-yellow walls. Dark shapes in the corner will become fluffy stuffed animals in daylight, remnants from when this was Dulce's room. So much better than waking to the hums of machinery and nurse chatter. The doctor said I'll be "good as new" in a few days.

The doctor is wrong. I am already new. Now there is hope and a future. A different future, perhaps, but one laced with endless possibilities. In another brightly painted room, next to ours, my children are sound asleep. The image makes me smile.

My future.

A porcelain cross hangs on the wall in front of me.

My hope.

Rob breathes deep in his slumber, one arm wrapped around me, his bare chest against the back of my cotton nightshirt. Through lemon chiffon curtains, a faint glow gives shape to objects veiled by darkness just moments ago. Go back to sleep, Mr. Sun. Grant me this moment for one more hour. Let me lie here feeling the warmth of his body against mine, the weight of his arm on my waist, lost in sensations more wondrous than any drug could evoke.

Mr. Sun does not comply. He continues to rise, filling the room with soft morning light as the faint aroma of Rosa's coffee wafts through the air. The arm around me tightens its grip. A warm kiss on my shoulder confirms Rob is awake.

"Mmmm." He yawns. "Let's live here forever."

"In Cielo Azul?"

"Right here in this bed. I love this bed. I love this room." He squeezes me again. "I love you, Jo. You know that, right?"

"I do." I turn so we are face-to-face, eyes gazing into eyes. Hearts clinging to each other. Whatever happens next, tomorrow, or in twenty years, will not come between us.

"I never want to lose you again."

His words are a serenade. A waltz to which my heart dances. My fingers caress his cheek, his brow, then disappear into his hair. He is mine, all mine. "You won't."

"You promise?"

"Robert Caruso, I promise to be by your side until death do us part, and in heaven as well."

He smiles. We kiss. "That works for me."

For the first time since arriving in the Keys, I am in paradise.

Rosa is setting a bacon-and-egg casserole on the table as my sleepy troop enters the kitchen. Orange frosted sweet rolls and a platter of fresh-sliced pineapple add their delectable aromas to the mix. My children's eyes are the size of dinner plates. The unprecedented morning feast has probably made this their best day in many weeks… and we haven't even left the house yet.

I grab a dishtowel and a wet pot from the dish rack. "Rosa, you must have been working all morning!" The love behind that fully laden table is so much more than I deserve.

"My pleasure, Josie. Finally you are eating like a real person. It brings me joy. This egg dish is one of Manny's favorites." She removes a white casserole from the oven. Bacon and green onions peek out from the top layer. "I hope you like it, too." She tugs the towel out of my hand. "Now go. Sit down with your family."

"Smells great," Mitch says. Commendable courtesy, but I know my boy. Nothing matters right now except the sweet rolls dripping in sticky frosting.

Ashley plops a juicy pineapple spear onto her plate. "Can we go back to the beach today, Mom?"

"Today is our tour of the Turtle Hospital, remember? You're going to love it. We'll have to check on Rocky and see how he's doing since the operation."

The pineapple freezes in place halfway to her mouth. "Who's Rocky?"

"He is a lovely Hawksbill sea turtle," Rosa says. "Sometimes boats run over the turtles when they surface. That is what happened to our friend Rocky. He needed surgery to remove his mangled fin. Also to remove some tumors."

"Is he okay?" Ashley's brows knit together. Suddenly Rocky is part of the family. "Can we help him get better?"

"Sí, he is healing well, but he has to get used to swimming with three fins."

She nods as though confirming the validity of Rosa's explanation. "I definitely want to see Rocky. Then can we go back to the beach? Please?"

I need no convincing. Yesterday afternoon at the beach was joy in its purest form. Elation. Every expression, every laugh, surged life into my heart. Like standing at the altar saying, "I do," or lying in the hospital, holding my babies for the first time. Yes, Ashley, we can go back to the beach.

"Can we, Mom?" Mitch's sweet roll is nearly gone after two bites. He is already reaching for a second one. Not a healthy choice, but anything goes today. All that matters right now are those happy faces. "The beach is cool."

"Sure. First the Turtle Hospital, then we'll come back here to help with…"

"Oh, no, no, Mrs. Josie Caruso. You are not coming back here to do anything. We've got plenty of help today. I've got Mrs. Cohen, a couple of teen volunteers, and Owen." She sets a mug of her cinnamon coffee in front of me. "Go. Spend this day with your family."

"But…"

"No buts. If you really want to help me, take those ostriches back home with you."

Rosa and Ashley share the same feelings about the large beaky birds. My daughter's eyes double in size. "Not the ostriches! Can't we take something else? Anything?"

Rosa laughs as she wheels toward my horrified girl. She places her palm on Ashley's cheek. "Oh, querida, I only kid. The ostriches are going to a sanctuary in Kentucky very soon. But...I do have a little something in the barn for you, if your mother approves."

Excitement replaces horror quicker than a shooting star. "Really? What?"

Oh, please, not the cat. Poor Clover would have a heart attack.

"I hope it's the black goat," Mitch says, eyeing the rolls for a third time. "He's pretty cool."

Rosa smugly smiles, the sole keeper of the secret. "Eat your breakfast, then we will go see."

Half an hour later, we are in the barn, where Sunny snuggles against Ashley, her long ears flopping over Ashley's arm. "Clover's going to love having you to play with. Isn't she wonderful, Mom?"

I look at Rosa, my friend, who can do more heart mending from a wheelchair than most people can with fully functional bodies. "She sure is, Ash. Absolutely wonderful."

Rosa turns toward my son, who is sitting on the edge of the donkey pen, alternately clucking and whistling in a futile attempt to get their attention. "And for you, Mitch, I have something, too."

Rob looks at me, rolls his eyes. "Uh, Rosa, I'm not sure what it's going to cost to fly animals back to Illinois. I'm thinking maybe they can just share the rabbit."

"Not to worry, señor. What I have for Mitch can go right in his suitcase."

Rob leans over and whispers, "Please tell me it's not a mouse."

From inside the storage room comes scrapes, bumps, and bags rustling, followed by, "Now where on earth? I put it here just the other day. Ah, here we go." She emerges with a large mound of bubble wrap and starts unwinding. "I hear you have an interesting rock collection, Mitch. Is that true?"

"Yeah. I've been collecting since I was a kid."

Rob and I share a smile.

"I have a lot of cool ones," the no-longer-a-kid adds.

Rosa finishes unwrapping an oddly shaped tube, its hollow inside coated with smooth glass. The smoky gray outside is rough and grainy with three small branches that shimmer like quartz. She holds it out to Mitch. His mouth opens, but no words come out. Eyes sparkle. If I didn't know better, I'd think she was giving him Luke Skywalker's light saber.

"Is that? Oh my gosh! Is that really...?"

"Fulgurite."

"It *is* fulgurite. I knew it! It's in my rock book. Saw it on the Internet too. Mom, this is real fulgurite!"

"Wow!" I have no idea, but he's excited, so I'm excited.

"It's what happens when lightning strikes sand."

The things this boy knows. If only they would test him on obscure facts, he'd be an A student for sure.

Rosa hands it to him. "Would you like it for your collection?"

"Really? Awesome." He holds out his hands for the grand prize. His wide eyes radiate a joy I haven't seen on him since...before. Before our world fell apart.

"Thanks, Rosa. This is great." He brings it over to Rob. Together they examine every inch of the foot-long tube before carefully replacing the bubble wrap.

We are a family again. But reality awaits me back in Riverbank. There are conversations to have, relationships to heal. This day is an oasis, cool and green. We've got each other for the first time in over a month. We've got palm trees, sun-kissed beaches, and a barn full of animals. Day after tomorrow, that jet will fly beyond the oasis, into the blistering desert. Our cab will cruise past that little white cross and into our driveway.

And then what?

The air around me thickens. I grasp the wooden beam next to Lightning's empty stall as my knees threaten to fold. No, it doesn't have to be this way anymore. Breathe in, Josie. Breathe in and remember you are not facing anything alone ever again. Not the memory. Not the nightmares. Not the empty places that Carmie and Ana used to fill.

I release my grip on the support beam and wrap an arm around my daughter. She responds by curling both arms around my waist. Whatever happens next, we will face it. Me and my family and God.

"I wish we could take Rocky home." Ashley had fallen asleep after the Turtle Hospital tour and hours of snorkeling. Half awake now, she clutches her bucket of shells as the rental car rolls into Preacher's driveway.

I reach back and pat her leg. "I don't think he'd like Riverbank too much, sweetheart."

Mitch can't resist the open door. "Yeah, Ashley, he's a sea turtle. And guess what we don't have in Riverbank."

"I know, Mitchell. I was just saying I wish. A person can wish anything, right, Mom?"

"Absolutely. No boundaries on wishing. Except for bad things, of course."

I wish, I wish, I wish I could go back to Halloween day. No, Josie Caruso. Wish better. Wish for something that has, at the very least, a remote chance of happening. A glimmer. I close my eyes.

I wish…that Ana will forgive me someday.

My sandy troop waves to Preacher as we pull up to the house. He is bringing Diego and the donkeys back in from their lazy day in the sea grass pasture. Diego stops as the car approaches, completely ignoring Preacher's demands to move forward. Mitch and Ashley laugh at the sight. Such sweet music.

"Look, Preacher!" Ashley bounds out of the car holding a bag of seashell treasures up high for all the world to see.

"Ah, shells! As soon as I get this stubborn llama into the barn, I want to see them all." How many seashells has the man oohed and aahed over in his life? But he will do it again for Ashley…and whichever children come to him with their jewels of the sea.

Mitch clutches his bag of beach rocks, far too cool to show them off. But he showed me.

Ashley strokes the cream-colored curls along Diego's neck. "Can I try, please?"

"Sí, *señorita*. The obstinate creature is all yours."

She places her hand on Diego's halter and Preacher lets go. My little girl whispers to Diego he is the "handsomest" llama she's ever seen. With a few more compliments and a scratch between the ears, Diego takes a hesitant step, then lets Ashley lead him right to his pen.

"Would you look at that?" Preacher slaps his cheeks. "How did you get that smelly beast to go with you? You have a way with animals."

"Thank you." Ashley basks in the compliment, her flip-flopped feet floating an inch or two off the ground. "Can we tell him the surprise, Mom?"

"Sure, honey. You go ahead."

She grins at the man who has just given her the greatest accolade of her life. "You get to have a free day tomorrow, Preacher."

Preacher lets out a hearty laugh. "A what?"

Rob chimes in. "She's serious. We're giving you a day off. Rumor has it you could use one. It's the least we can do. Grab yourself a reel, some worms, or whatever catches fish out here, and hit the water."

He's shaking his head as Rob finishes. "No, no. I've got two appointments tomorrow. One of the donkeys is limping. Saturdays are our busiest day." He looks toward the beach, the longing visible in his eyes. "A free day. Very thoughtful, but no."

A flood of determination sweeps through me. I have no other way to thank this man who has opened my eyes, my heart. Brought me back to my family. Back to life. This will happen.

"It's all taken care of," I say. "Owen is handling the appointments. Dr. Mike is coming at ten o'clock to examine the donkey. I'll write down everything he says."

"I don't know. It sounds wonderful, but I should be here on a Saturday."

"We've got it covered, Preacher. Please, after all you've done, let us do this one tiny thing for you. It would mean the world to me." I pause for effect, pleading with my eyes. "Call your friend James and go fishing."

"I don't know, I still have to look over Owen's sermon for Sunday."

"Just go. It couldn't possibly be as powerful and awesome as the last one you gave, but it will be fine, and you know it."

His dark eyes smile at me. "Powerful, eh? You said it was nice."

So that bothered him. What was I thinking? I wasn't thinking. I was too busy suffering. "Said 'nice', meant 'powerful.' It reached in and grabbed my heart. Opened my eyes. Now please say you'll take tomorrow off."

He looks at each of us, then out to the beckoning gulf. "Well…if you are sure."

He seems to let the thought marinate for a moment before his lips turn up slightly, then break into a full-fledged smile. "My goodness. A day of fishing. I am going to call James right now, then check my reel, get some bait." The more he talks, the more his face seems to glow. "Maybe I will pick up a couple of cuban sandwiches for our lunch. And some chips. Rosa never buys chips—too unhealthy. Thank you, Josie." He hugs me. "Thank you too, Rob." Still grinning, he offers my husband a vigorous handshake. "I hope it will not be too much."

Ben and I clean out neighboring pens as Rob helps Owen repair Diego's broken gate latch. A burst of laughter tells me the young island pastor and middle-aged Chicago suit have found their common ground. Owen's quiet demeanor seems to disappear when he's with Rob. Maybe he just didn't feel comfortable around me. Who can blame him? It's not like I've been Miss Congeniality.

I survey the barn, stopping at the empty pen previously occupied by that sweet pot-bellied pig. The teenage boy who adopted him will be a good owner, I think. Actually wrote down the food and care instructions. Ben walks over to grab a bale of hay.

"I'm sorry to hear you're dealing with custody issues. I hope it's okay that I know." Ben's got enough to handle without adding a crazy ex-wife to the mix.

"Nah, it don't matter. Everybody knows everything around here."

He pauses. Does he know my reason for being here? Probably. A rush of warmth rises to my face, but I stand strong and let it pass. Ben sighs. "I'm not a big one for prayin', like Preacher and Rosa. But I do pray for two things: for Rosa's legs to heal, and for my Connor to have a decent life. Poor kid, he really got cursed with loser parents."

"Preacher says in heaven's eyes there are no losers."

Ben smiles, shakes his head. "He stole that line, ya know. Does it all the time. It's from a song."

Charro strolls up to me and rubs against my legs. I reach down, stroke her back, feeling the vibrations of her inner motor. "Stolen or not, I believe it's true. You're no loser, Benny. You're running a business and raising an amazing kid. That says a lot about you."

"You didn't think so your first day here." A teasing smile. "Nearly killed me."

The vision makes me laugh. "Well, you have to admit, it wasn't your finest hour." The barn incident feels like forever ago. Another world. Another life.

"True. Honestly, I don't know why they put up with me. They have every reason to hate my guts. I guess it's because they love Connor so much. Who wouldn't?"

"I don't think either one of them have 'hate' in their vocabulary." His words sink in, tingling my spine. Something's about to surface. Something that hovered beneath us the day we met. "Why would they hate you, anyway?"

"Don't you know?"

I shake my head. A wave of curiosity swells. Did he get drunk and hurt Connor? Does it tie in with his wife leaving? I picture him and Rosa by the tree that first day. Ben tenderly helping her into her wheelchair. His head hanging as she talked. "I guess everybody doesn't know everything around here."

"That Rosa, I gotta hand it to her. She never tells nobody."

"Tells what?"

He runs a forearm over his sweaty brow, shoves his hand into the pocket of his cutoffs. "I'm the one who did it, Josie." Eyes that laughed only moments ago now glisten with moisture. Guilt tightens his lips. "I'm the reason she's in that chair."

This is where my jaw should drop open, or I should gasp in shock. Neither happens. Not that I knew, but a sea mist has hung over Ben's past. Now it is clear. Preacher's right. This place is drama central.

"You were part of the car accident? I thought it was just the two of them."

"Yeah, in *their* car. I'm the one who hit 'em. Ran a red light just a mile from here. Drunk as a skunk. That's why I don't drive. That's why I live in the trailer park, too. It's close to my business and Preacher's place." Ben spreads the clean hay around the goat pen. "It's all I could afford after the legal fees, even though they didn't press charges."

How do you get your legs crushed and not press charges? How do you get trapped in a wheelchair and care about the well-being of the man who put you there? This level of mercy is beyond understanding.

"Ben, it's none of my business, but…didn't that make you want to stop drinking?"

"Heck, yeah, it did. I was sober for over a year after that. Fell off the wagon a time or two, then stayed off the stuff for another six months. Until you came along. Not that you had anything to do with it. Naomi called the night before. Made me crazy."

Naomi could make anyone crazy. Don't know her well, don't want to, but I could see where she might drive him to drink. "I heard about that."

"I'm sorry you had to deal with her, Josie."

"You don't have to keep saying it, Ben. I know you are. Really. It wasn't your fault."

Lucy goat follows him like a white shadow as he finishes his task. "Wacko woman. I hope she stays in Key West for good this time."

No one can understand his feelings better than I. And yet…

"You know, I'm a little new at the whole Jesus thing, but here's what I'm thinking. If Rosa could forgive you for crushing her legs, shouldn't you be able to forgive Naomi?"

"I'm no Rosa. And I ain't no Preacher, either."

You have to appreciate the man's honesty.

"Good point, though." He stoops to give Lucy a scratch behind her ear. She thanks him by chewing the edge of his T-shirt. "Something to think about, I guess."

The sun has nearly disappeared for the night, its top rim glowing red just above the horizon. Pink and purple clouds streak the dusky sky. We stand at the pier railing, watching the remnants of brilliant color melt into the gulf. Preacher was sweet to take us here after stuffing us with his catch of the day. Now *that* was fresh fish. Rosa sits back down, her muscles exhausted from standing for the past ten minutes. And yet…she smiles. The others don't notice. They are too wrapped up in nature's amazing sky show. Something tells me this was her longest time standing since the accident.

Please strengthen her legs, Lord. She works at it so hard.

He has already heard me say it countless times. I can't imagine how often he hears it from Preacher. And Ben, of course, who lives with the guilt, which makes him want booze, which caused the accident in the first place. Talk about your vicious circle.

I abandon my spot at the railing to stand by Rosa. I reach over, squeeze her hand. "You doing all right?"

"Just a bit tired. But what a wonderful day, thanks to you and your family. I can't remember when I last had a whole day out. You should have heard us ladies at lunch, laughing like teenagers. To top it off, I stood through the sunset without feeling wobbly."

"You did great, Rosa. I saw. You outshone the sky."

"No, no. That's not true. But I am happy. For awhile I was making no progress. My hope was diminishing. Still, I tried. Each and every day. Finally, the miracle. I stood for thirty seconds, then a minute. Longer each week." Rosa gazes at the twilight sky. She reaches for my hand, squeezes gently, like I did with Melissa the day of the doctor appointment. "I am filled with hope, Josie. Maybe I will get these legs back. We will see."

"There goes our last sunset." Ashley steps off the overturned bait bucket she used to inch closer to the watercolor sky.

"Oh, querida, I hope your future will be full of beautiful sunsets. And sunrises. Remember, the sun sets and rises wherever you are."

"But it's not this pretty in Riverbank."

Riverbank. My home. Will it feel like home tomorrow? Picturing myself in Riverbank feels as foreign as this place did five weeks ago.

Music from Rosa's phone interrupts my thoughts. She glances at it, then places it back in her pocket. "My friend Nancie," she says. "I'll call her when we get back to the house. She is coming to the Keys in two weeks for a book signing, and she'll be making her lovely coconut cake on our local cable channel. She is such a beautiful, vibrant person." Rosa gazes at the remnants of pink and gold still gracing the horizon. "Oh, Josie, how I wish you could meet her."

"Me, too. I'd love that, but I have to go. It's time." Meeting Nancie McDermott would be such fun, especially after using her cookbooks for years and watching the uplifting videos she posted during the Coronavirus pandemic. Her fame sure hasn't stopped her from caring about people. And with that thought, another idea strikes with lightning speed. "Do you think Nancie would wear one of Marisol's necklaces on the show? And maybe even mention it?"

Rosa takes my hand and smiles. "You are a genius, Mrs. Josie Caruso! Nancie loves helping others. When I tell her Marisol makes the necklaces to earn money for her daughter's medicine, she'll be on board for sure."

Back at Rosa's Haven, we pack our belongings. Rob and the kids had left home in a hurry when they got Preacher's call. Only a few essentials fill the suitcase they share. All I have are thrift shop clothes, the sea glass necklace, and what I tossed in the car that day. A hundred lifetimes ago. And Sunny, of course, Clover's new friend.

A restless night gives way to an early morning. I gaze out the bedroom window for the last time, watching the sunrise, the birds, the palms dancing with the ocean breeze. Atlantic waves lighten from indigo to sapphire to azure as the sun climbs into a cloudless sky. Today will be predictably hectic, full of airports, cabs, unpacking. What will tomorrow's sunrise bring?

Muffins, toast, and bacon await us as we dive in for a quick breakfast before the two-hour drive to Miami. I drink in the scent of Rosa's coffee, wondering if I will ever savor it again. Something tells me I will, but thank God, not as the Josie who first sipped it a month ago. It seems a second "reinvention of Josie" has taken place. I wonder…will there be more?

Ashley leans over and whispers, "Mom, are you okay?"

"Yeah, honey. Why?"

"You were staring at your coffee like, well, like you used to before you left."

I kiss her ponytailed head. "I'm all right, Ash. I was just thinking about some things." I give her the reassuring smile she needs. "Don't you worry, okay?"

"Okay." She smiles back. Oh, what a beautiful sight. "We're still stopping at Shell World, right?"

"Of course!" I say it with enough drama to let her know she'd be crazy to think otherwise. "We can't miss Shell World. I'd rather miss our plane."

She giggles. "Me, too. I'd rather miss a chocolate peanut butter sundae from Frosty Freeze."

Rob tucks the last item into the trunk: a thickly padded box of Marisol's sea glass jewelry and picture frames. The old Josie would have relished the thought of a sea glass party, and maybe that will happen…eventually. For now, selling it for Marisol on the Internet sounds like the best option.

"Everybody ready?" Rob asks.

Rosa and I look at each other. The painful moment has arrived. Her face muscles tighten as she pushes herself up and out of her chair to hug me from a standing position. My arms wrap around her five-foot-two frame. The world stops. I breathe in her clean, soapy scent and the heavy island air, wishing she could be part of my daily life. Knowing that once this hug ends, it could be years before we see each other again. But it is time.

Rosa's cheeks are wet as she settles back into her wheelchair. She reaches into the colorful pouch attached to her arm rest, emerging with a new Bible.

"For you, querida."

My thank-you sticks in my throat. I nod. She understands. Swiping my own wet cheeks, I move on to Preacher. He pulled me from the depths of the sea, from the depths of despair, from a life void of what I needed most. He filled my emptiness with grace, compassion, hospitality, and hope.

"You saved me." It's all I can say.

"God saved you. I swam through those waves like Michael Phelps. Look at me, Josie. I am no Michael Phelps. I am honored the Lord used me for the task."

I smile. "Who better? Just wish I knew how to thank you. No words, no gift, could ever be enough."

He places a gentle palm on my cheek. "You still do not understand. Thanks is not what I want. And remember, you gave me a wonderful gift. A day out on the water…who could ask for more?"

"But there are still things I don't understand, and this sadness…I fear it will never go away."

His hands grasp my shoulders. Brows crinkle. He seems to search his heart for the right response. Eyes brighten as he finds it. "Martin Luther King said faith is taking the first step even when you don't see the whole staircase."

"I like that. He was a very smart man." My eyes slowly sweep the unusually quiet grounds that have been my home for a short time. The "Closed on Sundays" signs hang on the gift shop and barn doors. The donkeys stand motionless in the shade, probably asleep, while Diego stares at us from behind the pasture fence. Lucy munches on some sea grass, oblivious to her role in leading me to this place. I wonder if she misses Melissa, back in Michigan by now.

Cloudless and heavenly blue, the sky above Cielo Azul does justice to the island's name.

"It looks like you and Rosa will finally have some quiet time."

The two exchange a we-know-something-you-don't glance. "Looks can be deceiving, Josie. Ben and Connor will be here tonight. Before that, our next guest will arrive." Preacher glances at his watch. "Goodness! She will be here very soon."

I look toward the outer fence, but don't see the "Help Wanted" sign posted. "Who?"

The rumble of a motorcycle increases in volume as a skinny, dark-haired rider cruises up the driveway. We all turn and watch her park next to the house. She dismounts, brushing off her cut-offs and tattooed arms. She looks toward us, stays put. I turn back to Preacher.

"You're kidding."

"Naomi waited for me after church, the day after Ben got shot. She called me again on Thanksgiving and asked to meet with me on the beach."

"So that's why you disappeared."

He nods. "She wants to be a mother to Connor. Seeing you in the car with him that day...it did something. She wants her life back. Her boy. There are many layers to Naomi's problems. We will begin with her addiction and, with God's guidance, go from there. Your prayers will be most appreciated."

After a pause, I say, "I can do that."

"I know." His eyes smile at me.

Mitch appears at my side as if by magic. "Cool motorcycle. Can I go check it out, Mom?"

Prayers I can do. Letting my son get one step closer...I don't think so. That encounter with Naomi was enough to last a good long while.

I grab Preacher's wrist, pretending to study his watch. "Look at the time! We've got to leave now if we're going to stop at Shell World." Quick hugs all around before we pile into the car. Preacher and Rosa wave as we head down the drive. Turning halfway around in my seat, I see them stroll over to their new arrival.

In less than a minute, Rosa's Haven is out of sight. I open my new Bible and look in Mark for the verse I saw on Beach Man's T-shirt.

Daughter, your faith has healed you. Go in peace and be freed from your suffering.

Chapter 26

Josie

Ashley smiles even while munching her cereal. The child is so happy I'm back that it's hard to remember why I ever thought it better to leave. How could something so wrong have felt so right?

The devil lies, Josie.

Lie all you want, evil one. I've got my armor now, and while it may be rusty in some places, cracked in others, it's getting stronger.

A kiss on the head widens her cereal grin. How I long to keep them home with me today, but they've missed too much school already.

Mitch gallops down the stairs just as his sister goes up to change. I reach for a bowl, then realize he's making toast. "It's okay, Mom." He pushes down the lever and searches the fridge for the raspberry jelly, his favorite. "I'm used to making my own breakfast now."

"Oh."

I stare as he pours juice, wondering how he went from little boy to teen in just a heartbeat. A line of blond fuzz already covers his upper lip. I'd swear he grew two inches in the five weeks I was gone. That juice he's pouring used to go into a sippy cup, then a Power Rangers glass. Before you know it, he'll be grabbing a coffee mug. Pride tangos with a longing for yesteryear. My muddled-up heart doesn't know whether to sink or soar.

Comfortable in his routine, he plops down with his buttered toast and…what's this? Bows his head before eating. I sit across from him, coffee in hand, gathering the guts to ask the question that's been burning inside me.

He looks up, catches me staring. "What?"

A month ago I may have said, "Don't talk with your mouth full," but it doesn't matter at this moment. Not at all. I swallow a hot gulp, feeling it singe the entire way down. "Are we okay, Mitchell?"

He cocks his head like a puppy, letting the question mull until its meaning is clear. A slow nod precedes the "yeah." A blob of jelly plops off the toast hovering in midair and he swipes it with his pointer finger before turning his attention back to me. "Really, Mom, we are."

"You want to talk about anything? Ask me anything?" Does he still think of leaving home? Are kids still making mean comments? Does he know…how much I love him?

"I don't know. Not really."

I wrap my fingers around the hot mug, somehow finding courage in its warmth. "You were pretty mad at me before I left. Mad enough to run away."

"I'm done now. I'm not mad. Running away was a stupid idea."

Rather than take another bite, he politely waits for me to respond. Ah, company manners. I'd rather have him talk with his mouth full.

"Why? What changed?"

He looks out the window in search of an answer. Finding none, he sighs, searching his plate instead. "Church and Carol, I guess. The pastor said some stuff about forgiving people that just made sense, you know? And he said sometimes people don't even know they did something to make us mad. That's why you have to talk about it. But I couldn't really talk to you back then, Mom. It was like you were totally different."

Wow. A lot more than his body has grown. "You're right. I was different." His honesty inspires me. My turn. Can I be as brave as my son? "Mitch…the accident with Carmie, it was…more than I could handle. Can you understand that?"

"Yeah. Kind of for me, too."

"I know, honey. I'm so sorry. I thought I had to always be the one to take care of everybody. It never dawned on me that, if I needed help, you guys could take care of me, too."

He nods, somber eyes adding twenty years to his thirteen-year-old face. "I guess I kinda get that."

"I'm sorry I left, Mitchie. At the time, I really thought it was the right thing to do."

"It's okay."

I set down the coffee, lean over, and encircle my son in my arms, remembering when I felt incapable. Remembering when I wished my arms could stretch fifteen hundred miles to feel what I'm feeling right now. That shaggy blond hair on my cheek, his favorite blue T-shirt touching my skin. His warmth. His scent. I let go, knowing his hugs have limits.

"So who's Carol?"

His face relaxes, happy to be on to a different topic. "She's a friend of Aunt Theresa's. Sort of like a counselor or something. I met with her a couple of times to talk about stuff. You think that's weird?" He returns to his toast, probably cold now, and takes a bite worthy of Lily.

"No. I think it was a really smart thing to do. In fact, I'm planning to meet with someone too. Maybe it will be your Carol. So...she really helped you?"

"She's not my Carol, Mom. She's just...you know...Carol. And yeah, she did. I thought it was stupid at first, so I didn't talk to her much. But she just kept being nice. Sometimes later I'd think about the questions she asked. Then I started talking to her a little." He washes down his toast with the rest of the juice. "She said maybe you left because you loved us so much and you believed we were better off without you. It didn't matter if it wasn't true. If a person believes something...how did she say it?"

This is getting interesting. Again, he turns to the great outdoors for an answer. This time he finds it. "If a person believes something, then it's true to them. So in a really weird way, it was nice of you to leave."

I sip my coffee, completely blown away that a total stranger explained me to my son, blown even further by his understanding. "She sounds like a smart lady." Actually, Carol sounds like Wonder Woman, Superman, and Dr. Phil rolled into one. I think we should meet. But first, there is someone else I must talk to, and it needs to happen today. I take another sip, laced with a hint of cinnamon, and think of Rosa. What will that conversation look like?

A knot begins to form inside me. Twisting, tightening. Threatening to chain me to the chair, keep me from walking out that door. But I am not the friendless girl in the library anymore. I am a new creation. Wounded and worn, but loved beyond measure. Funny thing about love—it is tender as a rose petal, but tough as a grizzly. And definitely stronger than my fears.

Ana opens the door and I stare as though I've never seen this woman before. The curvy figure I envied for years is shapeless, covered by a baggy sweat suit. Sadness shadows weary eyes. There is no remnant of that contagious smile. Something needs to come out now—hi, hello, how are you? But it doesn't. I am as mute as the day I left. She stares back, tucking a loose black tendril behind her ear.

"Hello, Josie." It is Ana who breaks the silence. "I'm glad you came back."

"Thank you." Was that the right response? She waits for something more, but everything I planned to say has flown from my brain.

"Can I do something for you?"

"I just wanted to…"

She waits. I take a breath. "I just wanted to…"

"Yes?"

You can do this.

"I just wanted to tell you that I loved her and I'm sorry. For Carmie, for leaving…for everything." Saying the words seems small and insignificant. "There are no words, Ana. Nothing could ever convey what I really want to say. I loved her so much." My throat begins to close, but there is one more thing to say. "And you."

She nods, glancing down. "I see."

I see, too. The tears pooling in her eyes. The pain in her heart. My turn to wait now. Her face tightens as she purses her lips.

"Did you think I didn't know you loved my Carmie?" Quietly powerful, spoken with no emotion. And yet…it is there. "Each time she came back from your house, I would hear, 'me and Mrs. Caruso planted flowers,' or, 'me and Mrs. Caruso played with Clover' or baked cookies or drew pictures. Sang songs. Did you think I didn't know?"

"No. I just needed to tell you."

She looks up, deep brown eyes piercing mine. "You know what I needed, Josie?"

For your daughter to stay alive.

"I needed my friend here when the worst possible thing happened in my life. But I didn't get what I needed, did I?"

Harsh words combine with a calm, tired tone. The contradiction confuses me. "I don't understand. Didn't you hate me?"

A heavy sigh escapes lips that used to shine with Raspberry Dream. She looks like she should go to bed and sleep for a week. "I hated you and didn't. Blamed you and didn't. Wanted you here and wanted you gone. My child died, Josie. My little girl. I was crazed with grief, not thinking clearly. My feelings changed one moment to the next." Her voice ragged now, Ana no longer contains her pain. It spills down pallid cheeks, chokes her words. "Can you even imagine how it feels to lose a child? The only thing I was sure of that day you disappeared..." she stops, struggling to push out the rest, "was that I did not want you to leave."

I am lost. There is no point of reference for this, no one who might have tutored me in the proper response. Her words are pure crazy. "But I'm the one who made it happen! Leaving was wrong, I know that now. There are better ways to handle things. But Ana, can you imagine how it feels to kill a child? A child you love?"

"Maybe more than you know." She looks down, lips taut, battling an unknown force. "That night, just before she ran into the street, Carmie asked if we could stand together on the porch. She liked the fog. She grabbed her kitten and we were heading out the door when the phone rang. I said, 'I'll be right back, Carmie,' and went to answer it. I thought it might be Savanna, but no. It was a solicitor, Josie, asking me to take a survey about household cleaning products." She stops, takes a breath and looks past me, toward the street. "In the time it took to say no and hang up...it happened. I saw the glow of your headlights through the fog. Heard the thump of her head hitting the street. I knew. She lived for another hour, but not really, you know. If I had just ignored that damned telephone…"

In my dark fantasies, replayed a thousand times since that night, I imagine someone else was to blame. Someone else stole Carmie's future. Someone else ruined Ana's life. It was all I wanted.

Until now.

"No, Ana. It wasn't you. I was the one behind the wheel. Me, not you."

"There's more, Josie. I might as well tell you. Before asking me to go outside, Carmie asked Emilio to play Candy Land with her. He was looking up the price of snow blowers on the Internet. 'Give me five minutes,' he told her. Five minutes. So you see, Josie, you are not alone. We form a circle of guilt, the three of us."

Be careful what you wish for, Josie Caruso.

I do not want Ana and Emilio shouldering the blame, not even part of it. God and I will handle this together. My best friend has a heavy enough cross to bear without adding the weight of blame.

"Ana, please don't do this. Those things just happened—the kitten, the fog, the stupid phone call. Everything. I hit Carmie. I will spend the rest of my life wishing I could take back that moment. But I can survive with God's help. And so can you."

Ana purses her lips in an all-knowing Mona Lisa smile. "This is something I've always known. I am glad you know it now as well. But you have to understand, my daughter has been in the ground less than two months. My pain is still fresh. I still catch the scent of her in this house. Hear the echoes of her laughter and tears and silly songs."

And now for the hardest question of all. I grab the porch railing, holding on as though a tsunami may sweep me into oblivion any minute now. "Can you ever forgive me?"

It is a lifetime before she answers. Her eyes pause on the wooden cross at the curb, no longer covered with flowers. Faded from weeks of sun and rain. Dead leaves gather at the base where Ana's sister placed a white wreath a lifetime ago.

"I already have, Josie. Even before you returned. But our friendship…" she shakes her head. "I just don't see how. I miss it, though. I miss us."

Oh, God, please give her back to me.

I swallow, hoping to open space for words to slip through. "Me, too."

Ana swipes the single tear sliding down her cheek. "I don't know how to get from here to there. Does that make sense?"

"Yeah." It makes sense, but sense is not what I'm looking for. I want a miracle, nothing less. I want afternoons on the porch with a cup of coffee, seats together at school concerts, homemade enchiladas on my birthday. There is only one thing I want to do at this moment, and right or wrong, it's going to happen.

I wrap my arms around Ana's neck. "I'm sorry, I'm sorry, I'm so sorry." She stiffens. What did I expect? But I do not let go. Her arms encircle me. My miracle. Not what we had, but a sign, a message. She really does forgive me. I'm still there, occupying a small part of her broken heart. We sob together in the doorway, crying for Carmie, our friendship, and all that was lost on that Halloween night. My sleeve grows soggy and warm from her tears; still we hold each other, knowing we may never be this close again.

A wail emerges from the nursery, causing her arms to loosen from around me. No, Ana, don't let go of me.

"Juanito is hungry."

I nod. It had to end. "Yes, you go." I squeeze her arm, needing one last connection. "Congratulations. I've heard he is healthy and beautiful."

"Yes. He really helped me get through…everything."

My heart hopes she will invite me to come see him, but she sadly smiles a goodbye and shuts the door.

I breathe in a lungful of fresh icy air and take my time walking back home. Boots crunch on the thin layer of snow that fell as we all slept beneath soft fleece sheets. Christmas lights dangle from roofs, awaiting the cover of darkness so they can announce their glimmering beauty. On the lawn next to Ana's, a deflated Santa lies pathetically on the frozen lawn, grounded until the owners return and flip on the air pump. But it is the sight across the street that grabs my attention, though it's been there year after year. In a manger tucked into a snow-covered flower bed, Joseph and Mary gaze lovingly at the Babe in the wooden trough. An angel guards from atop the simple structure, lightly dusted with sparkling snow.

Epilogue

Josie

Emily Rose giggles at the pink party balloons bouncing in the Michigan breeze. Just hearing her laughter was worth the six-hour trip from Riverbank. In one hand she clutches a slightly frazzled bunny while the other wraps tightly around the gold wedding band on her mommy's finger. Lily stands watch next to her; ready to pounce on anything that remotely resembles a threat to her young mistress.

"Wee Wee!" Emily points at her furry guardian. The monstrous black head turns toward Emily with smiling eyes.

"Yes, that's Lily!" Melissa beams at her daughter, clearly delighted with her extensive vocabulary. "Okay, Punkin, you have to let go of Mommy so I can cut the birthday cake." She hands off her baby girl to David and heads across the spacious back lawn of this enormous ranch-style home. The proud daddy kisses his princess on the head, then does what daddies have been doing since Adam; tosses her up in the air, catching her in strong, loving hands. We all laugh at her happy squeals, each of us knowing how easily this moment might never have been.

Our gathering place is a natural wonderland. Emerald green grass bathed in dappled sunlight from the apple, peach, and cherry trees nestled along a sparkling spring-fed lake. A month ago, those trees were a twenty-five-acre fantasyland of pink and white blossoms. I could almost smell their heavenly scent from the photos Melissa emailed to us. Wish we could have been here. Even now, the earthy fragrance of grass, flowers, and pristine lake water fills my senses. This is what the earth should smell like. Organic, green, pure. What a wonderful place to grow up.

"Whose birthday is it?" Rosa lets go of her walker long enough to place a party hat on soft blond curls. "Such a big girl. Pretty as your mommy. Look how smart she is, Manuel, just look at her eyes. What do you think, Josie? Is it just me? Don't you think she looks extremely intelligent?"

Before I can answer, David sends Emily sailing skyward again. "I think she's a genius," he says.

"Me, too." I readjust the glittery hat that slid over her eyes in mid-flight. "Rosa's right."

"I think it is time for cake. Come on, we have to sing for our little birthday girl." Preacher leads the way as Rosa and I walk together at a slower pace. Before the day is out, she'll get tired and resort to her wheelchair. For now, she walks beside me, clutching her walker, but upright.

"Josie, reach in my purse, grab the little photo album. I brought it just for you."

I comply, pulling out a small vinyl "brag book" and flipping it open. First up is Dulce with her toddler and brand new baby. Is there anything more beautiful than a young mother's smile? Next is her son's wedding photo, followed by Melissa's. Number four is Connor's school picture. I can't resist touching his freckled face. "Awww, look at him. They change so fast at that age. Wish he could've come with you."

"Oh, he would have driven us crazy all those hours in the car! Plus his mother didn't want him missing school. He's struggling a bit in math."

Ahead of us, Preacher reaches the cake table and places the large "one" candle in the center while Melissa sets out plates.

"Is she really doing as well as you say?" Please let it be so.

"Turn the page."

Naomi's smile is nearly as big as Connor's, their faces pressed together cheek to cheek. In another photo, they are joined by Wagger, the half-lab, half-mystery puppy Connor got just after I left. The puppy is licking Connor's chin, but it is Naomi's face that draws my attention. With her hair pulled back and her eyes free of smudged eyeliner, her green eyes are actually quite pretty. Vampire girl has left the building.

"Wow, I never would have recognized her."

"Quite a difference." Rosa stops and lowers her voice. "But I have to be honest, it hasn't been easy. Especially the detox." She shakes her head, shudders. "Horrible. Thought we might not survive. She went from violent to sick to begging. There was crying, screaming. Ay, yi, yi. It felt like we were in a horror movie those first few days."

"I remember your emails. I was so worried she was going to hurt you." We start walking again, enticed by the sweet scent of strawberry cake wafting on the country fresh air.

"Well, thankfully, we had plenty of help. Michael, Ben, even Marisol."

"How is Marisol?" I've loved being her sales person, knowing each seaglass purchase buys medicine for her little daughter.

"That woman is so grateful to you, Josie. You have turned her life around with those Internet sales. And when Nancie wore one of Marisol's necklaces on TV, dozens of people came to the gift shop to buy them. Her daughter is doing much better now."

She motions for me to flip the page again, where I see a family photo of Ben, Naomi, and Connor. "As for Naomi, the worst is over, but still there are many wounds. She is going for counseling. And I'll tell you what; she adores that little redheaded spy. She's gotten a second chance at being his mom and does not want to blow it."

"I know the feeling."

Rosa smiles at me and, as if on cue, we look toward the corral, where Rob, Mitch, and Ashley are feeding carrots to a huskier, happier Lightning. I wave them over and they join us as Melissa lights a candle on the pink bunny cake.

Nancie McDermott's Turtle Mocha Brownies

(Referenced on page 128.)

For the Brownies:
1/4 cup butter
2 oz. unsweetened chocolate
2 tsp. instant espresso powder (optional)
2 lg. eggs
1 cup sugar
1/2 tsp. vanilla
1/4 tsp. salt
1/2 cup flour
1 cup coarsely chopped pecans

For the Caramel:
5 Tbs. butter, cut into 4 pieces
1/3 cup brown sugar, light or dark
2 Tbs. evaporated milk or half-and-half

For the Chocolate Icing:
1 1/4 cups semisweet chocolate chips
2 Tbs. evaporated milk or half-and-half

Heat oven to 350 degrees and grease 8-inch baking pan. In small pot, melt butter and chocolate over medium heat, stirring until melted. Stir in espresso powder.

In a medium bowl, beat two eggs with whisk or mixer until thick and lightened to a golden hue. Add sugar, salt, and vanilla and continue beating until volume increases. Add melted chocolate-butter mixture and stir well. Add flour and stir, scrape, and mix well. Scrape batter into prepared pan, spreading evenly. Bake 15 minutes.

While brownies bake, make the caramel. Combine the butter and brown sugar in a medium saucepan. Whisk constantly until melted and combined. Bring to a boil, then add evaptorated milk or half-and-half. Cook 1 minute and remove from heat.

Remove brownies from oven (they will not be done yet) and scatter pecans evenly over top, then cover with caramel syrup, spreading gently to cover pecans. Return to oven and continue baking for another 15 minutes. While brownies bake, make chocolate icing.

Combine chocolate chips and evaporated milk or half and half in a medium saucepan over medium heat, or in microwave. Cook until chocolate melts, then stir into a smooth icing.

Remove brownies from oven, spread icing evenly over top, and cool to room temperature before cutting.

About the Author

Faith, family, and a passion for nature, writing, and photography nurture Susan's soul. She loves to visit the world's amazing places and has a travel bucket list that includes the Northern Lights, the wild horses of the Outer Banks, and New Zealand's glowworm caves.

Susan worked as a Chicago-area newspaper reporter, then as a television reporter in Albuquerque before returning to her home state of Illinois. She currently works in public relations, teaches writing workshops, and gives travel presentations throughout the Chicago suburbs. Susan is president of the American Christian Fiction Writers Chicago chapter and a member of the Society of Children's Book Writers and Illustrators.

Acknowledgements

No book is written alone, and for every person who contributed in any form, I am truly thankful. As always, my gratitude goes first and foremost to God, who blessed me with the opportunity to take this story from idea to published work, and gifted me with amazing people throughout that journey.

My incredible family and friends are my cheerleaders, my inspiration, and sometimes my toughest critics during the writing and publishing process. And...they are all securely nestled in my heart.

Authors Lisa Samson and Patti Lacy, gifted writers and sisters-in-Christ, were nothing less than essential to taking this novel to a far higher level than its original version.

Cookbook author and anti-racism spokesperson Nancie McDermott graciously agreed to be the fictional friend of my character, Rosa, and share her delicious recipe with readers.

Ana A. Steele, internationally renowned anti-slavery spokesperson and former president of Dalit Freedom Network, provided powerful insight into the plight of Dalits and others facing various forms of slavery and trafficking. Her long ago presentation at my church sparked a passion for this issue, which I infused into the character of Mike the veterinarian.

The Turtle Hospital in Marathon, Florida, heroes to countless injured sea turtles, was the inspiration for the fictional Sea Turtle Rescue Squad in this book.

And finally, I am forever grateful to the awesome CrossRiver Media team—Tamara, Debra, and DeeDee—for great editing, a beautiful cover design from Carrie Dennis Design, and for believing this story should have a place in the world.

She turned to
him for comfort.
Now she's discovered
his dark side.
Finding
Beth
Available in bookstores and from online retailers.
CrossRiver Media
www.crossrivermedia.com

Discover more great books at
CrossRiverMedia.com

LOTTIE BRAUN SERIES

She's a little girl with a big gift. Lottie Braun has enjoyed a happy childhood in rural Iowa with her father and older sister. But the quiet, nearly idyllic life she enjoyed as a child ended with tragedy and a secret that tore the two sisters apart. Forty years later, Lottie is a world-class pianist with a celebrated career and an empty personal life. The Lottie Braun three-book series includes *Lottie's Gift* (Bk 1), *Lottie's Hope* (Bk 2), and *Lottie's Freedom* (Bk 3). If you like the Mitford series, you'll love Lottie Braun.

WILTED DANDELIONS

Rachael Rothburn just wants to be a missionary to the Native Americans out west, but the missionary alliance says she can't go unless she is married. When Dr. Jonathan Wheaton, another missionary hopeful, offers her a marriage of convenience, she quickly agrees. But she soon finds that his jealousy may be an even greater threat than the hostile Indians and raging rivers they face along the way.

DESTINY SERIES

This gripping, award-winning saga spans the Antebellum Era through World War II and tracks the lives of the McConnell family women. Award-winning inspirational historical fiction author Catherine Ulrich Brakefield weaves fiction with real life events to create this antebellum romance. Series includes *Swept Into Destiny* (Bk 1), *Destiny's Whirlwind* (Bk2), *Destiny of Heart* (Bk 3), and *Waltz with Destiny* (Bk 4).

THE UNRAVELING OF REVEREND G

When Reverend G hears her diagnosis — dementia with the possibility of early-onset Alzheimer's — she struggles with the fear of forgetting those she loves and losing her connection with God. But she soon discovers there's humor to be found in forgetting part of the Lord's Prayer and losing a half-gallon of ice cream. And she finds while the question she wants to ask is, 'Why,' the answer really is, 'Who.'

Should she help
an enemy soldier
or let him die,
cold and alone?

Road to Deer Run

IGNITE YOUR FAITH

Join us online...

CrossRiverMedia.com

Facebook.com/CrossRiverMedia

Pinterest.com/CrossRiverMedia

Instagram.com/CrossRiverMedia

Made in the USA
Monee, IL
19 April 2021

64933027R00144